T0209957

Praise for *The Physics of Sunset*

"*The Physics of Sunset* is a gorgeous poem to human and physical observation. Reading it is like being given the gift of second sight."

John Burnham Schwartz

"Set against the low-key affluence of the Berkeley hills, *The Physics of Sunset* is like the fusion cuisine served at her characters' parties. By boldly ignoring the incongruous, Vandenburgh successfully mixes nostalgia with satire and melancholy with hot sex. The result is an original and worthy follow-up to her acclaimed first novel, *Failure to Zigzag*."

San Francisco Chronicle

"A flawless tapestry of verbal imagery . . . a *novel* novel about a time-honored subject, adultery. *The Physics of Sunset* is unlike anything you've read before in this vein."

Donald Harington, *Arkansas Democrat-Gazette*

"Jane Vandenburgh knows these people. She knows how they worry and how they kiss. She knows how they buy their cheeses at Andronico's but get their toilet paper at Safeway. She knows how they take their coffee. Most of all, Vandenburgh knows how Berkeley people think."

Contra Costa Times

"[*The Physics of Sunset*] admirably grapples with the idea that doomed passion can have a place in our lives. . . . A curious mix of . . . breathtaking erotic defiance and unabashed romantic existentialism—much like adultery itself."

New York *Newsday*

"Right from the start you will realize that this is not a book to be raced through, but rather, to fully appreciate the author's amazing skill and talent it should be carefully and slowly savored. . . . Rarely will you find another author who so clearly takes the time to write each sentence exquisitely and with such profound insight."

Rapport

"Vandenburgh's meditations on such diverse subject as physics, architecture and nostalgia enrich this regional tale with shimmering metaphysical depth."

San Diego Union Tribune

"An impressive novel about husbands, wives, and destructive self-indulgence that originates from an honest quest for meaning, *The Physics of Sunset* suggests a raw tug-of-war between intellect and emotion, family and independence."

American Way

"Since her highly praised first novel, Vandenburgh has kept readers waiting a decade for this second effort. A smart, witty, sadly ironic novel about neighbors in Berkeley who become lovers, this is an even more elegantly crafted and perceptive work. Rich with intelligence and feeling . . . Vandenburgh's depiction . . . is scaring and poignant. Intensely erotic, its transports are tinged with pain—physical and emotional—and the knowledge of finality . . . Vandenburgh has created a memorable portrait of fulfilled love and bereavement at its loss. Her compassion infuses this story with insight and grace."

—Publishers Weekly (starred review)

The Physics *of* Sunset

ALSO BY JANE VANDENBURGH

Failure to Zigzag

The Physics
of Sunset

JANE VANDENBURGH

COUNTERPOINT
BERKELEY

Library of Congress Cataloging-in-Publication Data
Vandenburgh, Jane.
The physics of sunset / Jane Vandenburgh.
p. cm.
ISBN 1–58243–100–0 (alk. paper)
1. Architects—Fiction. 2. Berkeley (Calif.)—Fiction. 3. Women poets—
Fiction. 4. Adultery—Fiction. 5. Marriage—Fiction. I. Title
PS3572.A65 P48 2001
813'.54—DC21
00–065867

ISBN: 978-1-58243-100-0

Cover design by Wesley B. Tanner / Passim Editions

COUNTERPOINT
2560 Ninth Street, Suite 318
Berkeley, CA 94710

www.counterpointpress.com

For Jack Shoemaker

There was never any more inception than there is now.
Nor any more youth or age than there is now;
And will never be any more perfection than there is now,
Nor any more heaven or hell than there is now.

WALT WHITMAN, Leaves of Grass

I.

Queens Rules

That one body may act upon another at a distance through a vacuum without the mediation of anything else, by and through which their action and force may be conveyed from one to another, is to me so great an absurdity that, I believe, no man who had in philosophic matters a competent faculty of thinking could ever fall into it.

SIR ISAAC NEWTON,
in a letter written to Richard Bently while
Newton was working on the
Philosophiae Naturalis Principia Mathematica

— 1 —

Outdoor Survival Skills

V<small>ERONIQUE</small> C<small>HAKRAVARTY</small> <small>GREW</small> up in a little town in the south
of France—she called it my *vee*llawwge. The sun rose there
over golden hills to shine on a river crossed by a Roman bridge.
The scape of land eees similar to theees one, Veronique said.
She pressed her lips together, looked out from her hill above the
water of San Francisco Bay, then gestured in the dismissive way
that showed she, being French, was superior to either of the two
perfections.

The light, she asked. And this air? Veronique smiled at Anna,
who examined the atmosphere as if it were gauze between her fingertips. The light was clean and white, the air soft to the point of feeling powdery, as if it contained particles that multiplied light's
brilliance. California was dry, Mediterranean, and shadows did fall
in that sharp-edged, bluish way, but it was the molecular density of
Veronique's soul that had allowed her to be transported intact to
her new land from that more ancient one, Anna knew, and allowed
her to feel at home.

Springtime, a bright morning, the air cool on Anna's naked

arms. The past winter had been rainy so the hills were lushly green. A soft breeze moved up the Chakravartys' canyon.

Veronique had attacked the landscape like one of her Roman ancestors scooping out irrigation ditches, adding sand to the clay soil of the deep beds she'd dug into the terraced hillside. Her kitchen garden contained the same herbs and vegetables her mother grew: *tomates, aubergines, persil, asperges.* Veronique came, behaved as a conqueror, the earth responded, was changed by her.

And the local idiom was being altered by the force of Veronique's will. Anna Bell-Shay was a poet and had a hesitation in her own speech that encouraged her habit of listening carefully. Head down over the basting of a satin blanket binding or in the active grief that had yawned open for no good reason in the middle of her life, Anna attended her friend's various beats and breaths and emphases, unreasonably imagining Veronique Chakravarty was somehow teaching her fluency.

English was becoming ever more complex to Anna as she grew older. In the matter of a dash, for instance: how much pause might a dash be asked to carry? The dash was modern, also seemed to contain all of history. All her favorite writers seemed to balance there and so exist in the tentative.

Veronique didn't worry about this kind of thing. She went crashing off through the underbrush of everyday speech, imagining, for instance, that people rushing to their therapists were going to see their shrimps. This was Berkeley in the 1990s, where everyone was, or had been, or soon would be in some variety of therapy, the latest being traveling to the far-off reaches of the world to walk the most famous labyrinths. Veronique's husband, who was from Delhi, had an almost better than perfect English. It was elegant, carefully nuanced, slightly archaic. Because of Ravi, Veronique said *cawn't* and *shawn't*, she rode a *lift*, lifted the *bonnet* of the *caw* she'd *hired*.

Ravi's was a high old culture, his wife's more new and raw. His eyes gleamed, were deep-set, thickly lashed, so brown his dark glance might catch, take hold. His gaze possessed a person—Anna felt it grab the muscles of her lower belly in a cramp that was frankly sexual. Ravi and Anna sometimes locked eyes at dinner as Veronique plunged on and on—he might lift a brow or move his full lips slightly at something his wife just said. Ravi very pointedly did not correct her, seemed also arrogantly to defy anyone else to do so. Anna understood this. She suffered the same attraction. Veronique's being so noisily alive being why each was drawn to her.

The Chakravartys lived up the hill from Anna and Charlie, whose older house lay in the flats of Berkeley in the section of Northside called the Gourmet Ghetto in the real estate ads. Anna and Veronique had had babies within weeks of one another, their friendship—Veronique called it *free*-end-ship—had deepened over upchuck and earaches.

Nearly all aspects of early motherhood were without intellectual challenge, they soon discovered—even talking about children was often boring in the particularly overeducated way of the developmental psychologist, whose clinical language made Anna feel she might need to shoot someone. She might feel better, she often thought, if she killed something. She would probably need to commit one small crime some day soon. She needed to turn criminal or she needed to go book an hour in a Tokyo sleeper. These were the modular sleeping capsules she'd just read about. Japanese salarymen rented them so they could power-nap on their lunch hour in order to be rested enough to go out drinking with their bosses again.

Anna's own mother confirmed it: infants are no more wonderful than any other subset of humanity. God does, however, make all small mammals look cute and smell good so you'll want to nurse them, Margaret Bell said when she telephoned. Also make you less likely to toss them out a window.

Anna and Veronique sat together on the Chakravartys' wide deck, their children playing nearby. The light shone on water radiant as aluminum—they seemed to sit in a bowl of noon. With pregnancy Anna, who was blond and fair, developed new sensitivities; she now had a form of sun allergy. She wore big loose dresses and a wide hat and huge, very dark dark glasses to protect her pale eyes. Charlie called this Anna's Edith Phase—Edith was Anna's own unlovely middle name. He sometimes said to people that if life was a costume party, his gal Edith was going to come dressed as the *echt* artist/mental patient. She'd arrive with her head swathed in bandages, ear gone, her face all smeared with white stuff, dressed as Mrs. Vincent van Gogh.

It was the chemistry of pregnancy that changed her, Anna thought. Her mind turned dull as her skin became more sensitive. She was a prism now through which light fell and broke apart. If what Anna was experiencing was a natural splintering of focus, as her mother suggested, when was it that she might begin to pull herself back together? Anna had once been smarter—of this she was nearly certain. She recently called her mother to ask if this wasn't so. Margaret Bell now lived year-round in upstate New York in what had been their summer house.

It was natural, her mother said, that the soul of a female person should be riddled by empathy. This was a natural adaption. That mothers were porous to the wishes of those around them was what had kept humanity lurching from meal to meal all down through recorded history. She was herself now finished with that portion of her life, Margaret said, having relinquished responsibility for the heavy organs of appetite to the new generation. This new lightness was one of the surprising and very wonderful things about being a grandmother.

Days ticked by. Anna's daughter was one year old, now turning two. The photosensitivity began to ease. Anna often wanted nothing more than to go alone into an art museum, to stand in front of a great painting and be sliced apart by all the levels and degrees of silences. A great painting made its own quiet room. What she disliked most about poetry, she'd discovered, was that it seemed to so depend upon the noisy apparatus of language.

Until Anna witnessed it from within—experienced in her body the nubs of what might have once been deemed a *personality* being so rubbed down and burnished—she'd never been so attracted to people as ardently selfish as Veronique sometimes seemed.

Anna became so diffuse at times that she felt intoxicated by the mere presence of any other stronger individual. She experienced this as a profound psychological calamity, a loss of self. The experience felt tidal, she became rapt, went *out*, it might take days or even weeks for her to come back in again. This happened both with women and with men. Writers, in particular other poets, in particular other women poets of about her age, were most necessary to avoid, particularly those who were beautiful or might turn out to be honestly talented or to exhibit some originality. It wasn't the threat of her own plagiarism, so much as Anna's worry that she might be swept so easily into their sea, actually begin to be subsumed by them.

Anna loved Veronique because she was French and the French are a stubborn race that refused to be eradicated. Veronique also refused to kneel and worship at the altar of maternity. She said the things that Anna needed to hear in order to keep her sanity: that playing Legos isn't fun, that almost all children's literature is intrinsically inane.

The Chakravartys' house overlooked that of Alec and Gina Baxter. Alec was an architect and theirs was a famous house in Berkeley, poised on the opposite side of Ravi and Veronique's canyon. Very chic, Veronique said sometimes, looking down her French nose at it. Very BCBG, I suppose, but do you actually *like* eeet?

Anna was too porous to decide. The house was clean and modern. In a certain kind of light at various times of day, its surfaces became invisible, the glass side going sun-gone, the tint of the walls inside matching that of a whitish sky. The house shifted, changed size and shape, was sometimes nothing more than the reflected patches of scrub oak and evergreen standing against a brushy hillside.

The house was large enough to have been imposing except for its tendency toward atomic dissolution. It was also somehow a little out of place in Berkeley, Anna thought, as if it landed there not from the future but from another parallel reality, the lost world that would have taken the place of this one had things gone slightly differently. It was there, in the world beside the world, that Anna felt she actually resided rather than in the real town of Berkeley, California.

And while this town, with the university at its heart, harbored more Nobel laureates than any other and there were other major and minor geniuses of every kind all up and down its social ladder, Berkeley had the pretense of hating pretense. It preferred its geniuses dead, its great houses to be wooden and old, foursquare and democratic, like those designed by Bernard Maybeck.

I ated that ouse, Veronique said to Anna one day, ated them for making it. Then when the lorry comes and I see they ave that what eees theeeese thing? theeeese baby swing? and my hurt breaks for them and my ope flies up again.

So it always honestly did come to the same sad questions, Anna realized, the ones all the interesting women they knew struggled with: How to negotiate the inward and outward currents, when the job of making a household ran against the pull of a worldly ambition? How was anyone to accomplish this once mute and simple act, that of raising children? And how, in the face of the awesome privilege she and her friends enjoyed, to justify these twin burdens of despair and jealousy?

The disappearance of the mass of the Baxters' house seemed to be a poetic technique Anna might study and employ if she ever wrote again. She envied the painters, like Gina Baxter, or the architects, like Alec Baxter, those who made wordless physical objects, who put walls up, hung paintings there, things thick with dimension, dense objects that didn't depend upon the little markings that made letters that stood for sounds upon a page.

She and Veronique drank wine as the sun went down, Anna watching the Baxters' house as its essence changed. How to be completely and truly present on the other side of the work, she wondered. How to give away nothing yet still speak with intimacy?

How to become spare and empty without indulging her own strong impulse toward self-annihilation?

Anna had done her graduate work in Emily Dickinson—she hadn't finished her dissertation. Not finishing her Ph.D. now seemed emblematic of everything that was turning out to be wrong with her, motherhood being corollary to that earlier vanishment. When she was in graduate school, she'd once attended the reading of a paper called "On the Anonymity of Mothers," concerning the mothers of various early presidents of the United States about whom almost nothing is historically known, often not even the dates and places of their birth.

Anna, who was tall, had been taught by her mother to stand up very straight. Forgetting herself as completely as she did, she remembered the length of her body sometimes only when she abruptly stood and was made dizzy by the altitude. As she stood to ask a question at the end of the paper's presentation, and an old embarrassment swept through her, that of the big, shy, sweating girl, the awkward adolescent with enormous feet who'd always tried so hard to stay anonymous. She began to blush, to stammer, spoke softly, haltingly, then sat down, having become too nervous to even listen to the answer. And so it was, she saw, that self-consciousness might prove terminal, the inescapable gravity of constant self-reference. She was flame-faced as she left the hall, ashamed, ashamed too of being ashamed. Her hot face pulsed with every heartbeat going *me, me, me.*

Ravi traveled; Veronique was stuck up the hill at home with theee keeed. She now had two babies, but Veronique didn't bother with an *s* to form the plural. Veronique, who was bored, sometimes watched her neighbors with binoculars. The Baxters had uncurtained windows. They were an attractive couple, one so big he was almost lumbering, the other diminutive, each dark-haired but with mysteriously fair-haired children, all moving through the spacious wood-planked rooms as if on their way somewhere. Alec was well over six feet, so tall he needed to bend over with his face gone grave and solemn to listen as his wife spoke. Gina was stylish, antic.

She talked and talked, Alec listened. Gina had stopped growing quite early in adolescence, Veronique said. It was all her various tragedies, she added, somewhat callously.

Gina Baxter was now very busily accruing some notoriety, having recently gone beyond painting to work both behind and in front of the picture plane. This was her return to realism. Gina did seem poised on the brink of something—her friends had begun to eye her cautiously. The odds against her turning out to be any good at all were, of course, absolutely astronomical, Anna knew, the Bay Area being something of a backwater in the plastic arts. The lucky people, Anna thought, were people like Veronique who never noticed the difference between what was good enough and something that might actually matter. That was art's secret trick, Anna thought, that so few did it well, that no one knew exactly why.

Ravi, in electronics, was getting quietly rich. Veronique had never been more miserable. Come up *ere*, Veronique demanded. Bring that one up ere to play with theeees one. Stop and buy me a pack of cigarette. Do this, Awe-naw, or I *will* keeeel myself.

Veronique, who'd quit, was now back smoking Marlboros—she called them theee Red Death. She smoked as she painted cowboys and Indians in oils on the walls of one bathroom. She painted *faux naif* tepees and saguaro cactuses, all of this awkward, childlike. She used unmixed colors straight from the tube—raw umber, burnt sienna, cadmium red—and as she painted er ope rose up again.

It was art that did it, Anna knew, the act of being within the moment of creation, that lit the dim places in the brain with the thought of the other, better, more fully imagined West, the place the real desert sun still rose and set. It was there, in art, that the neurons gained the power to come alive and fire across the great bow of eternal darkness.

Despite herself, Anna found her own hope rising too. She had Maggie, the little girl born as a kind of miracle so late in her marriage she had already lost all hope. Her book of poems would be published by a respectable press in a year or two. She had a marriage that was probably as good as most, at least as good as the one her parents had—she thought of her own marriage not as a deepening spiritual bond, rather as a kind of equity of all the many years she and Charlie had each put in.

Anna believed in making poems as anyone might hold to any religious faith, that a hurt and broken world was made more whole by these irrational acts of faith. God existed, if He existed, in all enactments of love and grace, in every gesture made toward creation. Anna believed this. She also believed writing a book of poems was almost exactly like lighting a box of kitchen matches, one by one, and pitching them down a well.

They sat out on the Chakravartys' deck in good weather while Veronique, who had never heard of sunscreen, became tan, and their children grew and Anna basted satin binding onto the quilted baby blankets she made for charity. Maggie was getting bigger. A poem, or some lines in one, sometimes broke free, ran wildly, then came back to her in snatches, like the lyric of a song she was only now remembering.

Anna slept with a handsome man who, while mocking, was nice enough. He was reputed to be her husband. Charlie Shay was an experimental musician who taught at a women's college in East Oakland. He was startlingly good-looking—she'd recently begun again to notice. He was even better-looking than he ever used to be. This was not a man who was going to lose his hair or thicken around the middle. Charlie got on his mountain bike nearly every morning and rode it straight uphill to Grizzly Peak, his bright cheeks there cooled by the dazzling fog.

Anna's mother called to ask what fruits and vegetables were arriving in the market, to hear what Maggie was now up to. Margaret Bell fretted over her daughter's lack of happiness, more noticeable since Maggie had been born. It was a nullity that came and now resided. It manifested physically, an emptiness framed by the muscles of Anna's lower abdomen. She could never tell her mother this. She often felt a little sick, also ashamed of feeling sick. Her mother was Yankee, tough-minded, stoic. Anna had nothing real to complain about.

The Cold War had ended, the wall in Berlin came down, but Anna was still at times so panicked her hands shook, terrified she couldn't save her daughter from an ecologically imperiled world. She awoke in the middle of the night to the indelible vision of a black sun rising over a nuclear desert, the sky a cold and quiet blue. This was the color Georgia O'Keefe discovered by looking through the white eyehole of a sun-bleached cow's skull.

Anna still referred to her own husband by both his names, Margaret mentioned. Was it that Charlie's first and last names were like his longitude and latitude? she asked. Was Anna, after all these years, still trying to get a fix on him?

Anna was startled by her mother's comment. If she complained, she didn't mean to, as complaint made her feel petty and disloyal. She did lately worry that the man she thought of as "Charlie Shay"—this went back to their days at Stanford when there were several Charlies in their circle—might lack something that seemed increasingly essential, the vacuoles of irony that bubbled up in a personality at the level of the cell.

When, for instance, Anna told him she intended to call her book of poems *Outdoor Survival Skills*, Charlie lifted his clean, strongly muscled face and gazed off so intently that a hot saltiness rushed to fill the back of her mouth. She looked down at the uselessness of her upturned hands, long fingers that lost feeling in the cold or rain. The two were out to dinner, were having lobster and champagne. She swallowed hard against the same ache that rose from her belly and now settled in behind the muscles of her jaw. Her throat closed, she'd never known such emptiness. Would she ever meet a man for whom she didn't need to explicate?

Anna's throat ached, her heart ached. She was thirty-eight years old. She'd been married for more than fourteen years, and still hadn't found the road, she recognized, the one that would lead her home.

2

Important Documents

EACH HAD BEGUN to do things that startled her. He had their old house tented for pests, forgetting to mention it. Then the house was elaborately rewired, then wrapped in tarpaper and completely reshingled. Anna was trying to work. The hammering seemed to happen directly in her skull, within which Charlie's workmen had also come to take up residence.

He went to great expense to put in a security system, bought her a new computer as a present, had her files converted to its systems. Anna, who had been in the mountains teaching at a writers' conference, came home to this upgrade, found she had been too dispersed by traveling—she'd lost her watch, also a pair of sunglasses—and now possessed too little craft or gravity to bungle her way through all the new layers of complication. And so it was out of his great enthusiasm and generosity that her husband managed to bury her work in the deepest levels of some new electronic hell.

Charlie built the studio in the backyard against the fence in the footprint of what had been their old falling-down garage. Anna happened to miss the ramshackle building held together by the twining of wisteria, its shingles so weathered that thin yellow capillaries of electric light showed through.

Charlie began to send her flirty e-mail from his soundproof studio. She wouldn't answer him. It was the look of e-mail, the ugly way it printed out with its bulky dingbats and gizmos: its evanescent nature told her nothing lasts and nothing matters. E-mail was such an impulsive form, it caused a person to appear to be so naked, exhibited his weak spelling, also the twisted spine of his sentence structure. It made a person so easily rude.

There was always so much noise that surrounded Charlie. She hated the demanding little chime that said electronic "things" were in her "mailbox." Charlie sat less than fifty feet away from her, she had a deck off her study, he might simply open the door and let his voice carry. Instead he'd invaded Anna's one final secret place. At the jingle she could feel him on the other side of the monitor, Charlie's watching, breathing, waiting.

Something might be really wrong with her. Stalled, she began to watch her own long white hands with an air of detachment: were these the hands of a murderer? They seemed to now move independently, as if they might suddenly shoplift or begin to yank the cork from a bottle of cold white wine to toss back a quick one. She seemed to be sending out weak flares of defiance in no particular direction. She and Veronique drank red wine now in the middle of the afternoon, becoming more and more entwined in their mutual cynicism. They gossiped so destructively she came home feeling as sick as if she'd eaten a pound of chocolates. Veronique liked to talk about sex. Anna couldn't, wouldn't. Veronique wasn't verbally modest. Anna admired this but couldn't match it. She had nothing much to say. She'd known a few boys, but that was so long ago. Her marriage wasn't ardent. If her marriage, like so many others in the last few days of the American century, was guttering out, why should the cosmos care?

Anna shopped for groceries, lost interest, hated being made low, drawn down to gossip, stopped anyway to read entertainment weeklies in the magazines aisle, became filled with revulsion over the baseness of humanity, over her own shameful staring in bald fascination at the faces of all the famous people she could never get herself to fully recognize. She fixed on the unexpected deaths of famous people, how fame was intended to make one buoyant and large and therefore somehow inoculate against mortality—this was once religious faith's responsibility. A poet could not be famous, by definition. If Dickinson walked down the streets of this town, she wouldn't be noticed in any particular way. She would seem like any one of the legion of other neurotic women, all tight-lipped and sexually repressed, dressed in white, unfit to inhabit the physical world. Milvia had been designated Berkeley's Slow Street to make a place for them to walk.

Anna had always imagined vanishing, disappearing one day, then to come alive again, completely reconfigured in some lost future. It may have been this that prompted her to annex Charlie's last name, to give herself more letters. She needed consonants, she imagined—unlike the airiness of vowels, a string of louder consonants might add a little heft. What seemed to keep her in place now was her own place-keeping, that she stood in the pattern of generations—Anna bridged the moment between the two more luminous Margarets, the sun that was her mother, the moon of her own daughter's ascendancy.

Anna, stuck in this earthly paralysis, stood fixated in the magazine aisle of the grocery store, suddenly unable to buy any of its garish items. There was so much wrong with food these days, no one knew where anything really came from. She decided most food was unappealing because it contained no particle of God. There was no God at all in the particularly American habit of eating way too much, then dieting. Anna took her purse and left the grocery store, abandoning her half-full shopping cart. Charlie complained that she had no other job but couldn't keep milk and eggs and bread in the house. When was it that Charlie's demands had become so childish?

The cultural moment now carried a waft of incense, a mood toward a paring down, a spiritual simplifying. Anna wanted to become a Buddhist, but her friend Serene Hoberman was already one and she didn't want to emulate. Serene made an altar in her bedroom to remind her that every act of sex should carry God within it. Anna imagined her own Zen existence, how she and her daughter could make do on the $423 per month in income she received from an annuity her father left. She wanted a life filled with right action, so unlike the life she currently led. It was wrong, she thought, that she and Charlie bought so much and owned so much and were so dependent on his parents. They had no money of their own. They lived beyond their means because his parents were much too generous, really. Anna needed to simplify, she believed, to get back to whatever was essential. She had never felt so tight, so unloving. There was nothing she needed, nothing she could get herself to even remotely desire, yet she had begun to charge random items to the Amex card, things she could not imagine owning, merchandise she barely recognized after she brought it home.

Anna now sometimes caught herself in rooms into which she could not remember going. She stood at the window of her study, looking east, watching her fingers lying along the windowsill. These fingers trembled slightly. She had come searching for important documents.

She was staring up toward the houses that had been built back into the shadows of the hills. These hills burned completely in 1923 in the fire that raced down the canyon and took half the buildings on the campus. Now the windows of the houses up by the Chakravartys glinted, caught the sunlight, tossed it back at her somewhat knowingly.

Anna studied the hills as if they were more than a lesson in geography—an old volcanic uplift and wear-away, of granite outcroppings and of what was changed by heat and what was laid down by sediment and how over history topsoil ran off those old burns and into the gushing mocha-colored creeks that boiled out into the alluvial marshes rimmed seasonally by fire, and that on these trembling flatlands her house had been built. In an earthquake the ground her house stood on experienced liquefaction.

Anna had come to unreasonably believe there was something to be learned about happiness by studying these hills, that people with good houses somehow had a better chance at decent marriages.

She lost things, bills, money, pages of manuscript. Charlie made love to her. Was there God in it? She couldn't force herself to pay attention. She had her thirty-ninth birthday, two months later her book was published. She held her breath, listened carefully, but no phone call from Heaven came. Anna felt oddly vindicated, as if she had run for her life through a thunderstorm and had somehow made it indoors, even if she was completely soaked.

"A poet lives nowhere, knows no one," she said aloud. Someone—another poet—once leaned across two empty chairs at a reading at Black Oak to whisper this to her. Anna turned forty, promised herself she would never write again.

She wasn't altogether certain she had ever loved her husband or that the man named Charlie Shay was someone she'd ever known or that she would even miss him if he left. She developed the unnerving habit, he said, of distractedly asking "Excuse me?" whenever he spoke to her.

They should have divorced that year. Instead they embarked on a complete remodeling of their kitchen, borrowing tens of thousands of dollars from Charlie's parents. Their architect was Carlo Empy, the other partner in Alec Baxter's firm.

3

Bodies at Rest

I T WAS A few minutes after five on a warm October afternoon, the first unremarkable day in that remarkable week, the only one in which Alec Baxter's whole evening had been laid out pleasurably and he knew just what to expect. The A's were two games up. Instead of sitting shiva on the cardboard boxes the rabbi dropped off at the house on 219th Street in Queens, instead of observing phone silence, staying home in order to say prayers and light a memorial candle for his father, Alec flew right home. Back at work, he seemed to have forgotten all about it.

A brilliant California day, with the sky towering up into great struts of cumulus. Alec was happy, was walking free, had come out the other side of the worst of the suffering.

He was free, also hungry. He was out on Solano Avenue going into Zachery's to pick up a couple of half-baked pizzas. He was making his way to Fran and Jerry Bloom's, who lived above him up the hill on Descartes. It was at the Blooms' that the members of their two families would convene to eat stuffed pizza, Chicago-style, and worship in the Church of Baseball.

The streets were strangely empty. Thinking of nothing so much as his hope for a Giants win, he heard the clap of its coming before he even felt it. This was just as he walked through the open door of the pizza shop. It slammed in, faltered, then seemed to renew itself by taking hold of the ground where he was suddenly rooted.

There were two girls at the register, each one gripping the countertop. "Get down," he ordered them. He bellowed this as if to steady not only them but the entire world. Their open faces emptied of expression—girls with big eyes only staring up at the place where the pendant lights were swaying. These were jokey Tin Man light fixtures, ones hung on long attachments, galvanized, swinging in a perfect description of the waves of shock.

His heart went out to them. All these loud and buoyant girls— were they all to die like this with their hopes unmet? He thought of his own daughter, his son. Parents in Berkeley sometimes dreamed their children's names, so the children were named with hope for an imagined future—the parents' own longings and wishes written out in a way that was achingly transparent.

The interior walls were eighteen feet high, the ceiling open to the metal roof, its members cross-beamed by structural steel. There was such a hollow at the core of so much in California that even the word *building* didn't necessarily mean what it might have in the East. Stores and even schools were cheaply and idiotically made of unreinforced masonry—these were the very places his wife and children spent half their waking lives. Across the room the ten-foot stacks of cardboard pizza boxes began to shake apart, slick white boxes skewing out across the tile floor, as if an imperious God was giving a demonstration of the verb *to undulate*. The boxes, two-feet square, tumbled out, strewn like a deck of waxed and magnificent cards.

The floor was cool, smelled of bleach. It was concrete, scored to resemble bricks and dyed Tuscan red, so well waxed it looked like tanned leather. Materials were a matter of life and death to Alec—you could literally die here of the shoddiness of the solid world, of the duct-tape-patched-together life, the one lived on the cheap. Concrete was one substance he ardently loved; this love gave him solace now. Alec let his cheek rest on the floor against the hard chill of it. He loved its pliability, how it started out as such thick liquid to be molded, poured, pressed, shaped, scraped for texture—a stone that could resemble anything, depending on the craftsman's artistry. Concrete had such flex before it hardened, such give, like a young person's life. Now it was only the fragile skin beneath which beat the heart of the living world.

The quake boiled for a good fifteen seconds. Plaster, already brittle, cracked. The high walls that had been sheared shook but held. They were stabilized too by the grids of the brick-red metal roof.

Tears had suddenly come to him, began to stream his face. It wasn't grief that rocked him, rather the keening disappointment that his evening's selfish pleasure had been so quickly wrecked. What was wrong with him, that his best and truest feelings were left like luggage in the East? It is by losing faith, his father said, that a Jew becomes American.

Alec was alone except for the pizza girls. He was hungry and he was tired; he'd wanted only such a simple thing: to go up to Jerry Bloom's. Jerry worked at the Lawrence Berkeley Lab. He was a Bronx Science whiz kid, a type of goofy genius—he and Fran always laid out quite a spread. Jews knew a thing or two: the close relationship between loss and gluttony; also, the way you had to bury quickly to get it done before sorrow annihilates.

Jerry always kept a fifth of Stolichnaya in the freezer. The two might have taken that bottle and tiny glasses stuck like thimbles onto Jerry's big cartoonish fingers and gone alone out onto the deck into the fading light to smoke cigars. They would look out over the water as its color deepened and the bay filled with dusk; they might speak with hushed voices while staring off, speak of Ted Williams and John Coltrane, then offer a few toasts to Alec's father as the sun went down, never mind they lacked a minyan.

Alec lay with his palms flat, his rough cheek against the cool floor of the pizza shop. The girls called out to him, asking if he'd been hurt. People came out from the kitchen, streamed around the counter, Alec wrongly becoming the focus of their attention. Had he been hurt? they kept asking. He struggled to sit up. He was weeping; he couldn't answer them.

Later he came to think it was the earthquake that had broken him, that in that moment the abyss had opened and he glimpsed the moment of his own death. He had been terrified. He saw that he lacked a certain structural integrity. He thought of himself as morally scrupulous—Gina called it rigid. Alec had always been more strict with himself than he was with other flawed and more primitive beings, a group that included his wife and children. The rules with women were more fluid, he felt. Women were hard on one another, yet made allowances. They were more elemental, less high-minded, which is why Alec had been able to forgive Gina for her crimes against him.

He raised his palms, which were bruised from the panic with which he suddenly hit the floor. He was shaking his head to try to say it: my father is a few days dead; I don't know where my family is. He was a man who never wept, who hadn't cried at his father's funeral. How many days now since he'd eaten. How long since he'd slept. Alec was hardly recognizable to himself. He needed something to eat, needed also to sit quietly for another minute to adjust to this world, the new and vaulted emptiness in which no father stood above him.

4

Closure

In architecture, this term refers to the property of perception which causes the tendency for an open or incomplete figure to be seen as a closed or complete and stable form.

FRANCIS D. K. CHING,
A Visual Dictionary of Architecture

WHAT THEN WAS Alec guilty of—that he was a less-than-perfect husband? That once, in the long distant long ago, he made his wife Gina suffer a specific cruelty for which she then very amply repaid him? That the last time he saw his father Alec had gone out of his way to fight with him?

Stuart Baxter, once a man of sophisticated political opinions, seemed in old age to become more and more simplistic. In the last few years of his life, Alec's father began to rigidly divide the world into what was Good for the Jews and Bad for Them. Stuart began to loudly admire the Hasidim, to go on and on about their purity. The Hasids of Brooklyn were notoriously wealthy as diamond merchants, and were often robbed, yet they walked to *shul* on Shabbat without carrying money, not even a fake wallet to give up in case they were hit again.

"Which," Alec mentioned to his father on his last trip to Queens, "*might* be viewed as being a simpleton."

"Now Alec," his mother said.

"It causes war, Pop," he told his father. "Remember *war*?" he asked. "W-A-R? And that it's usually the religious fundamentalist who's happy to kick it off." He felt like he was talking to a four-year-old.

When had his father become like this strict Jew off a TV sitcom? The house where Alec grew up on 219th had aluminum siding. Why? Because, as Stuart said, paint costs money! And their interior decoration ran severely now toward the *Oi, Gottenyu!*—with everything done along the lines of his parents' cultural allegiances: brushstroke prints of kitschy Chagall-like brides flying upside down, or the made-by-kibbutzim crap his parents got in the airport shops in Tel Aviv. *Oi*, Jesus! the jumble of occasional tables for which there was no occasion. Hadn't their parents once been more aesthetically interesting than this? he asked his sister Betsy. Now their reading was of the most pious kind. The silver-bound Israeli Hagaddah sat out conspicuously alongside their book club books, nearly every one of them written by a conspicuously Jewish author and very often on Jewish themes.

For the rest of that visit his father was polite if cool. First Alec insulted the Jews, then he criticized Stuart's driving. It was Betsy who asked her brother to speak to their father—their father stopped listening to Betsy when he turned into what she called the Jewish Mr. Magoo. When he got lost or confused, Stuart now impulsively braked to a stop, never mind that he was on the turnpike. Their mother, who did not drive, encouraged and colluded. "You can go now, Stu," Vivian chirped. "The coast is clear," she said. Stuart yanked the wheel, making an abrupt left in front of three lanes of oncoming traffic.

"The coast is *not* clear!" Alec bellowed from the backseat. "Pop! What's going on here? Are you trying to get us killed?"

"Will you look at that?" his mother asked as Stu pulled ahead and blandly kept turning. Brakes squealed, horns blasted, curses were hurled at him. "See?" she sniffed. "They won't give an inch!"

Alec and his father quarreled in July; Stuart Baxter died of a heart attack on a Saturday morning in October, no angina, no prior history. Alec flew out on the next plane east feeling only mildly startled. Their father died while praying, Betsy said. Stuart was wearing his white and ivory prayer shawl, his wrist and hand were wrapped in phylacteries. Could this be literally true, Alec wondered, or was his father really somehow alive and still manipulating, going into disguise as a thoroughly pious man in order to become the stuff of family legend?

Alec got off the plane to discover that the sunlight and all colors had gone watery, that the whole of Long Island seemed bent and drenched and held underwater by the enormity of this news. His father had really died and so was really dead. Grief twisted him, might have broken him, had he had no give. The look of the world changed; objects seemed to float just as Alec too now did. He took a cab in, went right to the funeral home, bent to kiss his father's face. Stuart lay in a plain pine box, his beautiful head wrapped in the same silk shawl he'd had since he was a bar mitzvah boy on Oak Street in New Haven. The skin was cold to the touch of Alec's lips, his father's features so pure and still.

"Oh, Pop," he said. "How I loved you. I am so sorry I was rude to you."

Alec flew home, staring out the window of the plane, went right back to work in order to forget himself, to forget the ways in which he didn't live by the other nine of the Ten Commandments. Then just as everything began to settle back and coalesce into the ordinary, Alec's whole bright world again began to shift and buckle, as if without the rules given by God to Moses, the earth would never again be stabilized. Thou shalt honor thy father and thy mother, the strata thundered. This quake measured 7.1, lasted a full fifteen seconds.

Earthquake time is like all other kinds of time that lie within a frame of violence. A second goes on and on, trails away as far as one can see into the future. One reasons that the moment now must end but it doesn't end and even when it then does end, the event is never really over with, as both history and the future are bent at that point, and all of time is therefore altered by what has just transpired. This is known in physics as the Frozen Accident.

It is chaos, Fran Bloom told him—if the quantum works for

anything, it's to prove there is no cause and effect, no way the world reflects the inner state except that we view it intrapsychically. The cause and effect of guilt was a human construct, a mathematical calculation, she reminded him. It happened in the one-and-one-equals-two of the realm of the superego, which—in Alec's case—was becoming strangely harsh and punishing. Fran Bloom was a psychoanalyst, one of the old-fashioned Freudian, lying-on-the-couch school. She did the talking cure, left off with the pharmaceuticals. Alec admired that, admired the fact that Fran Bloom still used both names to identify herself when she called the house though he'd known her for years. The name Fran Bloom, he thought, was as comforting as the lub-dub, lub-dub of heartbeat.

He sometimes wished he had married a woman who possessed such wisdom, such certainty. Alec had begun to go up the street in the evenings to visit with the Blooms because he needed now to actively obsess and they were older and would listen patiently. Alec had to go over and over the various events to find his place in them. He went back mentally, a bit forward, then back again, all the way back past Peter's birth, back before Gina went to finish her schooling, back to the winter Cecily was conceived in his office at Cal. The redwoods were hung with glittering raindrops. Had there been some kind of entrapment for which each of them secretly blamed the other?

Alec seemed to be fingering a chain of evidence: here the fight he and his father had, here his father's startled look that his son could so caustically talk back to him. Alec was simply hurt that his father turned away from him, that when Stuart rejected his earlier liberalism to return to the warm comfort of the fold, he left his son's children outside in the chilly zero.

Buried in the past were all those hurtful things that Alec had almost entirely forgotten—such as that when Gina was finishing her schooling she'd once known someone named Timmy, known him much too well.

The quake struck like a hammer drop, centered near Santa Cruz, its shock waves radiating outward for hundreds of miles.

The shifting occurred on the Loma Prieta Fault; this was part of the same splintering system that includes the San Andreas and the Hayward, the strike-slip fault that ran directly beneath the Baxters' house.

That was October 17, 1989. The clockwork of events might have been constructed differently, might have sprung out and dinged and been plotted to produce a different result. Alec might have been at the ball game at Candlestick Park, might have taken his son Peter with him. He loved this boy so much it made Alec much too vulnerable to loss.

They might have gone with his partner, Carlo Empy, who had tickets, might be stuck there in the darkened stadium with fifty thousand others, phones and bridges down or clogged and no way to get word home to Gina and Cecily. They might have driven there and have parked and gone in and might have therefore lived, but it was also conceivable that they would be running late since they were with Carlo, who ran late. Carlo was half Italian. They might have been rushing to the game and so just hitting the upper deck of the Bay Bridge when the slab fell in. They might have hit the connector just there where it pancaked, at the I-880 interchange, killing forty-two people. The Cypress Structure stood only two or three minutes from Alec and Carlo's Fourth Street offices. Before that day, no one knew such a thing as the "Cypress Structure" even existed.

This would have happened because Alec had Peter with him, Peter had psychic vulnerability, might be charged, even, in the particular way that draws lightning down. Alec was meant for nothing, he often thought, aside from keeping his children safe in this shifting world.

Alec would have taken his son to the Bay Bridge World Series game—he seemed to need to repeat this for weeks to anyone who would listen—except his father had just died and Alec was just back from his trip east, was home without eating or sleeping, was bordering on near exhaustion. "You don't border on near exhaustion,

Alec," Gina mentioned in bed one night. "That's like your saying *dethawed* when you mean *defrosted*."

He made only the slightest little grunt.

"You might begin to feel a whole lot better," Gina was going on to say, "if you went out and got a little strenuous exercise. You need to eat more greens, lose a few pounds. You need to drink more water and a lot less coffee."

Alec was lying in bed with his hands behind his neck studying the shifting gray geometries of shadow and deeper shadow on the ceiling. These came from moonshine caught in the light well he placed at the center of the house. Light invaded each upstairs room at night by falling through the transoms in luminous Rothko-like floating rectilineals. He was guilt-wracked, vexed. Just when Alec relaxed, settled in to witness the many and very obvious pleasures of his life, a word or phrase (such as *Timmy, the fucking boychik*, such as *Despite his better nature, my father had come at the end to perfectly despise the goyim*) would bubble up to punish him.

"Know what Voltaire said when they told him he was killing himself with coffee?"

"What?" Gina asked. She was falling asleep.

"I was born killed."

She made some small sleepy acknowledgment. "Know what U.S. Grant's last words were?"* Alec asked. He was a specialist in this kind of knowledge for which he had yet to find any real application. Gina's breaths slowed, evened out; she was lost to him. Who or what was it Gina dreamed of these days?

Never mind, he told himself, I'll go find someone else to tell.

---

* U.S. Grant in a note written to his doctor on the day of his death from throat cancer, July 27, 1885: "I do not sleep though I sometimes doze off a little. If up I am talked to and my efforts to answer cause pain. The fact is I think I am a verb instead of a personal pronoun. A verb is anything that signifies to be, to do, or to suffer. I signify all three."

5

Celestial Elevations

H E HAD KISSED another woman once, someone he hadn't yet known well enough. Anna Bell-Shay was shy, squirrely, a close friend of their neighbor Veronique. Anna and her husband had come to dinner a couple of times at Carlo and Julie's. She was a writer, a poet, one of the vague women Alec thought of as being members of the Horizontal School.

He'd found Anna sitting outside on a low stone wall at the party of friends in the neighborhood. This was after the earthquake when whatever held Alec attached to the earth had begun to let loose of him. For a week or ten days when rescue teams were still pulling living people out of the rubble, everyone exhibited a great capacity for joy. People were talkative, briefly united by the shared catastrophe that seemed to reach so deeply into every aspect of their lives. This was later in November, the Bay Bridge had been reopened, things were settling back: modern life again began to atomize.

It was a big party on a mild night. She had excluded herself and was sitting alone in the quiet dark, drinking wine and staring in through the big window of the dining room at the crowd around the buffet table.

Anna and her husband had the lookalike marriage Alec called the Bub and Sis, like a type of deli sandwich. Each was tall and blond, each had a wide angular face, strong, purely American features. Her eyebrows were so pale they scarcely showed. This was an endogenous marriage, like that of first cousins, rare in California, more common in the East.

Bub was of one type Alec actively despised—Columbia had its share of these. They were feckless, good-looking, rich—they never balanced their checkbooks. Blue-eyed, ankles tanned, they golfed, went sockless, came mewing around women who seemed to like them, though what was the exact appeal? Bub, in Anna's case, was a musician who taught at Mills. She was clearly too smart for him. He was charming, nothing more. At dinner Alec had been bored and more than a little annoyed that men of this type exhibited such ease in getting good-looking women.

Anna patted the spot on the low wall beside her. Alec sat. It had been a clear fine day and still was warm enough that they could sit comfortably outside. The evening was peaceful; light through the window pooled on the flagstone and moss just beyond their feet. Neither felt moved to speak. The clouds above were still brightly lit, but here below in the shadow trail of the house next door, they were sequestered by the quiet and by the gathering darkness.

The sun was going down and the last light glinted like hammered copper along the rippled glass of the upstairs windows. This was a big hills house, a Maybeck, brown-shingled, effortlessly perfect and of its time. That he be half as good as Maybeck or Julia Morgan was all a man might really hope for. Birds were screaming raucously. This was only a few blocks below Descartes—Alec had come out the kitchen door to see if there was a way to sneak home by going over a back wall or up the path past Indian Rock. He could go home and sit in his car for a little while, read a couple of paragraphs of physics—this was the end of the eighties, so he'd have been reading *A Brief History of Time*, which was simply too difficult. Or he might go home and listen to the ball game on the car radio, drive back down to get her. He could be gone an hour before Gina even missed him.

"Nice party," Anna said.

"Tip-top."

Each fell silent once again.

"Actually," she said. "I left because I couldn't really stand another second of listening to the sound of my own voice."

"That's the one good thing about smoking cigarettes," he said. "It gets you bounced right out of a place like this."

"Do you have a cigarette?"

"I don't smoke."

"Neither do I," she said. "But I would if you happened to. If you smoked, you might have run out and you'd have to leave to go buy some and I could get a ride down the hill with you."

"Too bad about cigarettes," he agreed. "I liked it when there were cigarettes."

They were both quiet again. Alec felt compelled to add: "There isn't anything that's come along that helps so much with social awkwardness."

"Don't talk if you don't want to. What I hate most about parties, really, is that everyone nervously talks so much." He nodded, each was silent. They stayed that way for a little while, then Anna said, "I was stuck in a corner with people discussing the homeless, and someone said they'd been put on earth to teach the rest of us gratitude."

"*Gevalt.*"

She smiled at him. "The whole discussion began to make me so angry I started stammering, and I tossed my drink back so fast my brain felt like I'd been given a lobotomy with an ice pick." Her face was now alive with self-amusement. "Then someone else told *that* person to stop calling them 'the homeless' since this term can be seen as one of derogation, both fixed and judgmental. I honestly could not stand it. So I came out here in order to drink anti-socially." She swirled imaginary wine in a glass that was now completely empty. "God, how I wish there was still *something* at times like these. Hashish was great—I wish there was still hashish. People were no less stupid when there were drugs, but at least we didn't have to notice everything stupid everyone said and then remember it in such exquisite detail."

Alec groaned. "Christ," he said. "I'm just too old to be doing this again—my memory's shot. I honestly can't remember the names they changed everything to the last time. I can't even remember that they changed the name of Grove to M.L.K. The whole title of that street is now written out 'Martin Luther King, Jr., Way (Old Grove Street)' on the plans at City Hall. It happened ten years ago, more! I should have adjusted by now. My father spoke Yiddish first, then English, but at least he only had to learn his second language once. And now my nine-year-old daughter comes home to inform me in her superior nine-year-old way that I have to upgrade to the new format."

"Format?"

"She tells me I have to go out and rebuy all the music I own on records and on tapes or I'll die without getting to ever hear what music really sounds like."

Each was silent, each thinking about what music really sounds like.

"Life does sometimes seem like it's becoming one constant upgrade," Anna said. She sighed. They were quiet, then she said, "It was better when there were cigarettes."

The birds had quieted. The night was so peaceful, they both heard it when his stomach rumbled. "Are you hungry?" she asked. She dug around in her bag and brought out a packet of airplane nuts. Anna handed these to him. "The crowd's gone from the table. We can go back in if you like." She said this, but neither of them stood. She dug around in her bag again, pulled out a tangerine and a pack of saltines, handed them to Alec.

They spoke quietly for another little while, had those few moments full of humor and good will. He kissed her when they each
stood to say goodbye and go back in. They kissed, this felt perfectly
natural. They may have lingered slightly, but not long enough that
anyone watching them through the window would have been able
to really tell.

6

The Parts of Speech

Wasn't life its own grand and spacious miracle? That she who needed nearly perfect silence in order to work had somehow married a musician? This had honestly never before occurred to her. Being weak-minded, Anna was as bullied by music as she was by being in the room with an attractive person. Music approached her, tried to get inside her just after she'd gone numb. Music wanted her, wanting her to become lost to its fluency.

Fluency was what Anna always lacked. She had, in speech, not so much a real stutter as the need to halt, wait, pause at the blockades put up by any kind of disjunction. In high school this evolved from a slight stumbling to a need to fully stop at any kind of punctuation so she could peer out cautiously over the line to see what lay ahead of her. The speech pathologist taught her how to slow down, press her lips together, focus, breathe, go on.

The whole course of her life now seemed to come down to these matters of hesitation. It wasn't that Anna hadn't been able to finish a dissertation as much as she hesitated to even really start one. She always felt the need to eliminate as silly or wrong or

clichéd or probably more untrue than true more words and phrases
than she could bring herself to produce and so ended up, year after
year, with fewer and fewer pages to show to her advisor.

This man came to her wedding, held Anna's hand for a long
time at the reception, staring down into her palm as if reading her
future. He was more than a little drunk, became too effusive in
praising her interesting mind. He wanted to ask something of her,
he said. He wanted to ask Anna to not go into the house and never
come back out again.

But what did she have to say about Dickinson that hadn't already been better said? And why should anyone whisper another
syllable about this poet, surely our most silent and importantly
vanished one? Could Anna's thesis be only two lines long, say just
that? Could she submit one holograph page of her own loopy
handwriting marked by her own wavering and infinite dashes?

She became perversely proud of it, the Ph.D. dissertation that
went backward year by year toward its own inevitable nonexistence. She fell out of touch with her department, then with her advisor, finally deciding she was incapable of inflicting any part of her
critical stammerings on an unwaiting world. The universe would
be a better place, she knew, if less of this was written. The world
also required fewer books of poetry. It wasn't that poetry shouldn't
be made but that no one else should ever be made to actually look
at it.

At forty Anna still dreamed guilty dreams of what she'd left un-
finished. She dreamed of her advisor, that she saw him in the library and tried to hide within the stacks that were not stacks because
they changed into the showers in the women's gym. Through the
warped optics of the glass bricks, Anna became poisonously objec-
tive. She watched her own naked body go cubist, breaking apart in
a shower stall.

Why had Anna married Charlie? Was it that she once imagined
Charlie's happiness was like a language that he would be able to
teach to her and that it turned out instead to be an aptitude? Like
perfect pitch in music, some people had it, while most did not.

They married, made accommodations to one another, grew older, had a baby who then became a toddler. Then they went to Europe late one summer.

This was the third or fourth of the recent honeymoons given them by his parents as anniversary gifts. The two of them were sitting in a café in Prague eating dinner when Charlie decided it was time to say he'd been having an affair with one of his graduate students.

Anna licked her lips, steadied herself. It wouldn't have been entirely honest to say she was completely shocked by this revelation. Because her sense of smell had become hyperacute when she was pregnant with Maggie, she had on occasion detected a kind of perfume on the tweed of Charlie's jackets that smelled quite a bit like Play-Doh.

She studied the laced fingers of her hands that lay in her lap, palms upward, then looked over Charlie's shoulder in order to catch the eye of the waiter. If this was to be another of those everlastingly introspective evenings, they were going to need another bottle of wine in order to get through it.

This was exactly what he had always loved about Anna, he said, this great calm of hers, her maturity, her self-possession. He didn't actually say "Old Girl," but that did undoubtedly occur to him. This was a crisis surely, but it need not be the end of them. Their baby was two and a half years old—they needed to consider, he supposed, a separation if that's what Anna wanted; they would do whatever Anna wanted, but he wanted really to think long and hard about Maggie. There was the new study on the children of divorce, its long-term consequence. As for the student? Charlie was embarrassed to say he hadn't been in love with her, nor she with him.

Anna was too astonished by all this to know exactly how to respond. She was suffering from a kind of aural reverberation, a bounce, then delay, then echo, that came with extreme self-consciousness in which she had to hear everything she thought of two or three times in an outwardly transmitted ripple.

She might say this or she might say that. If she heard herself speak, she might be able to determine what she actually felt. She thought of saying this: Well, that's good, or she might say, Oh well, too bad, then, for each of you—Anna's tone might be either blithe or sarcastic. What she really wanted to know, of course, was had there been God in it, but this question seemed much more personal than any she might ask about their specific sexual customs and/or practices.

There were gas lamps on the corner and there was hokey Czech folk music tumbling from a staticky speaker and an old Michael Jackson song blasting from the open door of the disco across the cobbled street. This was the New Czech Republic, Anna struggled to remember. All the old names of the same old countries had gone away into the Dark Zone behind the Iron Curtain but now were coming back, just as heroin was back and crack cocaine was back—she'd just read this news in one of her several trashy magazines. Whole countries were rematerializing with the New Nationalism—some had been submerged for generations—yet a blanding was happening in Europe so the countries now seemed to her to have been transported from the different parts of Disneyland.

Anna was having trouble listening. She was thinking of swimming in Sand Pond during summers when she was little and how she had always known beneath knowing that her mother took Anna and her brother Davis up there sometimes to punish their father for things he'd done. She also knew without knowing that it had to do with sex.

Sex was the Dark Zone, was buried in the layers of what was known and what was not known and what was spoken and was not spoken and in this was like the distinct layers of temperature of the water in the pond. The water was meant to remain cold, the dark and secret place. The warm layer was clear; through it the shallows displayed their golden pebbles, and that was where the reeds grew and the babies sat.

The warm layer of water was never more than a foot deep even in August at the peak of summer. The X-shaped insects skated, balanced their infinitesimal weight, the bubbled X's haloed, echoed, on the sand below, held aloft by pods of surface tension—because of waterbugs, X was still one of Anna's favorite letters. Through the clear water the exaggerated shadows of the water-skaters bumped and abruptly moved. It was easy knowledge that lay in the shallows, and this easiness lay atop the deeper water of the quarry. The deeper things were cold, were dangerous. Sex was dangerous, was singular, was why you learned to swim, why you were frightened, why you jumped off the raft and why you disappeared into blackness as you went off and into it.

She was thinking how very much she now wanted to take her own baby daughter and go home to East Eden, except that Anna was ashamed to have made so little evolutionary progress and to do so would mark her forever as her own mother's girl.

She was ashamed of herself, also ashamed of Charlie for being unable to keep his word. He'd promised to change when Maggie was born—she more than half believed him. She forgot the most basic truth of what it meant to grow older: one does not change except to become more intensely what one has always been.

"You're not angry then?" someone asked. It was Charlie. He was here. She'd forgotten all about him.

Angry? Anna wondered. She turned the word over and over, counted its various letters, rubbed it until it became as polished as a river rock. What was he talking about again? She was remembering something else. This was a huge man, both tall and fat, who once danced with her at a roadhouse. This man was maybe forty or even fifty—Anna was not yet seventeen. It was upstate near the border of Canada. She and her mother driving north in her Grandmother Rutherford's big old-fashioned boat of an American car, having left Rhinebeck abruptly. Neither Davis nor Anna's father was with them. They'd been driving aimlessly, heading toward the border, flying northward as if it was as "up" as the way it lay on the flat of the map, having lost all sense of internal gyroscope and with it the natural horizon.

The big man spoke to Anna in French as they danced, spoke suggestively of the things he'd like to do to her. He could not have known how completely she understood him. They danced and Anna was beautiful to him, no longer the tall shy girl with the frizzy hair, no longer awkward in speech or tripping on her size-ten feet. Dancing with that elegant man was like being danced with by the ocean.

Had he simply led her away with him, she would have gone. She would have gone anywhere that night to escape getting back into the car again with her mother's desolation.

"Well, good," Anna told Charlie. She heard the word recede in reverb, going *good! good! good!* This might be a kind of echolocation, she guessed, like the system of sonar used by bats.

She reached over to borrow his reading glasses to look again at dessert—the waiter had taken her plate and she was suddenly starving. "Good," she said again. "That's settled then."

She squinted, looking for a list of pastries—she wanted something *gross*, something that came served *mit Schlag*. Some unspoken cue caused her to look up. She peered over the readers to look at her husband. Was there something wrong with him? There in the *Weinstube* in Prague was the first time Anna could remember ever seeing Charlie look actually frightened.

There was more, evidently, that needed to be said: Charlie hadn't brought this up in order to hurt Anna or cause her distress but because she was going to find out anyway. The girl told her parents, who had threatened Mills with a lawsuit. Mills was arranging her admission at another school, one that was, Charlie said, *really* first-rate, one she probably wouldn't otherwise have been admitted to.

Anna positioned her tongue and lips. She breathed. She was experiencing a moment of hesitation. She needed to spend a couple of moments organizing herself, her internal pacing, commas, periods, and the question marks, how they might pose what kinds of expectations. She was also deconstructing this last part: this current girl's various chances and hopes for advancement and future happiness. And the strange twist of her good fortune. The bend this girl's life road took there when it came to Charlie, that there was this small thing back then that her parents made into this big legalistic deal—though not *serious* in that it barely mattered since no one's heart was broken, the one small irony being that what wrecked her professor's marriage turned out to be her trampoline.

Charlie was going on. The lawyers for Mills were talking to the parents' lawyers and both were talking to those of Charlie's parents. It was Charlie's parents who came up with the idea of the cash settlement for the girl and endowing Mills with the practice rooms.

Anna's mother was a handsome woman, an accomplished pianist and a sophisticated milliner. Margaret wasn't beautiful but was tall and thin and she carried herself well. She had a kind of wry solemnity, Anna thought, as if she had secret value.

Anna was thinking of her mother, how each seemed somehow fated to stand in the rising damp of a cabin in a logged-off hardwood forest picking men who turned out to be as useless as this one. Men like this were nothing special, men like this were a dime a dozen. Anna felt very close to her mother then.

Anna quietly gathered herself, as her mother might have, and stood up from the table. The night was warm. She remembered to take along the cardigan she'd hung on the back of her chair. This sweater had been crocheted by her mother. It was a creamy white and had tiny buttons made of pearls.

Charlie began hurriedly throwing money down on the table. He threw down great bunches of large bills printed in blue on pale pink, and green on pale blue. The paper was as crinkly and thin as the tissue used to wrap Italian almond cookies. These were made of egg white and air and sugar, weighed next to nothing; these, with Jordan almonds, were Anna's mother's favorite sweets. The look and feel of money was simply better in Europe, Anna thought. There were so many kinds of currencies, so many shapes and weights, bills printed so beautifully on so many kinds of paper, yet the global commerce was soon to convert it all to MouskaDollars.

Anna—tall, proud, chin up, back straight—stumbled slightly on the uneven cobblestones. She had gone a ways down the block when he caught up to her. Charlie reached to take her elbow, leaned in, needing to confide something. He needed to tell her this: if Anna was set on walking back to their *pension*, she was going in the wrong direction.

She steadied herself, licked the dryness of her wine-tart lips. Anna too had something she needed to confide. She leaned over to whisper it: "Fuck you," she said.

They were a handsome couple, or so they were always told, and they did mirror one another in a certain way. She saw the two in her mind's eye: blond, large-faced, freckles scattered across their good cheekbones. The clinical name for what was happening to her, Anna remembered, was *disassociation*. Anna and her husband turned, she thought. Anna and her husband began to walk the cobbled streets of this ancient capital back toward their room, which lay in the Dark Zone beyond the thumping disco.

"Excuse me, Charlie?" she asked after another moment. "But do you know what?" His head was down to listen carefully—he was clearly penitential. "You?" He nodded. "Your parents—her parents— that whole sad story?" He nodded. "It's completely sordid." She listened, heard her words veer off, going clipped and strange.

This old and dignified capital had been so carefully rendered in this phony theme park of this jigsaw Europe that the phony flickering gas lamps were turning out to be real. She watched these lamps as they begin to halo. There was a shine on the street and on the sidewalk and on slick wet roofs, which were made of what? Some kind of slate or tile? The shine began to blur, certain places in her vision began to bounce and magnify. She put one hand out, long fingers facing up, to feel if anything was falling. Had it been raining? Anna couldn't remember. The water shortage was so extreme that year in California that half the counties ended the summer in emergency rationing.

"Charlie?" Anna asked after another moment. "You know what else?" He nodded a little too eagerly. "My mother has never liked you." Then she leaned over and, as if to make a physical point of this, she threw up onto his shoes.

7

These Shades Of

Frustrated by the melancholy traces left by his faithless pencil while sketching on the shores of Lake Como. . . .

FILIPPINO LIPPI,
exhibit caption at
The Metropolitan Museum of Art

Ev-ven-ning, Veronique said. Eeeeev-ven-ning, as if it was an even-ing out, the place where light came to its great pause, a halt, a shift, a place the world balanced, waiting before it went ahead and plunged headfirst into

Dusk
Dark
ness

The shades there
of

— 8 —

Laws of Return

ONE SUMMER ALEC and Gina moved with the kids up from Oxford Street; then almost immediately his parents came. The
new house, built only a quarter mile from the strike-slip fault, was
bolted to bedrock, as he pointed out to Stu and Viv. Its idiom was
postmodern, Alec said. Its materials, he told them, were *Wrightian*.
He enunciated as if his parents were hard of hearing. The two of
them were small and sweet and clean; they blinked in stupid uni-
son. The house had been shot for *Architectural Record*, he embarrassed himself by mentioning—this didn't impress them either.

The house was simply perplexing to his father, hidden as it was
up a drive in the center of a block so it didn't even seem to sit on a
real street and did nothing therefore to proclaim itself. Alec could
see Stuart struggling to find adequate words of praise, saying it was
unlike any house he'd ever seen, more like an art museum with the
big rooms and Gina's work put out on the floor around.

"What's the matter with them, Stu?" he heard his mother whisper. "That they don't own furniture? No furniture, no drapes or
curtains, but they have these naked women sitting on the floor with

their legs spread wide?" These were abstract landscapes, actually, hills, valleys, new mountains, the more ancient ones. What threw Viv off was that Gina called the pieces, which were done in rough plaster, *The Great White Nudes.*

It was August, yet his parents went around bundled up indoors, shivering dramatically. Alec once found them sitting in his car, where they had the motor on and the heater going, reading the travel pages of the newspaper as if plotting their escape. They found their son residing with his family in a hardship post, Stu said, in his most smug and jocular tone, the one he got with his degree at Yale. This was Alec's father's little joke; he repeated it to Viv nearly every single day. Ulysses S. Grant's proclaiming San Francisco a hardship post meant he and his men got extra pay when they were stationed at the Presidio. Stuart found this fact by browsing in Alec's life of Grant. Stuart was also reading whole stories from the *Chronicle* aloud to Viv at breakfast so they could laugh together at the ridiculousness of Californians, never mind these were Gina's people. "Oh look, Stu!" Viv said one day. "That must be the mayor!" They were on Telegraph Avenue on their way to a concert at Zellerbach Hall. She was pointing at a barefoot, obese, homeless man sleeping on the sidewalk.

Alec's parents, who once traveled and were sophisticated, now spent their time whispering between themselves about anything unfamiliar—what was the strange orange meat in the Chinese food? They shielded their eyes dramatically from the glare of the afternoon sun glancing off the too-bright bay. Because the house followed the hill's slope, there were a few steps between the two main rooms. Alec's parents couldn't go up or down between the living room or dining room without remarking upon these steps, always in new surprise. More disturbingly, Viv had begun to keep her pocketbook clasped tightly to her side indoors, as if she expected to meet muggers in the hallway.

"That's Mount Tam, Grandma," Cecily pointed out helpfully. "And that's the Golden Gate Bridge." Cecily was so little then, her beauty seemed heartbreakingly pure to Alec—why didn't her grand-parents seem to really *care* for her? Had they become utter narcis-sists, entered the mirror world in which no one else any longer exists? They did now look almost exactly alike. Vivian couldn't get over Cecily's long blond hair, kept asking and asking when she was getting it cut, couldn't believe her granddaughter was allowed to keep rats as pets.

"Oh, I know, dear," Viv sniffed. "And believe me, by my age, if you've seen one mountain, you've seen them all."

His folks sat overbundled with their hands clasped in their laps, bolt upright on the plain, straight-backed Stickley furniture in an attitude of bland endurance. Alec squinted, tried to see the place as they saw it, a trick he used with clients: a house built of rocks and metal and glass, as cold and blinding as a snowstorm. Home, on their tree-lined street in Queens, people sat out on the stoop in shirtsleeves on a summer evening to escape the air-conditioning. Home, there were lightning bugs, robins, real blue jays, the air was thickly humid. In Queens light was soft, old green trees overarched the pavement. The ice-cream truck would be along and Stuart would buy her one.

This was in 1987, a couple of years before the earthquake com-pletely wrecked the transportation systems of the Bay Area, both freeways and public transit. Peter had just been born. Alec had never known such joy as that event aroused—their little family now was mathematically balanced in a way it hadn't been before, and Gina had the second child she so desperately wanted, the baby who canceled the bad reproductive luck she thought she might have in-herited from the unbalanced equation that was her parents's tragic lives.

The house faced the bay, one blank wall sitting recessed behind an apron of glass panels facing the fall-away into the steeper part of the canyon. Alec called the entry the Water Room. He remem-bered the words etched on the first sketches he ever did of this house. The room preexisted in a Platonic sense, it seemed to him—he had simply been always striding ahead into the future in order to discover himself within the room he would one day make.

The room was positioned to catch sharp-edge morning light that poured in as the sun rose over the shaggy treetops. Light pooled, spilled back into the house from a line of interior dormers that ran just below the roofline. The floor was slate, stepped up from the entry door along the angle of the hillside. You stood in the entryway and saw the little creek foreshortened as it came at you, its streamed lined with rocks. The water was then pumped back up again out of the pond, which—he wished he could tell his mother this and have her understand him—said something about what might be known about eternity.

In this pond Carlo's girlfriend, who then became his wife, had planted water lilies. Julie Empy was a landscape architect who had trained with Garrett Eckbo. The entry was an empty box. It held nothing but light and air and the sound of the flowing water. It was in this pond that Alec kept his three meaty carp, large fish that were each astonishingly individual and petlike. The arc of their flashing colors, a yellow gold and a reddish gold and a white that was opalescent, often made Alec feel he was present at a moment of creation.

His mother frowned at the whiskered ones, waved her tiny hand before her face as if to wipe the wet away. She was terrified of rats, fish, all of wild nature, of snakes and bugs and of the savage giantness of a redwood tree. This was the reason Alec and his sister were never allowed a dog when they were growing up, nor a cat, nor even a parakeet. Water running within a house? Viv asked, the baby might totter in and drown.

Alec's house was as pure as koi, he consoled himself. His real father might have admired it had he lived past 1974. His true spiritual father—Alec often almost actually believed this—was the visionary Louis Kahn, the most important American architect since Frank Lloyd Wright, as he tried to instruct his parents. They nodded, their faces poised and blank to show they weren't actually listening. Why was he not Alec Ben Kahn or Alec Son of Rothko (who was born killed) or of Charles Moore, with whom Alec had briefly worked when each of them was at Cal?

His parents liked Alec's house, they said—it just wasn't particularly homey.

"Homey?" Alec choked. This was years later, years even after his father died, but Alec found he was still stung by his father's saying this. He was on the phone to Betsy. They were laughing at their parents. Laughing at their parents was the way the two of them had always kept themselves from going straight to Queens to kill them.

"What can I tell you, Alec?" Betsy asked. "It's ten, eleven years and she's still fussing about the wall-to-wall. She thinks you don't have drapes because you ran out of money." Betsy and her husband lived out in Riverhead. Betsy and Ben had the wall-to-wall. "She worries people across the way could look in and see her use the toilet."

"Homey?" Alec said again. Tears of sick mirth stood in his eyes. Alec objected to just exactly that blend of schmaltz and wishfulness. The experience of *home* or *homeland* might come to those who were particularly blessed. Jews, however, had such a talent for exile that the memory of loss seemed to him to be embedded within their bones. Everyone in Berkeley, aside from Gina, had moved here from somewhere else, many from far-off countries.

Alec hated the way a word like "home" or "family" was warped the way a logo was by computer graphics, twisted, whizzed away by clients who were veering off into the purest state of self-delusion. Clients came to him insisting on a *study* in which they would never read a book or even manage a moment to quietly sit. Everyone these days was too busy being gone, out making money or writing the screenplay for the movie of the story of their own lives.

Alec was a big man, nearly six feet three. He often scaled rooms outward from the sense of his own anatomy—he made rooms big enough to accommodate his stride and physical restlessness. This was to relieve him of the Queensish feeling of having the ceiling come down on him. He and Gina furnished the rooms of their house slowly, sparingly, with a few good things that having little kids wouldn't immediately wreck. Alec needed the sense of open spaces, needed to continue to witness the terrain and vistas, access, egress. These were what Moore called the spiritual matters of architecture, those concerning *path* and *axis*. How people might come and go within a room, how they might actually sit and breathe and read and be alive in one.

Try as they did, his parents were too old to ever learn the map of his house and so seemed to wander in that place as if they'd been lost for days.

Alec had always been a good student, never got in much trouble. He was a citizen, a mensch, had always been their good and loving son who was dutiful and never fucked around much but had kept his head down and had worked hard and had achieved much of what he'd set out for himself—his work and getting to see something of the world. He married, had two children, including the son that would carry on his father's, okay goyish, name. He was hardworking, a good provider, had stayed married when it might have been easy enough for him to have found the reasons not to, but all this just wasn't *homey* enough for Stu and Viv? It occurred to him he may have stayed with Gina in order to somehow spite them.

The two always subtly blamed Gina for whatever lack of the domestic touch they missed, usually something as cornball as tea towels embroidered with the Hebrew letters *"chai,"* or that there were the wrong birds on this side of the Rockies. This was because Gina was an orphan and wasn't Jewish.

Or there may have been some tiny precipitating event, something about how Gina had once worn a sheer nightie down the hall on 219th to use the toilet without pulling a bathrobe on—his parents were both dumbstruck by her immodesty. "Oh hi, folks," she said sleepily as she passed the open door to their bedroom. She was full-bellied, hugely pregnant, exhibited no shame in it.

"What can I tell you?" Viv told Alec's sister. "She's from *California*." Betsy, who may have been ambivalent before, became, at that moment, Gina's most staunch defender.

The house was acclaimed both for the purity of its design and for the theoretical efficiency of its energy use. It was heated by a system of water pipes running beneath the hardwood floors. The designer of this particular heating system was Frank Lloyd Wright, but Alec's parents had already dismissed him from any importance since, unlike Kahn, he lacked the requisite Jewishness.

The house was cold because its systems worked imperfectly— Alec went back to the drawing board, above which he had push-pinned this, his own carefully written-out motto which was DON'T SELL THE BIKE SHOP, ORVILLE. He worked patiently. Alec was nothing if not patient, if patient in a few matters only. This was one: the time and money and psychological distance it took to build a real house, a real house being one that actually *deserved* to exist and take up space in an already too-crowded world. A real house was one that had achieved its own perfection. Often it was very simple. Alec didn't actually believe in perfection but thought of it as he did the Unified Field Theory—he'd bet a lot of money the Unified Field was never going to happen.

Alec saw the house broken back down again into its elements: the softest graphite riding the smoothest sheet of vellum. As long as Alec lived and drew breath, there was still the possibility of actually achieving an exquisite balance of planes and shapes and formulae, and this lay in the same place off where the quantum met the Theory of Relativity, Hawking and Einstein touched, meshed. Everyone would know the moment though no one would at first believe it, just as Newton didn't actually believe anyone sound of mind could believe in the Laws of Gravity. The truth in math could, however, be proved and proved and proved. Jerry Bloom said they'd most likely find the Theory of Everything by looking in an unlikely place. How Alec loved all math, particularly geometry and trigonometry, how he hoped to believe these manmade languages spoke of rules that accurately described the structure of the universe, as gravity did, in that it could be proved and proved and proved. It was this he loved, the theoretical rush of a torrent of light just as it struck the three-dimensional.

He imagined the house just as he had once dreamed it: a simple set of luminous volumes floating behind the oaks as seen from the road downhill. The house showed only on the private side, turning its back to the public street in a manner that was both Mexican and Japanese. Descartes looped up around the hill behind his house, dead-ending at the Blooms' and the Chakravartys', whose houses sat on the cul-de-sac.

He saw the house to be as elemental as the perfect chair he had not yet designed but might one day, the old joke being that the most brilliant of architects was incapable of making a chair that not only looked good in a room but was actually comfortable for a human being to sit in. A chair had every physical and aesthetic problem pared down, reduced to simple form: context, balance, materials, scale, all the problems in the physics of stress and of fabrication. Most chairs, if not purely imitative, were simply breathtaking in their ugliness. The comfortable chair often looked as ridiculous as a Laz-E-Boy.

Perfecting the systems took Alec and Carlo almost eighteen months. Carlo was a saint; he had also trained at M.I.T. in structural engineering. The floorboards came up; the pipes were then relaid. He and Gina and the kids camped out on the lower level during the mess of reconstruction—this space would later replace the place on McGee Avenue that she was using as her studio. McGee was Gina's house when she was growing up.

Finally, the concrete was poured again, the floorboards reset. It was a wonderful house, was acclaimed as such. People wanted one—this surprised him since Alec had such a generalized contempt for so much of the taste of his fellow man. He and Carlo went on to build similar houses in the hills of Oakland and Orinda. There was one in Marin County, another larger one faced north in

Encino, overlooking the San Fernando Valley, this one done for a movie star. The glow at night could be seen for miles.

The Baxter House had been perfected, but that ruined first visit was the last trip his father ever made to Berkeley, a place so Bad for the Jews that Stuart would evermore refuse to come.

Irrational Numbers

ALEC CLIMBED THE slow slope of his hill, thinking of the beauty of the most simple physics, of how he might have built his house before the Industrial Revolution, before the Age of the Machine, how the pharaohs had built the pyramids using only levers and the inclined plane and the sweating deaths of a million slaves.

He was walking home from the bus stop down on Shattuck Avenue as he did every evening—he walked in order to keep his heart and lungs in good working order. He also liked the speed of walking, that it took his mind home at the same slow pace as his moving limbs so all of him arrived more or less together. The wisdom of slow locomotion, Alec knew, was what the Amish practiced. Stuart's mother, Grandma Leah, born in Minsk, once traveled to Lebanon, Pennsylvania, and there mistook the Amish for Orthodox Jews and so spoke to them in Yiddish.

Alec was fit but not lean, as Gina recently told him. She went to the gym to work out to get the job more quickly done. His wife simply had *no time*, as she had started to exclaim. His wife, these days, had infinite things to do on her path to some kind of high art righteousness.

Alec had a Fiat Sport in the carport but didn't drive it much. The model was no longer imported from Italy, so its parts were hard to come by and the car was now so old and frail it seemed increasingly precious to him.

His house sat at the end of the curving drive, lying above a line of trees—stands of pine and oak and eucalyptus—in the cleft of two small rises. It was built back into the hillside on two pieced-together lots, lots so steep they were hitherto deemed unbuildable by the City of Berkeley. The house wasn't so much on the hill as of it, as Wright would say.

Alec and Carlo had to work for more than two years in order to get a variance. "All right, Alec," Carlo said at one point. "You're American, you tell me—who is it I must sleep with in order to get this done?" Carlo, half-Italian, half-British, was born in Surrey, educated at Oxford. He was likable and handsome, the shining, affable partner who presented well, leaving Alec to loom and brood, bite the earpiece of his glasses, grunt, yank his hair.

The glass panels hung before the concrete like a curtain. The concrete walls had been tinted Haze Blue, the surface then burnished to a sheen like the final bright etch of sun clearing away the last licks of fog. Alec had always loved this color. It lay, in both hue and saturation, very close to the metallic paint on the undercarriage of a B-52 bomber—Gina called it camouflage. The house was best at night with everyone at home, when the gray was warmed by incandescent floods. He imagined swooping in, flying toward it, seeing it as another might.

When he was able to imagine it like this, Alec could almost believe in its reality, could imagine it did cohere and that it was more than the sum of the materials and labor costs, that it did rise up and look effortless. It looked effortless, he thought, to everyone but him. Bolted to bedrock, safe as a bunker, he wanted his house to seem to accelerate.

Alec stopped on Spruce to look up past the treetops to pray, Please, God, might I get liftoff? He didn't believe in God any more than he believed in perfection or the answer at the end of the square root of two, yet did half-expect God somehow to signal him, for his house to appear to magically levitate as the Taj Mahal is said to do at dawn.

The house was dark, heavy, his dread set in. His mother was in there, visiting. This would be her last trip west. His mother was a nightmare, a sump hole in the Universe. The evening before, upon arriving, she started right in. Viv tipped up her long beak of an aristocratic nose, sniffed at the barrenness of floors, the old and threadbare kelims, the bayside wall of windows. She had been a redhead and her nose was still dramatically freckled. It had grown such knobs and knuckles it now resembled one of her twisted fingers. Herself the daughter of a prosperous butcher and more than a little spoiled, Viv pitied Gina for being an orphan, an urchin, but once kept this more to herself. The night before at dinner, Viv began to rehearse the old complaints, that Gina hadn't even owned a good winter coat until Alec came along and bought her one. The kids looked startled; Gina smiled brightly, bitterly, at Viv's condescension.

With the New Haven relatives, Betsy said, Viv could really get going, that Gina went barefoot in all weather—not her fault, no one raised her, what with the mother dying when she was young and the father being a drunk. And this was why Gina didn't know any better than to nurse the babies in public restaurants.

Alec let himself into a darkened house—Gina clearly had taken the kids and fled. The kitchen was cold; it smelled of apples. Why couldn't he and Betsy have had a dog when they were kids, why couldn't they have had real parents?

He found his mother in the living room staring bewilderedly out the window, back on the drapes again, wanting him to help her with the measurements. The sunset across the bay was gaudy and lovely, exactly the kind of thing Viv would somehow find offensive. Viv asked after Alec's *girlfriend*—girlfriend or boyfriend is what Viv called Gina or Ben when she, for whatever reason, preferred to pretend not to remember the names of the people her children had married.

"Ma?" Alec asked. "This isn't about Geee-nah." He said it very carefully, letting his hand sweep through fading light. "Ma? This is how we like it. I mean the both of us." His chest felt so constricted with anger he could barely manage to let the words go.

Viv squinted, peered up at Alec. How could two neat, nearly matching people have produced this hulk? At thirteen Alec towered over them. By fourteen he was so tall he'd begun to shadow corners. It was then Alec had begun to feel hunched and odious in his little mother's presence, as if he bore no physical relationship to her tidy person. Alec very much wanted her to talk about something, anything, aside from Gina, so he wouldn't have to hate her. New Haven in the old days when she went to the movies at Jimmy's Nickolette?

Stuart was dead, the house completed years before. What was wrong with his mother that she had to keep having the one same conversation? She kept complaining about Cecily having rats when she hadn't had rats for years.

"Hey, Ma?" he asked. "How long have you and I been acquainted?"

"Oh, I don't know, Alec," Viv said. She seemed irritated at being pinned down like this. "Maybe a dozen years by now?"

Alec was forty-seven years old. He guessed Viv was kidding, though his parents were too carefully behaved and Yaley to have ever come up with much of a sense of humor. He walked quickly to the study, where Betsy was on autodial. He wanted to tell her he figured their parents were clinical narcissists, that this is why the two of them had to raise themselves. He also wanted to check a few things out with her. There was the matter of Viv's sense of time, that it fell away into absurdities, that she seemed so out of context. He also needed to ask his sister if her little girls had helped with their grandma's packing.

When Vivian arrived the day before, Alec hoisted her bag off the luggage carousel at SFO, making the exaggerated grunt meant to impress his mother with how hard he always worked and how well he had succeeded against such great odds. She hummed to herself tunelessly, as usual, stared off, as usual, in her superior rich girl's way.

Alec hoisted the bag. It was huge yet weighed next to nothing. It came off the carousel effortlessly, wanting to fly into orbit in an arc way ahead of its plastic handle.

Once in the parking structure, he stashed his mother in the front seat, leaning forward to belt her in when she couldn't work the mechanism. Her bad breath had taken on its own menacing proportions. He shut the car door, went then to shove her luggage into the back of the station wagon.

These were old-fashioned hard-sided bags made of cardboard printed like leather, then plasticked, both cases now badly gouged and dented. The basement on 219th was full of cheap crap like this—Alec's father would buy set after set of luggage, essentially throwing away his money, refusing to ever invest in a single handsome piece. Why? Because, Alec, if you have something good, they know by that and *that's* when they rob you. These had to be the oldest ones, suitcases with steamship stickers that showed they'd taken Stu and Viv to pre-Castro Cuba, to Bermuda and to Europe when it was cheap, more places than Alec would get Gina to ever go.

They were Road Runner cartoon bags, weightless as Wile E. Coyote before Isaac Newton came to believe in gravity and therefore defiant of all haptic expectation. Her luggage, made of paper, was filled with nothing.

Alec clicked one case open to make certain his mother's things had not actually been stolen. In the overnight bag were a few old underclothes, a strange spiderwork of twisted and yellowed bras. In the other, bigger suitcase someone equally demented had packed a few old towels wrapped around a red-waxed ten-pound brick of Poverty Program cheese, date stamped from when Stuart was still alive.

"Mom?" Alec said.

—— 10 ——

Robbing the House

THE EAST WAS thick with humidity and guilt. In Berkeley, you
didn't go by that. If you were guilty or felt ashamed, you just
spent more money on therapy in order to get over it.

Alec had himself recently done a few bad things, but because he
had Fran Bloom to confess to, he didn't need therapy. He had, for
instance, started stealing from his parents' house on 219th whenever he went home to visit. He'd taken a crystal decanter from his
mother's sideboard just the week before. This wasn't something he
could really tell anyone.

He and his sister had each agreed to reclaim the book or clock
or the milkware pitcher they'd given their parents as presents over
the years. They accomplished that much, then stopped, so much of
the stuff in their parents' house being so bad neither of them really
wanted it.

But this was new, Alec's stealing his parents' actual objects. It
started when he realized his mother no longer possessed the self
with which she might really own something, either to keep it or to
give away. In this she was like an infant, or less than an infant,

really, since a baby would still be attached to its mother or bottle or blanket. Viv was out there now floating umbilically in the ether of disinterest. She still had style, gesture, but lacked the weight of ego heavy enough to achieve either desire or possessiveness.

"I guess I'll take this then, Ma, if you're sure you don't need it?" He waved the decanter her way, nonchalantly. It was dusty, filled with soured wine.

Viv had come downstairs while he was robbing the sideboard and was staring at him from the living room, needing . . . ? she stopped, moved her hands up and down in front of herself in order to try to complete the faltering thought. She seemed bewildered by Alec's question, both bewildered and annoyed. Why was he bothering her like this when she had more important things on her mind?

Her modesty having left her, Viv now stood before her son in only a bra and a pair of torn and baggy pantyhose held together at the one big rip in the calf with a rusted paper clip. She had on lace-up walking shoes. He tried not to notice how the see-through nylon matted her thin gray pubic hair. When Alec mentioned that he thought she *might* have been looking for her dress, she stared at him dismissively. "What I need," she said, "is my nightingale." Her hat, as always, sat at a jaunty angle.

He and Betsy had been interviewing people to live in. The women who wanted this job appeared to each of them to be so obviously bored or criminal, so emotionally ill or mentally deficient they seemed of a lesser order than those who make a life's work of passionately grooming dogs. His sister found someone who was adequate, and in so doing redefined the word *adequate*.

Alec flew home sadly, carrying the decanter on his lap. He and Carlo had been using the Duct Tape Airline because their offices had become somehow entwined in the complications of its frequent-flier program. They found themselves, therefore, flying in and out of the most cracked and broken parts of airports, places that seemed much less than First World. The Employee-Owners of TWA had also just added another row of seats, he noticed, making the cabin so small Alec had to get a bulkhead seat in order to fit his legs in. He was going to have to begin to upgrade to First Class. This would cost him some of the miles he'd been trying to save for a vacation.

He'd only set the decanter down on the floor for a single moment to go to the toilet, but while he was gone one of the Employee-Owners rammed the decanter with her drink cart. She'd smacked it, took a chip out of it; still, it hadn't broken. It was good stuff, cut crystal, heavy, leaded, not pressed glass. His father came up a bit in Alec's estimation.

Home, Alec filled it with a good amontillado. He liked an excellent sherry now and then when he came in from work.

It was Alec's now, yet his father hadn't actually given it to him. He drank too much one evening while brooding on the death of cities—Gina was out at an opening, Cecily gone, Peter on an overnight—why was no one ever home anymore? He needed to call his sister, needed to have a nice long talk with her. He had this specific guilt: his grave-robbing, his vulturing of the not-yet-dead. He hit her button on autodial, then—realizing how late it would be for her—began to hang up, but Betsy had already answered.

"You what?" she asked.

He began again to recite the story—it was circular and he hadn't quite come to the point of it—when his sister cut him off. "Alec, do you understand that you just woke me up in order to tell me something so trivial that it is putting me back to sleep just listening to it? Where's Gina? Tell her to make you go to bed."

"But it's probably *worth* something," Alec whispered. "This isn't the usual junk Pop would get. It's nice, maybe even a gift from somebody high up in Housing?"

"Alec, listen to me carefully. This is anxiety talking. Anxiety is the modern malady. My doctor suggests half a Xanax, a cup of hot tea, two cookies, to be followed by a good night's sleep. My doctor talks like this." She was talking very fast. "You're my brother and I love you and I honestly mean this so listen to me carefully: *I don't care*. I have three kids, plus Ben, plus Mom, plus the girl at Mom's who isn't fat like we thought but is soon to become what used to be called an Unwed Mother so I don't want anything else, all right? So you have Pop's whachacallit, so keep it, all right? So we settled that, so I love you and now I'm hanging up."

Alec listened to the dial tone for a little while before remembering what it was he had meant to say. The curt voice of the woman he most especially hated came on to nag and vex him: *If you wish to make a call, please do so. Please hang up and dial again.*

It was so simple to dial Betsy, he felt so close to her—just the single button, the long-distance dialing system beamed up and down from the satellite. He admired the way it worked instantly, gathered no time to it, took nothing like the decades that used to erode when he was leaning over his desk, frowning down, patting his head and various pockets to try to find his glasses, laboriously dialing this number and then this number on the rotary—years fell away while he waited for the return after a nine or a zero.

Alec punched, got the little snatch of now-familiar music that spelled his kid sister's number out. He'd made her life miserable when they were growing up. He was so sorry now—he was a nice person, a good person, he adored his little sister. He was proud of her and grateful—how had he forgotten to mention this? Betsy was curly-headed, tomboyish, a little bug-eyed, smart-mouthed. Growing up, she'd hung around him all the time. He was constrained by his father from ever belting her, though it often occurred to him. He had swatted her a few times; she had always yakked at him, talked with her mouth full. She also lied. She had actually been as annoying as an insect.

He was talking into the lightweight plastic of the handset—the phone felt ridiculous in his clutching hand. "But she might miss it," he whispered. "Since it was Pop's," he added.

"Know what, Alec?" Betsy asked. "She doesn't miss anything. She doesn't miss you and she doesn't miss me. The other day when I took her grocery shopping on Hillside Avenue, she tried to pay the cabbie with the red of her dialed-out lipstick. Only, know what? I'm telling you this, then I'm hanging up. The cabbie was Ben and the taxi was our station wagon." She hung up.

Alec held the buzzing nothing of the (*wait, wait*) telephone.

He was remembering the last time he took his mother out to lunch at that fish place in Queens Village he'd been to a hundred times, the name of which now escaped him. She shook out her napkin, placed it in her lap fastidiously. His mother still had lovely manners. She looked around the room in her superior way, then leaned forward confidentially. She reached out one hand, Alec took it.

It was a strange object, this hand, large and out of scale against his mother's shrinking body. The fingers stuck out almost directly from her palm, which emerged flipperlike from her wrist, each segment going off at what seemed like an increasingly useless angle.

She pressed her lips together, nodded at what the waiter had set before her, winked to show Alec she was no one's fool. This was a plain salad of lettuce and tomato with Thousand Island.

Viv watched the waiter leave, then leaned forward to ask Alec something. Her face was humorous, even wise. He leaned forward eagerly—now she was going to tell him something. "Alec," she asked, "say again? What's the name of what I'm eating?"

11

Chemical Sugar

TIME FELL AWAY in chunks big as islands, the globe was warming, Antarctica's ice shelves breaking off entirely and floating away so the microscopic life forms might try all over in order to get it right this time. Alec sat in his Le Corbusier chaise in a darkening room, thinking of various women.

He thought of women in the East, how they softened and their hips spread, how they had once seemed so womanly to him. In Berkeley, women remained tense, wise-mouthed girls of forty, who all seemed poised in the act of still becoming. They were all potential runaways, all still climbing out the bedroom window of their father's house on the way to meet someone down at the 7-Eleven.

Women had certain problems. It was up to Alec and Carlo to listen very carefully to these problems, then offer the wise solution. It was the duty of the architect to find the artistic answer, then express it in the practical world. These women wanted certain things, got them, wanted other things. They wanted an entirely new house that would contain no impress of the controlling fuckhead they'd just been married to.

Alec looked away from this client—rich, beautiful, under-dressed, and over forty—to glance at Carlo. Carlo would not look back at him. Each had learned not to move a muscle of his face when one of their prospective clients made this kind of announcement. A woman such as this did not need to be encouraged to elaborate. She elaborated. In her new house she needed a special nook in which to achieve her yogic moment. She crossed and uncrossed her long, very well tanned legs. She leaned forward to tell them this: she now found exercise to be more pleasurable than sex ever had been.

Houses, kitchens had now achieved a pushed and stagy valence, with black rock and pink marble and wild cutaways done in the dulled and gorgeous shine of the newest metal, which was titanium. The kitchen was one topic that often came up hot. No longer was it necessarily a woman's job to cook for her family—she might become offended if this was even suggested. One was not to assume, however, that she wasn't an excellent cook. She was very good at cooking, at household, at everything, and she was going to come back and cook very brilliantly again right after she lost those last few pounds.

Gina's own meals had become like art lately, taking on a certain As-If quality, while having departed the realm of taste and sustenance. This came from working on the Video Family—her love for this project—she called it "Bungalow"—was so intense, her love for her own family paled by comparison. The muscles in his face grew so heavy when he gazed down at Gina's food that she snapped at him. "Stop that, Alec, it's just insulting."

"This is good," one of Gina's women had recently said about whatever it was Gina was currently passing around at one of her many parties.

"It is not," Alec countered. "It isn't *good* and it isn't really food. It's much too vivid to be food. It's a Serving Suggestion, it's made of Animal Screams. Time goes, *et voilà!* We are arrived at the *heure* of lay DIN-nay. It's the Dinner Hour, so get the fuck out of my house." Alec did not, of course, actually say any of this aloud.

Animal Screams were the simulated, very lifelike recordings of the stuck-in-the-sludge woolly mammoths and saber-toothed tigers he and Peter heard at La Brea Tar Pits. These screams were activated by pressing an innocent-seeming button—the screams were so immediate and real it did seem to be a matter of life and death, and Alec's heart beat hard and fast in response to them. It was terrible to hear these mammals going extinct, mammals gone extinct being the animals with which Alec had always most closely identified.

Gina—who began art school as a printmaker, became a painter, then a sculptor of plaster and fiberglass and metals—was working in mixed media now. What most bothered Alec was that Gina had begun to incorporate "text" in this new project. The real meals she cooked had become something like text; they were like the food she might serve to the host of her simulacra, *les produits chimiques,* food styled on tape loop, cooked up of ephemera, done in the vast elsewhere, made—like the chemical sugars that Cecily wouldn't allow anyone to use since they were tested on animals—to closely imitate the Good and True. Was their marriage good and true? Alec could no longer tell.

Dinner had somehow turned into a joke on dinner. Peter dreamed off, ate nothing that anyone could discern, becoming quietly terrified of various mundane things that had always been around. Cecily was loud, her manners slovenly. Gina did nothing anymore to unite their household, was herself a vacancy. She was always rushing through dinner, it seemed to Alec, so she could get back to work. She was working on her installation, videoed faces shot from stills in ragged scrapbooks and projected on the stuffed heads of muslin dummies that had been positioned in lifelike rooms, was preoccupied, seemed gone before she was even gone.

"Mom!" Cecily would yell at her, "Hey, Mom! Remember me? I'm your daughter, you know, your *real* one?"

Gina was short-tempered, huffy about the needs they had—here she was trying to *do* something, and they kept treating her like the mother ship where they came to get supplies. Why weren't they becoming more self-sufficient? She was sick of being indispensable. Here were three able-bodied people who lived and breathed and spoke and ate, all sucking up huge quantities of food and milk by the way but increasingly unable to help around the house. When she was Cecily's age. So forth.

Gina recently weighed a bag of groceries on the bathroom scale, multiplied that by the approximate number of bags consumed per week over the years of their marriage, stuck her computations on a Post-it on the door of the Sub-Zero, her on-site mothering expressed in a matter of tons. Gina began to let houseplants die. She did this, it seemed to Alec, by aggressively withdrawing all nurturing. "You're supposed to talk to plants," he suggested. "You're supposed to give them a little spritz or something." She gave him a withering look, got up to leave the room— she had more important things to do. "Go spritz yourself," she said as much to him as to the ficus.

She was just on the verge of something. She had almost achieved something she'd worked so long and hard for—naturally this was the exact moment her family would decide to collectively decompensate. The kids were both awful, but Alec was worse, frankly, the way he sniffed a bottle of milk suspiciously before he poured, just as his mother always had to demonstrate her ability to *discern*.

She needed time, Gina said. If someone bumped into her in the house, she snapped, just a minute before the question had yet been asked. When Cecily went downstairs to hang out with her after school, Gina told her to go back up, to do her homework, to learn to work more independently. Peter was booked into infinite classes, had something going every day after school. Gina needed time, space. They were impossible to cook for, with Cecily, who was vegetarian, having to vet ingredients written on the side of the package looking for Pony Hoofs and Parts of Kitten, and Peter becoming phobic about the garbage disposal and afraid of clowns and of the shoe store and eating nothing, even rice, without considering each grain's place in the cosmic suffering. Was Peter going to turn out to be one of those spooky little Berkeley kids, Gina asked, who chewed the buttons off his shirts? If so, he was obviously getting this from his neurotic Jewish side.

"Clearly," Alec said, "since *your* family exhibited such a pure mental health pedigree."

Privacy while she worked seemed absolutely necessary. It was the constant interruptions, the phone, the vibes of people right upstairs just waiting to interrupt her. She needed to move off-site. She decided to rent studio space away from the house. She needed this space and much more uninterrupted time than had ever been allowed her. She needed to scale back, lead less of a big life. Alec didn't mention that the source of much of their big life was Gina herself. When Alec asked what she wanted for her birthday, Gina said: time out. She looked at him in her level way. I mean this, Alec, she said. I want the entire month of May.

So she rented a loft in Emeryville, a place where she could walk to get a latte at Carrera's. Carrera's had great panini.

And this broke Alec's heart a little—he'd already bought her an espresso machine for her birthday—it was hidden in the carport where he kept the regular gifts and the backup gifts for when she or Cecily didn't really like something. Alec could usually tell. Peter, being a boy, was much easier to shop for. The espresso machine was restaurant-quality, Italian, gorgeous really, and expensive, copper and stainless steel.

Time passed, Alec's life was falling away. He was lulled now, waiting, keeping the home fires burning. Marriage was a long-range bombing mission; he was listening to the drone of engines. He was actually proud of her and of this determination—it was the hallmark of Gina's character, had kept her going in circumstances that might have destroyed a weaker person.

Alec was proud of what they had, two great kids, this house, two full-blown careers. They'd survived Timmy, survived fifty-seven straight days of rain, also mudslides, earthquake and now the latest wildfire that might have taken their own hillside. If their house had been lost, as Carlo and Julie's was, ten years of Gina's artwork would have gone up with it. She was moving her art onto the flats, out of the fire zone, down to where the next big quake might bury it.

Alec settled in. He listened to jazz on the radio, to Coltrane on vinyl, to the hiss of the needle whispering across those ancient grooves of a record that he'd nearly played white. He waited for her in the living room as he watched the sun go down, thinking vaguely of other women.

— 12 —

Technically Daylight

W[HAT ONE DID] in order to demonstrate that you were a successful Berkeley couple, Anna noticed, was manage to stay together long enough to get the family's portrait done by Elizabeth Smythe and therefore have irrefutable evidence. Elizabeth Smythe was a good photographer whose work completely lacked the irony Anna believed was probably necessary to endure life in these last few years of the twentieth century.

Anna was getting a very good chance to study the work of Elizabeth Smythe as she sat outside across the street from the photographer's studio on Hopkins Street. It was four o'clock—for nearly two hours Anna had been waiting in the rain. She was on the sidewalk under the covered awning of the bakery, sitting on a damp wrought-iron café chair. This was exactly the kind of chair her mother had in the kitchen in the cabin at Sand Pond.

Sitting upright in the wobbling chair reminded her of the humid summer evenings when the cabin became unbearable and Anna's brother had taken the car somewhere and her father was still in town. The men in her family were usually out while she and her mother stayed home with their books and sewing. This seemed then like a matter of choice—each was socially reticent, each superior, believing they were probably at least as interesting as whosoever else they might have gone out to see and needed then to talk to.

Anna and her mother would drag the kitchen chairs out onto the screened porch to sit in the thick night air, to drink limeade and read companionably. They read Marianne Moore aloud or Pound or H.D., and Anna, who hadn't set out to be a poet, sometimes thought she'd been made into one by the strength of her mother's hopes for her.

Because her mother was Yankee and being Yankee was like religion, the chairs the Bells sat in were always churchlike and strictly upright.

The cabin was in what was left of a logged-off forest, the pond formed by the digging of a limestone quarry. The heavy air in the larch and hemlocks was alive with the rolling blink and scream of electric insects. Anna listened hard, hard, trying to pierce the deafening, straining to hear something beyond that mechanical whirling. The noises of the night seemed to be set out in a formal code.

Anna was on Hopkins Street waiting for Triple A, her old car having broken down once again. The battery was dead; she was also locked out of it. She had nothing to read, no money to spend on a coffee at the bakery, no checkbook to balance, no pen or small scrap of paper on which to write a suicide haiku. She'd been flustered by the engine's refusal to turn over, had left her keys and bag lying in Maggie's car seat when she went in to call emergency roadside service. She had locked the doors in the dazed automatic state she often found herself in *those* days. Veronique pronounced the phrase "*these* days" as "*those* days" for some reason no one had never been able to figure out. The phrase as Veronique said it did impart a funereal sense that seemed to Anna to properly fit the present moment.

She'd called Veronique for help, but she wasn't home or wasn't picking up. This meant Ravi was traveling—Veronique became mysteriously unreachable whenever Ravi was traveling. Veronique did this, she said, in order to heighten her allure.

If the pond of Anna's childhood once offered the temptation of nonexistence, she seemed to stand on that same sand these days, watching ripples of diamonds beckon to her. She had, at times, the most profound sense of being *no one* aside from her daughter's mother and her mother's daughter. Through the process of divorce she was losing the accouterments of Somebodyness—money, property, husband. Anna imagined this being *no one* happened to poets more easily than it did to other people—it was occupational, that poets remained permeable, open to their surroundings. Marianne Moore once wrote in a letter to Elizabeth Bishop: "Even just standing still and refusing to disappear is one's greatest triumph of fortitude."

The faces in the photographs across the street were having a too-strong effect on her, Anna noticed, reminding her of the strong ones who taunted her for stuttering when she was a kid. These portraits were big, self-congratulatory. It was color work, photographs of weddings, of new well-rested moms and dads with their tidy babies—everyone good-looking and happy and prosperous, it was a matter of Trickle Up. These weren't the kinds of people who would be susceptible to psychological disintegration—their flesh was ample, too well fed and solid. They undoubtedly owned the things they imagined might save them.

When was it, by the way, that everyone began to look so Republican?

"Large Bad Painting," Anna said aloud. It was the name of one of Bishop's poems. If her mother were there, she would understand exactly what Anna meant. If Margaret were there, she would arch an eyebrow and say, Nice enough, I suppose, if you happen to *care* for that kind of thing.

Anna stood up, forced herself to move, to go back to the real estate office to borrow the phone again. She called Julie Empy to say she was still waiting for the towtruck; Julie brought Maggie home with her from nursery school to play with her own daughter.

Anna stared at the snapshots of houses in the real estate display. All houses in Berkeley—and these houses were nothing special—

seemed to cost half a million dollars. This news gave her the same dizzying feeling she sometimes got when she stood up too quickly. She went back to sit outside under the awning to watch for the tow truck.

Their own house and the price it might or might not bring was a matter of contention in the divorce, as was every other thing she and Charlie had ever owned, including this old and broken car. This was a sixteen-year-old Suburban in two colors of dirt, a relic built to run on leaded gasoline. It was a heap, as everyone kept saying—still, Anna wanted it. She was used to this car, understood the kinds of demands it made—it suited her in the way her own clothes did. She didn't understand why she kept having to keep explaining this to Charlie and to Charlie's lawyer and to her own lawyer, all of whom looked at her as if she was childlike and hence pathetic.

Though it was technically daylight, the day was suddenly dark as Prague. Anna tried actively to believe in her mother's Episcopalian God. She tried to imagine the earth as her mother's God might see it—He lived off in the leafy precincts of heaven, out beyond any place so far detected by the Hubble telescope in its travels, in the spheres beyond the stars.

Anna imagined the spreading light of the world's cities, the glow made fuzzy by the glaze of dust and the smoke of forest fires and all the industrial pollutants—smog softened, made light diffuse, as did the ice on the inside of an incandescent bulb. This gauzy curtain would work both ways, she knew, as the combined lights of the world's merging cities worked to eliminate all visible starshine. What people did in the terrestrial realm would become increasingly hidden from His eyes.

——— 13 ———

Suicide Haiku

CHARLIE SHAY STILL stopped by without calling, entered without knocking. Oh, he might tap once as a courtesy before letting himself in with his own key. And why not? The house still legally belonged to him and he had maintenance to perform. His synthesizing and recording equipment was all still set up out back in his soundproofed studio, waiting for him to move it. Anyway, Charlie's wife had never been the kind of person who had anything much to hide, which was, Anna guessed, probably at least half their problem.

"How many feminists does it take to screw in a lightbulb?" Charlie asked her pleasantly. He was standing on the pie table in the middle of the kitchen changing the overheard bulb to a one-hundred-watt. Anna was watching from the doorway. She was wearing her bathrobe, had her arms across her chest in what she hoped was obvious belligerence. Her chest, her entire body, seemed suddenly light and huge, so filled was she with luminous rage. What if Anna preferred her kitchen dim?

She was having a very hard time not speaking out in defense of her costume, her wattage, her basal metabolism. It was the weekend, after all. She and Maggie slept in—what business of his was this? They slept in, then had a little breakfast, then Maggie sat down to watch cartoons while Anna went back upstairs to work. Her *working* explained why they were still in nightclothes though it was nearly one in the afternoon, not that she owed Charlie any sort of explanation.

"That's right, Edith," he said. "The right answer is, *That's not funny.*" Charlie pronounced the name Aay-dit, as in Edith Piaf. He sometimes called Anna his Little Sparrow to kid her about her height and that she had no singing voice.

She smiled up at him on the pie table in her most thin and brittle way. Charlie was such a good sport, he joked and teased, which he honestly believed was affectionate. During the week, Anna and Charlie were engaged in complicated and acrimonious divorce negotiations. During the weekends, however, when he cheerfully came over to pick up his daughter, they were still best of friends so he often stayed for a cup of coffee. They were best of friends though Anna couldn't actually stand the sight of him.

Charlie came, Charlie went—his life had never been so uncomplicated. Charlie was a twentieth-century man completely unburdened by the weight of an unconscious—he was pre-Freudian, as he was quick to say. He couldn't *see* the unconscious, wasn't literary, wasn't interested in pausing long enough to witness its effects. Charlie was simply simple, had no tragic flaw, spent no time and effort being in turmoil as Anna had always been.

Charlie was also as good at ownership as she was bad at it. And he was a man with those secondary sex characteristics and that kind of muscle mass, so it was Charlie who acted upon the mute objects of the household, imposing his will, doing the screwing in and hammering. This was probably why all the mutual tools of their community had been listed in his column on the draft of Schedule C, Personal Property. Schedule C was only one small part of the intimate and deeply embarrassing document that would someday end up filed in the courthouse of Alameda County as a matter of the public record—that is, if she and Charlie ever finished this never-ending process. Their divorce was easy compared to many, her attorney told her—a clean California dissolution without grounds, without matters of custody, without much real property. Still, it was seeming to take years and every cent they ever hoped to have.

Charlie got the tools on the advice of Anna's lawyer, George Beemus, who said getting her half of them would cost more money and more effort than it would take just to drive to Pastime Hardware and simply buy the various ones you needed all over again. So Anna acquiesced, though she didn't have the slightest idea of how to rebuy tools—where was Pastime? Did it have a parking lot? Did the lot require a validation?

George Beemus often took this tack with her, that of an understanding condescension: Why don't we let Charlie have this or that because it seems to matter so much more to him. Let's save our energy, he said, for the Big Ticket Items.

Anna smiled weakly at George Beemus. Nothing, frankly, aside from the person of her daughter, had ever struck her as being a Big Ticket Item.

She loathed her own attorney, loathed her husband, loathed the tarnished objects left from their sad marriage, imbued as they were with the sense of the profundity of their failure. She gave in also as a matter of breeding, having been raised by her mother to a habit of polite, if angry, relinquishment. Her mother found the material world to be tainted by the greed of men. Anna's father had been an insurance executive who worked in Manhattan during the week, insisting his wife stay home in the suburbs of New Jersey.

Anna had broken out of that paralysis, the particular stasis created by each bad marriage. She was no longer frozen, fixed as the sad-sack wife of the feckless Charlie Shay. She might, therefore, turn into anything. She might go live in Brazil like Elizabeth Bishop. She might turn out to be lesbian. She might begin to act any way at all, might—one day—yank on her clothes and pull up her boots and drive to Pastime, buy tools, become *handy* and thereby *really* shock her friends.

Many women in her caste and class, she knew, were very good at spending money. Anna had been trained by her mother to be frugal, however, taught that buying things wasn't a very good use for either the money one spent or the time a purchase took. Anna was now often in such a mindless panic about money that the job of shopping became increasingly difficult. It was never the clean transaction, rather became metaphoric. She wanted it to be as simple as it was in preindustrial times before the invention of inflation, when there were simple economics, a bartering, the plain trade of this piece of money for those goods or services. She had to think about all aspects of any deal she was involved in, so filling the van's gas tank or picking up the dry cleaning might take much longer than a day.

Anna had so long been the disembodied member of the Bell-Shay household she'd lost whatever corporeal edge she might once have had. She didn't quite understand the evolution, how over the years of her marriage she turned into exactly the type of female person she never much cared for: one of the women poets with three names, with an allergy to sunshine, the one bewildered by the complex trappings of upscale poverty, the frayed divorcee with an incipient migraine caused by drinking too much wine, the single parent summoned to school to get her child on account of head lice, who drives there and back on an empty tank, with the brake light flashing alarmingly.

This marginality was in her nature and so predated the divorce, as she and Charlie were both aware. Marriage was the long dark cave into which Anna had once been happy enough to climb. The world outside was bright; it hurt her eyes.

Charlie Shay had the habit of telling the same jokes over and over. "My wife's a poet," he'd tell someone needlessly. "And two poets don't make one entire person." Then he'd beam at Anna as if this was her finest quality.

14

Head of a Young Man Turned Left and Looking Down (Recto), 1504

S HE'D BEEN ALEC's student when he was at Cal, might have been good had she decided to go back and finish after Cecily was born. She certainly understood the goof on the middle class that ran faultwise across the warp of the postmodern, understood the bland and ugly path most commonplace building took in California after the end of the Second World War. It was here in the emptiness of the West that the fraudulent misapplication of Wright's aesthetics had produced such utilitarian miscreants they seemed like his legitimate offspring systematically poisoned in the womb.

Gina sat in the back of class turned away from her drawing board so she could rest back against the wall. Alec's nostrils flared when he saw her. She noticed, tipped her face up, her smile knowing, sardonic. She crossed one of her little hamburger bun shoes across the other knee the wide way—these were thoroughly beat-up oxfords. She was the only woman in the class; men teased her for the shoes but she didn't stop wearing them. She was friends with men, smoked with them, laughed raucously with them in the hallway—there were still so few women in architecture then. Gina swore rather remarkably in those days, humorously and loudly, and this did somehow contribute to the attraction Alec felt for her. He found himself listening for her barking laugh in the hallway, for her husky voice to carry down to him to alert his body that she was coming.

When she came in, her hair was often wet. She swam laps at Hearst Gym, he overheard her to say. Julia Morgan was *too* gay! This loud remark of Gina's once punctuated the argument she was having in the hallway. Her own sexuality was inscrutable. She wore the same clothes to class day after day: brown pants with a soft-looking feltlike surface, a big flannel overshirt. Her breasts were small, the nipples pointy. The fabric of her much-washed pullover was so thin Alec could make out the distinct geographies of skin and bra. She stood close to him in order to ask a question. There was smoke in the fabric of her shirt, chlorine in her still-wet hair. Her eyes were fearless as they flicked over him.

She came up, fell into step, walked out of class with him as he went back to his office. She carried an old-fashioned leather brief-case clutched to her chest like schoolbooks. She stopped to fish around in it, then light a cigarette. He watched her lick her lips, saw the shine left on the bottom one. She said she was born in Berkeley, that she had raised herself. Her face was virtually expressionless as she told him this. Life was rough. Gina glanced over at Alec to see if he was prepared for this.

He was so junior in the department he'd been assigned an office in the basement in old unsafe Wurster Hall that was to be torn down as soon as New Wurster was completed. The joke among architectural students was that New Wurster was built to be the ugliest on campus. It was huge and it was sprawling and visually incoherent—was it British Modern or somehow Aztec? It looked like it had been designed by a team of quarreling imbeciles. It had the grace of a prison, the obvious cheapness of cinder block. The words FASCIST ARCHITECTURE were regularly spray-painted onto its ugly walls all the time it was going up.

If the job of a building is to interpret a community to itself, the school that built this was in terrible trouble.

Alec came to Berkeley from the East imagining an Athens. He wanted only to sit in the same light as Charles Moore on the same hopeful side of the continent, but found a school riven by factions, a department torn by rivalry. Moore was already seriously disaffected—he was brilliant but was rumored to be queer, was denied tenure because of this. Moore resigned and was immediately hired to head the school at Yale.

Alec was retained but passed over for promotion twice—who could say why? The signals and signs of his department baffled him. He had never felt so lonely or as Jewish as he did at Cal among the fey WASP elite, many of whom had gone to Princeton. He was baffled by the mores and manners, their goofy WASPy bow ties, the complete incomprehensibility of the broad vowels and the flatness of what he guessed passed as jokes between them. Where, he wondered, did they even *get* these people? The only friend he made in the department was Carlo Empy, a fifth-year teaching fellow.

In the dank basement of Old Wurster, Gina used the men's room. So, she used the men's, so what? She didn't pee in the urinal but went right into a stall. So what if some guy was shocked when the stall door opened and a girl came out? That was his problem, wasn't it? Her eyes were brown, her gaze direct and challenging. She placed her lips together in a certain way. Her face was small, her chin pointy. Alec could have covered it with just one outstretched hand. He could imagine playfully doing this, her playfully biting the pad of muscle at the heel of his palm—his right palm looked bruised because of the smudge of graphite.

Gina was as tough in her way as his Russian grandmother, who came to this country as a girl and had broken English. Gramma Leah had no doubt at all about what was right and just. She was old-world, looked like Mammy Yokum. She once came into the offices of the New Haven Power Company and set her newsstand up.

Oh no, Madame, they said, you can't do your selling here. Vy not? she said, ven yesterday you people plant a power pole in the corner of my front yard vidout knocking the door to ask me?

On the way to his office, Alec bought each of them a tea brewed with powdered instant in a paper cup, then stopped to browse the Servomation snack go-around. This was the purest junk, Gina said, he really shouldn't be eating it. Alec smiled at her, bought a packet of six Oreos anyway, and—once in his office, with each of them seated—he opened the cellophane and divided the cookies equally, balancing three cookies on the soft brown fabric of her knee. Alec felt the heat of her skin beneath his fingertips. Her leg moved almost imperceptibly. His balls hardened, lifted.

Her still-damp hair dangled down, darkening the fabric of her shirt. She left the cookies on her knee for a moment, then moved them to the desktop, reached down into her satchel to get her cigarettes, tapped one out. She lit it with her father's silver lighter—she showed Alec the engraved looping intertwine of initials: JJT, III—John Joseph Tinnerley, the *Third*, she said. She half smiled, looked at him, appraising him from under the hem of her dark bangs. She squinted out at Alec through the smoke she blew. So a man's putting cookies on your knee was some new way of his coming on to you?

She smoked, watched Alec carefully. Her eyes were dark and darkly fringed. He was older and from the East. He heard himself begin to try to impress her. He'd gone to Columbia, traveled all around in Europe spending four months in Rome, three in Florence, had taught one year in Japan. He knew people, knew Moore, he said, though this wasn't strictly true.

She swept her bangs back out of her face. Her dark brows were thick and ran straight across. Her eyes were solemn, even when she was smiling. Men were weak, weren't they? They went bad on you, didn't they? She assessed him. She took her own drawing from him, holding it open to look at it again with his criticism in mind. He could see her mind work, the way she used his eyes as she studied it, looking at it hard again. As he spoke, she turned to watch him. She wouldn't say his name, didn't call him anything. They each mentioned their parents, the way they were all ridiculous, laughing at the way every family was so comic when eavesdropped on, when viewed from right outside the window. She was going to be different from her parents, she said, in that she was going to live long enough to finish a couple of things.

He heard the whole story later. Her telling of this tale was almost affectless, how Sylvia and Joe Tinnerley met at Cal, came from certain privilege, had promise, turned out to be charming, witty failures. Each wrote, each painted, each died with little to show for it. She called them the beautiful corpses, though neither death was pretty. Gina was twelve when her mother died of a swift reproductive cancer that mimicked pregnancy. Her father, having thought Sylvia was going to have a son, went into a speechless shock.

After that, whenever friends asked Gina what her father did, she said, He sits in a chair and reads. He read shelf after shelf of books from the various Cal libraries. By the time he died, Gina told Alec, her father knew just about everything.

Joe Tinnerley, who was alcoholic, died before Gina was seventeen. She was underage but needed only a year to finish high school. Her lawyer, the father of a friend, helped convince the county agency that Gina was capable of caring for herself, as demonstrated by her savvy in getting a lawyer to argue the case for her. As an emancipated minor, Gina was allowed to handle her own money. She got something from a trust her mother had, enough to pay the mortgage. She began to receive survivor's benefits from Social Security. She rented out one of the two bedrooms in the little house. She reminded him of Leah, who was a scrambler. Leah supported the family with her newsstand on Oak Street in New Haven. Leah's husband was bookish, a rabbi who taught one class in Aramaic at Yale year after year for which he never received a penny, each side being too gentlemanly to ever discuss the matter of money, Yale imagining its quaint little Jew was paid enough by the honor its name bestowed on him. Alec hated Yale for that.

Her motherlessness showed in the confusing way she dressed; the fatherlessness was in there too. She had the Little Man shoes, the big briefcase, his lighter, her watchfulness. Boys Gina's age didn't seem to interest her. They were too young, too unformed. She understood boys, the shallowness of their motives. She understood almost everyone. She had always known what people wanted, she told Alec soon after she'd met him, which is why she would probably have made a really great whore.

She flicked her eyes at him as she said this—was he a prude who might be easily shocked? She looked away, stared off. People had always been transparent to her, she said, which came, she guessed, from having ghosts as parents. She spoke out of the side of her mouth, like a little tough girl.

Her hands were small and bony. She had a bright patch on either cheek that looked like a hectic flush. She clearly smoked too much, was almost runtish. She looked starved but wouldn't eat. Never before had Alec become ardent about a student. There was no abuse of power—he had no power over her. He was the one transfixed, while Gina could come and go at will.

But his patience did feel grand, almost godlike. He didn't impose himself. Instead he waited for her to come around. Gina seemed already to exist for him as if she had been laid out on the high table where he stood to draw. He would tape a big sheet of thick vellum there—he never used a lesser sheet even for the roughest sketches. A plan was always already there. A plan lay beneath the surface. All Alec had to do was wait and the body of it would rise to him.

She was wary, an animal that had not been mistreated but left alone too long. She watched his mouth as he ate a cookie. He chewed. She watched his eyes as they traveled over her, the dampness of her shirt, how it stuck to her collarbones, the hardness of her nipples beneath the scanty fabric, and the cleft made by the soft brown of her pants where they shaped to her cunt lips. He wanted to get in there, at it, taste it.

She saw him looking, watched him in her level way. She wasn't modest, didn't cross her knees in order to keep his eyes off her.

It was weeks of his habitually buying them before she ate one of the cookies. He put the three on her knee each time, using this as his excuse to touch her. Sometimes she held them on her knee for a moment before moving them to the surface of his desk, where she stacked them up like poker chips.

Gina was laughing—she was very pretty when she laughed. They were laughing together at the ugliness of buildings, the new ones in San Francisco's downtown which were uniformly mediocre and hokey if not downright wretched. Architecture was such a public act, Gina said, weren't people ashamed of themselves for erecting such great huge shit that really messed up a skyline? Who would want to be the person responsible for something as bad as the Transamerica Pyramid? It was so bad it turned sentimental and over time people became *fond* of it.

Her cheeks were bright with the heat of feeling. He watched as she dunked her cookie into the tea and ate the soft wet part of it—she'd forgotten she didn't eat this. Alec's mouth yawned open. He had hardened, the warmth radiating outward across his thighs, flowing up into the hardness that was the flat muscle of his stomach.

She looked off—he thought Gina had forgotten him as well. Instead she seemed amused when she looked back. She fixed him with her large and steady eyes. So this is it, Baxter? she asked. This is where you fuck me?

15

Sundowning

H<small>E LAY IN</small> his Le Corbusier chaise, having a single sherry. The peace of the empty house had been satisfying for a little while but had now begun to plague him. He wanted something, needed something, couldn't think what it might be.

Alec was reading physics in preparation for a class he planned to take at the Lawrence Hall of Science. He needed a more active hobby, Gina had begun to tell him. He needed to get busy, to stop mooning around feeling sorry for himself. The physics class kept being postponed. So what? she asked. So why not sign up for botany?

He'd been in California all these years yet hadn't learned the names of trees. Out this window he could identify oaks, a bay laurel, two different maples, but what was the name of the one Peter called the shine-bug tree, big and flame-shaped, its leaves flicking from silver to green in Cliff Peech's side yard. Peter was still magical, still half-believed this tree was animated by spirits. He was a quiet boy, observant if fearful, good at languages, as Alec was. Small like his mother and, like her, adept at water sports.

It was only the shine-bug tree that guarded Alec's house from the snooping of Basta! whose house sat next to it on the street below, and the tree, being deciduous, worked as a curtain only half the year. Basta! was the too-loud city planner. Her lot was an aggressive wedge cut back into the block. Alec called her Basta! for the terrible way she screamed her cat's name right beneath his bedroom window. Her voice was industrial-strength, you could use it for spots on carpets.

The trouble with city planning, Alec and Carlo agreed, was city planners. Planners knew everything about human will and motivation, couldn't refrain from telling you. Berkeley contained literally thousands of people with just this kind of societal certainty. Planning meetings were a particular nightmare. Planners yakked and talked and yentaed.

His house staggered downhill diagonally too close to the Peeches' and to Basta! A big house like his in the East would have demanded a better margin in order to make the clear transition. What was lost in California was the stately middle distance, no time for adjustment of figure/ground or for gradual revelation. Wham bang! it was all immediate. It was because of the pretense to classlessness. It was also the fault of the society of women. His wife's friends all slammed right into intimacy, wouldn't identify themselves when they called on the phone, assuming their voices to be known by him when in fact he couldn't tell them apart. More than once he'd come home to find Veronique Chakravarty in his kitchen when Gina wasn't there. This was a perversity, he believed, the desire to overflow the banks of warmth, to fan out in one's closenesses and cover everything. Even men in California came to love this stylish blur of custom and distinction.

This polymorphism was political in Berkeley, it was philosophic. The town was invented as a place of egalitarian Arts and Crafts bungalows that all workers could afford, the modest well-made houses designed to fit a standard lot. Wealth came after the Second World War, with it scarcity. In the real estate boom of the mid-1990s, property had become so astonishingly expensive the town was threatened with losing its scholarly class as profs lost out in buying when up against the baby businessmen.

His windows stood open. Birds in the Peeches' trees were calling out raucously. The sun was going down. His house stood right at the Jay Line, where the scrub jays and Steller's jays overlap and vie for territory.

Birds become increasingly agitated and noisy at sundown. The same was true of their mother, Betsy recently told him. She and Ben had recently brought Viv to live with them. Alec's sister mentioned this when she called to give him the progress report.

"Progress?" Alec asked, his voice a croak.

The senile are disturbed by twilight—when the light thins and the vision dims, a person's sense of self diminishes, the margins between what is inside and outside growing fuzzy. Their mother was losing the haptic sense, the feeling of having weight in her own body, what it was to have an earthly presence that was held in place by terrestrial gravitation, something rooted by its mass, an object planted in the physical world.

Their mother's self was eroding. As Viv came apart, time became the thing subject to gravity. Time was the sandstone cliff that continued to give way beneath her feet. She panicked and her terror was made worse by her loss of the words with which she might express her helplessness. Light granulated after sunset. The minutes flew away, passed wildly, the moments quickly telescoped. As daylight leeched, the rooms of their mother's life compressed, each growing smaller with the duskiness, a set of darkening boxes, each one smaller, each one fitting within the one before. Light's leaving became a single terrifying rapidness. Daytime fell away. The rooms of night came increasingly to resemble life's final one, the plain pine box where her husband lay.

She might have wanted to go lie with Stuart except she could no longer remember him.

The magic of telling time has been so important to the ease of suffering that this power is described as the absolute work of God. But time is only the tale of human history told another way, the one pronounced in the language of numbers, another story mankind has invented to while away the hours spent squatting by the fire. Other animals have had no need to invent the timepiece that might chart whatever emptiness. Mathematics is only another of humankind's intricate inventions, yet we, as any band of faithful, believe in it, believe it stands above us and is overarching, and are unwilling to admit this to be no more true or beautiful than any of our other arts. It was when science began to rival the older forms of God sometime after Darwin that mathematics became a form of modern prayer, so absolute it is regularly viewed as something that exists outside human invention and so seen as a discovery, as real and infinite as stars. What did his mother have aside from counting, her past making her days add up, making this finite tally, each one made sacred by the fact that it is counted. Viv was Joshua, Judges, Ruth. She was Numbers, Deuteronomy.

And now she would, like any animal in a slow and agonized death begin to disconnect her consciousness from matters of her anatomy. She could no longer localize discomfort, had forgotten the word for hunger, misplaced the one for thirst. She still held her hands in her certain way to light the Sabbath candles, Betsy said, but now stumbled through the rhythmed mumbling in that no-longer-remembered language.

Sundowning is so common among the demented, Betsy told Alec, it's called a syndrome. How many parts did Alec imagine a thing had to have to qualify as a syndrome? His sister's voice sounded like she was fried, she was tense, short, brittle. Their mother's dying was taking so long, these exhausting days followed by equally exhausting nights. She had someone in to help with Viv, but there was no escaping the overwhelming responsibility, as with an increasingly babyish child.

"She only says pat phrases," Betsy said. "Her same old clichés."

"I'm so sorry, Bets."

"She still has her pert voice, her little robin's chirp. The songs are still in there sometimes, as if the music somehow helps her keep the words glued together. The other day she singsonged this out at me: *I don't know if I am coming or am going.* She chanted it like a cantor, Alec, but you could tell from the look in her eyes she knew what she was saying and that she actually really meant this."

"I'm so sorry," he said again, helplessly. "I wish we could do more to share this."

"We'll send her," Betsy told him. "How do you want her, Fed Ex or Next-Day Air? She weighs nothing, she's so skinny I could almost fax her. She's still stacked, though, and she still has her finishing school posture. You should see her, Alec, straight back, chin up. I put her ratty old mink on her shoulders when Ben and I take her for a walk, and the old guys driving by slow down to ogle. Maybe one of them will decide she's a wealthy widow and want to marry her. She always made such an excellent bride."

"It's really good of you both," Alec told her. "Betsy, you're a wonderful person. So is Ben," he added. "That Ben," he said. "He's one in a million."

Alec waited, waited. He said this and he meant this but didn't actually get the recoil of *feeling* it. His emotions were being effaced, just as their mother's had been. Her flatness of affect, her becoming increasingly self-involved and inward were some of the first of her symptoms.

"Oh, never mind," Betsy said. She said this after a long moment during which she may have been either laughing or sobbing in an air-gulping and almost noiseless way. "Okay, don't tell me how many parts a syndrome has," she said. "I'll find out myself. I'll call up the Car Guys."

"I just want to state how much I appreciate all this." Alec listened to himself, wondering where all this fulsome sincerity was coming from. They were true words, he meant them, but once uttered they fell away. My mother is dying, Alec told himself. He said it, then stood coldly at the door of that room. What was he supposed to be feeling. Alec was a mensch, well meaning, hardworking, had always been. He was an attentive son, a faithful husband. He was dutiful, also increasingly resentful of the dullness of a life lived by the rules of obligation.

Timmy—the word came unbidden. It seemed like a song drifting in from far away, one that might somehow free him. The boychik who painted with his clothes half off.

The next time Alec phoned, he found this greeting in Ben's voice on their machine: "And I quote," Ben said. "Nihilism leads to the wholesale warehousing of the elderly and insane."

—— 16 ——

Dreaming the Names
of the Children of Berkeley

SEE THE MOON, PLANETS, STAR CLUSTERS, GALAXIES
THROUGH ASTRONOMICAL TELESCOPES
SATURDAY EVENINGS BEGINNING AT 8 P.M.
THE LAWRENCE HALL OF SCIENCE PLAZA (WEATHER PERMITTING)

THERE WAS ONCE no one, nothing, that had ever come between them. It made his hands ache to think of how they were then, when his love for her was so large that all women seemed to belong to him. Women then were impossibly lovely, in that last season of their ease when the world shimmered under a great blue heaven, a vaulted sky patterned by green leaves and a moon etched in daytime. He and Gina could speak of anything.

Alec and Carlo were also working on putting their firm together. They were taking long walks in the cool evenings along Berkeley's streets, up past Indian Rock, then winding down to Solano to get coffee. They spoke of architecture in America, of which buildings they loved and which they loved to loathe and of what was wrong with cities and with residential building and who was paying for the new cathedrals, to which the answer was always either government or commerce. They were similar in their tastes, both being early admirers of the work of the two L.A. Franks, Frank Israel and Frank Gehry.

It was when Cecily was little, and he and Gina were still down on Oxford Street. This was before Timmy, and before Alec found the property on Descartes and bought it without her say-so. After Timmy, Alec knew one thing only: he needed to build this house. He bought the lots, then settled in to wait for the variance. He'd go there straight from work, sit straight down in the waist-high grasses, his body so suddenly heavy he couldn't carry the weight of it. He often forgot to eat, thought of it later as the Starving Time. He could no longer imagine what was going to happen.

"Know what you are?" Gina said then. "You are a *decent* man." She made it sound like criticism.

Before, when they were too poor to own anything but one beat-up car, Gina used that old Dodge station wagon to haul her canvases back and forth from the College of Arts and Crafts. She'd started casting the torsos of women in amber resin, half-bodies that hung flat against the wall. She—who had no mother and was scrawny as a kid—fell in love with the voluptuous, lay the forms on their side on the floor, turned them into mountains. She was in a group show; she sold a couple of pieces while she was still in school. She moved across the bay to finish at the Art Institute, where she studied with Joan Brown and Manuel Neri.

They had no money. Alec had failed at Cal, was in the process of leaving, was struggling to start out, to try to find commissions. She used the house on McGee as her studio at first, but they were so poor they needed the rental income. She moved her painting into the dankness of the basement apartment on Oxford. It sat right above the water table of an underground stream.

He was so in love with her then, he'd walk home from lunch on a sunny day in order to surprise her. He'd feel lucky if she and Cecily were alone, lucky too if she was out back in the garden with her women friends. The energy of his love for her radiated, pulsed, gave off. People knew. Her women raised their eyes to look at him.

The house on Oxford had a tiny backyard, half-shaded by a young redwood. Gina and her friends would be lying out on the chaises on the bricked patio, the kids from the neighborhood play group naked, splashing in the wading pool. The little silver sprinkler at the end of a snaking hose gushed against the sweet peas, the blooms standing out, stems bobbing all along the fence, the purest of pinks and whites and lavenders.

What a beautiful race the children of this town were. That neighborhood was less rich, less estranged than the one they found when they moved farther up the hill. It was more nicely integrated, with a Cal-based buzz of brains and cultures and languages. So many of the kids in Berkeley were ethnically or culturally mixed, and Alec's generation had rid the place of prejudice—these kids would grow up to speak all languages. AIDS, drug deaths, traffic accidents, the Twelve Steps, families in crisis—none of it yet pertained to them. Alec's generation had saved the world, now its children would go out and inhabit it.

They were naked, their bodies and minds as innocent as primitives, slick wet bellies sticking out, big eyes, big heads, their short arms and bowed legs, their little cocks peeing out, little cunts full as nectarines. This was before Calvin Klein, before kiddie porn on the Internet, when Alec could take photographs of the wet beauty of these children and no one would think of arresting him.

This was before the hole in the ozone layer, when Gina and her friends still went out to sunbathe. That was the last season of her laziness, of her yawning, stretching, and of the salads she sprinkled with petals of violets and the homemade pasta she flecked with basil and served with tomatoes still warm from the garden—he hadn't seen a tomato that red in years. It was when they drank white wine ice-cold and she might run her fingers back through her bangs, look at him frankly and ask if he was finished, and, if so, would he like to come upstairs with her and commit an act of sodomy.

It was before Gina and her friends got busy, packed up, before they began to watch carefully as others began to tote up their accomplishments. There were new girls coming in. They who once defined what it was to be young and promising were somehow no longer current, were suddenly shocked to realize they no longer knew the names of rock stars.

He found her outside in the garden. She was barefoot, without makeup. She'd let her hair grow long when she was pregnant with Cecily; it hung in a ponytail down her back or she wrapped it in her fingers, making a twist at the nape of her neck that she stuck with brushes or pencils. From this bun-thing tendrils fell. My wife, Alec thought. He yawned, slung his jaw out and around to move against the joy he felt.

One of the kids had splashed her. He witnessed her: long neck, declivity behind water-beaded collarbone, angle of her nose and chin. Then as he came out onto the porch, her eyes half shut: "Hey," she said, her voice low, intimate, though she had women there.

"Hey yourself," he answered her. "So how's your morning going?"

"How's *my* morning going?" Cecily put in, jealously.

Gina was hungry then, she was passionate. She had everything she wanted; she loved everyone and everything. She wanted to spend the day in bed with him, wanted too to get up and go back to work. She loved being home, also wanted Cecily in nursery school. She wanted another baby, the son her parents never had, the child Alec didn't think they could yet afford. She didn't want to wait— waiting would hold her up—she wanted to get on with it.

She was seated at the edge of the redwood deck. She was sun-bathing, lying back in one of the reclining chairs; the straps to her summer dress were undone and these dangled down. Her skirt was hiked up, her thighs spread so the long muscle along the inside showed. She got up, went out to move the sprinkler.

She sat at the edge of the deck, the air perfumed by sweet peas Cecily was picking and bringing. Cecily was softly counting, saying Same-same, each-each, one bunch for herself, one for her mother, dividing the beauty equally.

Gina's feet stuck out into the grass that was wet from the splash of the kids in the wading pool. The tops of her feet were tan. He loved her feet so much he told her he'd have them bronzed for the mantelpiece if something ever happened to her. She cast one foot in the resin she was working with at school; it was bubbled, as clear as honey. He took this foot to his office where he lay it on its side so he could look up and see the instep.

It was such a simple pleasure, to walk the twenty minutes home in the middle of the day from his new office down on University Avenue. The house on Oxford was so dark it always took his eyes a moment to adjust as he entered—he walked blindly through the rooms, as if in a railroad tunnel, made it to the kitchen, stepped out again into a wince of sun so bright it always took a while to find her.

She was down sketching at the table on the bricked-in patio, brought one tanned arm up to shade her eyes. Her chin was tipped up, her gaze as level as that from the back of the room when she was still a wary girl at Cal. Gina had hiked the hem of her dress up out of the water the kids made by splashing. The kids and their mothers all were gone, Cecily down for her nap.

Gina lifts one beautiful foot, then the other, placing each on the chair in front of her, toes curled. Her skirt is hiked and he can see the white of her underpants. She wraps her arms around both bare knees.

His heart catches. Gina smiles at him, her lips pressed together. She gestures with her chin to ask him to come on down to her.

— 17 —

The Center of Effort

A MILD FALL DAY stinking of geraniums and dust. They are driving downhill with the windows unrolled. The station wagon inside smells of dirt and gym clothes and of the hot bright stink of bubble gum, all stuff Peter's father cannot stand. His knuckles are white on the steering wheel as the car heads down Marin Avenue, as if the brakes are just about to go.

There are pools of fallen yellow leaves lying in quiet patterns that pop and stir beneath the tires of the Volvo. Peter turns to stare back uphill, where particles of crushed leaves lift and eddy.

They haul their bikes across the bridge to San Francisco, where a race has closed the streets to cars in the Marina District. They ride the wrong way along the race route to find a place to eat breakfast where the racers will pass by. Peter has on shorts and a tee shirt, but his father is dressed wrong for fun in a doofy short-sleeved sports shirt, slacks, the wide leg held by a bicycle clip, in the beat-up shoes he calls his "sneakers." Oh, my God, Mama! Cecily screamed when she saw their father. Can you please not let him go out looking like that?

His dad dresses as he does so he can move along the poles of melancholy, going from place to place in his life as if connecting the dots on whatever map might give him the sense of what is *familiar*. This is why his dad picks where he does to eat breakfast. Some dump, huh? his father asks, with his turned-down smile, as if he himself is proud to have invented it. A blue-collar café full of dock-workers at the foot of a pier, avec *pas* du Yuppies, he says, et *sans* le waterview. It reminds him of a diner on Hillside Avenue. All that grease and disappointment.

Peter's father gets a particularly long look on his face when he is thinking of the East. He eats hungrily, almost angrily, his head down gobbling biscuits with butter and jelly, eating the eggs and hash browns and bacon to show he's not afraid of dying the same way his own father did.

The two eat silently, Peter moving the scrambled eggs around on his plate—he ordered the same thing his father did, but the plate looks sickening. His dad hates Peter's squeamishness—Peter's trying to be a mensch. *Ein Mensch* means simply *man* in German, is something else in Yiddish—a mensch being a whole person, his father says, one who is complete.

They're watching the racers streak by in neon pink and orange and green out the café window, a close race among the first bunch of five or six. Alec asks Peter to pick the winner. He wants Peter to be a winner, to know a winner when he sees one, but Peter secretly favors the underdog because of what was done to Jews. His father gives him money, sends him to the register. It's easy to be a mensch, his dad says. You honor your father and mother. You stay married, you set your kids a good example, you don't lie or cheat or steal. And every once in a while, Cookie, you gotta pick up the check, his father says, then winks.

They get back on their bikes to ride the wide and empty streets along the water to the Marina so they can watch the winners cross the finish line, then they'll make their way back to the place they think they've left the car. Peter's good at directions. This comes from being native for generations by way of his mother's family, who came westward on the Oregon Trail. His father is often entirely turned around, which comes from being born in the East and having the ocean lie on the other side of you.

Peter is learning sailing in the Boy Scouts, is good already, has sailing in a kind of internal memory that seems more like instinct. His Grandfather Tinnerley had his own skiff when he was Peter's age; he kept it at the old boathouse at the Berkeley Marina. Peter's father gets seasick, doesn't understand the basics of navigation, that the Telltale Compass is made to be read upside down since it's mounted on the ceiling in a wheelhouse. He'd never heard of the Center of Effort. This is the point in the sail plan where you can visualize all the forces coming together to drive the yacht forward.

Peter knows his own coordinates, 120°20′, 37°50′, at the Jay Line, 103 feet above sea level. They called the Naval Air Station at Alameda so his dad could set the barometer Peter and Cecily gave him for his birthday.

San Francisco is particularly easy for them to get lost in, the steep streets dead-ending into walled terraces from which bright flowers overwell like a kind of brilliant trash. Peter is confused but doesn't want his father to know it. The alleys twist off, leading away uphill in two wrong directions past houses painted in slick pastels. They can't find the Volvo. Peter and his father ride steep alleys and flat places, crowded streets. His father yells at Peter to stay close, be careful. In North Beach along Columbus, traffic snarls and they are the cause of it and his father's clothes look ridiculous and his dad's face goes pale with the worry that looks like both rage and loss. Horns honk. Oh, bite me, his father says right into one driver's rolled-down window.

"It's towed," Peter says when they pull up, dismount. "She's going to kill us."

"They couldnda towed it," his father says. "They don't tow on a Sunday."

"It's towed or we'd've already found it."

"I don't think so, Honey," Alec says. "They don't tow on Sunday. The cops in this place are all Irish, like in Queens. They go to mass. Anyway, I parked legally. I'm pretty sure."

"No, you didn't," Peter says.

His father makes them look for another hour before they call the impound lot. They call, but the police have no record and they can't yet report it stolen since they can't say even roughly where they might have left it. "Why would anybody steal Mom's car?" Peter asks.

"Beats me," his father says. "You don't joyride in a Volvo, Peter. There'd be no joy in it."

"She's going to kill us."

"We didn't do it, Honey. Anyway, your mother's a reasonable person."

"No, she isn't," Peter says.

Her face looks flattened when his mother gets there, as if she's driven the top deck of the Bay Bridge in the Fiat speeding along without the buffer of the windshield. "Okay, okay, we know, so don't say it." His dad holds his hands out to ward her off. They chain the bikes to a downspout, take off their helmets, go climb in the little car. His mother is a small person, but she is able to completely fill any room with her furiousness.

Peter gets in back, his father in front. It is only then they dare to look at one another, to smirk their conspirators' smile. They are adventurers, a team, partners, they're Orville and Wilbur at Kitty Hawk.

"Why is it," she asks, "that no one ever remembers that I may have been doing something more important?"

"Because, Gina"—he says this *Gee-naw*—"you are *always* doing something more important. You have been doing something more important for the past sixteen years."

"I wish you would think about the kind of example your losing things sets for Peter."

"We will talk about examples *set*, and all that later."

She stares at him. "What is this, Alec, tit for tat?"

His father turns away, looks out the open window. "You figure it out," he says, then adds, "Now will you please settle down here now, Gina, and help us find the goddamned car?"

"Why should I?"

"Well, it's *yours*, for one thing. If you no longer *want* the Volvo, Peter and I'll take our bikes and make our way home by Bart."

"What? and leave me with some big car mess to straighten out? This is so passive-aggressive of you, Alec. You just never liked the Volvo."

"Gina," he says very quietly. "Gina, please, please listen. Listen carefully. This isn't the time or the place to be having the *car choice* discussion. Can we please have that discussion later? We can have it after we have the argument with Cecily about what hippies wore."

The virus for the flu shot is grown in egg yolk, Peter knows. He is staring off, remembering the eggs he tried to eat, remembering the ache in his bones the last time he was sick, how the cold and hot came in waves and his head hurt and his joints hurt and his skeleton felt as light as it might when death hollows a body out. His mother was there in the daytime, but it was his father who slept in Peter's room so he could hover with sips of water and a wrung-out washcloth, which is how to be a mensch.

"Don't sell the bike shop, Orville," Peter tells him from the backseat. This is what Wilbur Wright actually said to his brother after one of their many crashes. His father turns, looks into the backseat, his lips pressed into a little *oh*, cheeks sucked in and hollowed. Veronique the French calls this Alec's gaunted look.

Peter thinks of the silver metal being stored within the porous web of his long bones so they are mirrored with a lacy silverness like leaves eaten to dust by insects. He has always been afraid he might have to bite the thermometer and break it in his mouth, that he then wouldn't be able to keep himself from sucking the mercury out. Peter learned to sit quietly when he was little, learned to concentrate holding his teeth and tongue very still. He kept his eyes shut, watching his bird bones light up and become miraculous, watching how their hollowness filled with a million tiny particles of the silver heaviness.

Peter rides in back but can't buckle up because the seat belts are lost down the crack. He worries they'll notice he isn't strapped in, that they'll both turn and yell at him. His parents believe in seat belts; they are not the French. The French refuse to buckle, neither will they snack or queue, which is why Euro Disney will fail, Veronique always says. Veronique explains the French as she drives the carpool. She speeds, is reckless, which his parents do not know. They don't have Halloween in France, but in Peter's school they do. Christophe, the teacher Peter had when he was in kindergarten, came nearly naked one year, dressed as Christ crucified, on a cross and with his side stabbed. When asked at school what he was going to be this year, Peter told them a traffic light.

His mother drives, his father's face contorting, going "Easy, Gina, easy," every time she clutches or brakes or shifts.

"Oh, knock it off," she says. "I know what I'm doing."

"Well, it's old, Gina," he says. "It's a sweet old car and the transmission's fragile. Can't you be a bit more gentle?" His father can't get a new car, Peter knows, because his license plate wouldn't then mean the same double thing if he didn't have a Fiat. The license plate reads FIAT LUX.

"Why is it, exactly, that we have to go through this kind of thing?" His mother holds up one hand; it's stained mahogany up past the wrist from what she was working on. "Do you realize that no one in our family *ever* really even looks for something before asking me to come help them find it?"

"We did, Mom," Peter offers. "Mom, we actually really, really looked."

"And the one thing you two *may have noticed*, while you were really, really looking is that this particular item is much bigger than a breadbox."

"Know what I was always wondering?" Peter asks his father. "How big is a breadbox?"

"About so." His father twists in the seat to show him. "A little smaller than a microwave." They smile at one another, his father winks. They're a coupla comedians.

His father likes to give Peter the words he himself grew up on: arange, harror, armund, jukebox, icebox, breadbox, *shmata*, *mishuga*. *Tsouris* is one you'll need, his dad recently said, this being the particular heartsickness only your family can cause.

"And I want you to learn something, Peter, from this excursion," his mother is going on to say. "There is sometimes a deep and somber truth lying at the heart of certain ethnic jokes, such as the one where the punchline goes: *When Daddy's standing with the door open staring into the fridge asking Mommy, Where's the butter? and she's busy doing something in a completely different room.*"

"That," his father says, "will be about enough of that."

"Mom?" Peter asks. "Mom? Did you know that it makes it hard to understand a joke when you tell it backwards?"

"Daddy knows exactly what I am talking about."

"You're not supposed to get it, Peter," his father says. "Mommy only told part of the joke and the rest is anti-Semitic."

"That part goes like this," his mother adds. *"How can you tell a Jewish prince?"*

"Stop that, Gina," his father says. "That will be enough of your insultingness."

"Peter, listen to me—this is urgent!" his mother says. *"Insultingness* is not a word."

And then his father turns around to smile the turned-down smile to tell him the bickering is okay, even funny, and that they will never split up, never get divorced though they often fight like this. His father has promised this, given his solemn oath: Queens Rules. He holds two fingers up when he promises, like a Cub Scout.

The squabbling is meant to be amusing, but Peter's gone trance-like, off to argue technicalities with himself, how a half a Jew such as he will ever get into heaven according to Israel's laws concerning who's to be regarded as Jewish. Paradise is called Jerusalem, one place his father has never gone. Israelis speak Hebrew, which is written right to left. Yiddish looks like Hebrew, sounds like German. Since Hebrew is written right to left, the silver Hagaddah of his grandparents opens backward the way this joke of his mother's goes.

"The reason you can't find anything, Alec," his mother is saying, "is that you're made so angry by anything that's lost. To find something it is necessary to go down, get calm, be low. When you go low," she says, "it'll be like whatever you want came looking for you instead."

"Calm?" his father asks. He is looking out the window.

His mother has no religion aside from being from California. Californians are the best drivers in the world. Riding with his mother makes Peter completely confident. She goes fast and this causes a thrill to run through him. His father putts along like an old man. Could you pick up the pace? Peter sometimes says. He drives slowly because he respects crash energies, what he calls the Cold Laws of Physics. He recites the words of physics to Peter sometimes, *velocity, thrust, lift, acceleration.* He hopes Peter will be a scientist. He says he himself picked the wrong job because architecture is about finished now that nearly everything has been built. He's going to be a physicist in his next life, he says, freelance, part-time.

His mother revs, corners completely fearlessly, jams the gearshift forward, shouts out, "Oooops!" when she sees she has mistakenly turned into a one-way alley. "Okay, Peter. Now walk backward in your mind, like they used to do on Sesame Street. Honey, I need you now. Close your eyes. Let your heart speak. Let's go there, Sweetie. Let's go to the Knee of Listening."

"Would you please not teach him that kind of gobbledygook?"

She tips her chin up. "There is so much more going on here, Alec, than you will ever learn in science."

"So now we have something against the Scientific Method."

"Mom?" Peter asks. "Mom?" he says again, hearing his voice sound wheedling and babyish. He's going to ask if they can't go back and check the bikes when the Volvo rematerializes. The station wagon stands just where they both now remember leaving it, tucked safely up an alley between two dumpsters just where North Beach meets Chinatown. Peter and his father have ridden by the two entrances to the alley at least a half-dozen times. His father's face is so happy, so joyful, to have lost something so completely he had abandoned hope, then to have it come back to him intact. "See?" he asks as he turns around. "It's the Law of Return." And he reaches back and touches Peter's knee.

"That," his mother says, "is not a legal parking space, so you two must be blessed."

"Yes, blessed," his father says.

2.

Fiat Lux

Everything tends to become real; or everything moves in the direction of reality.

WALLACE STEVENS, *Opus Posthumous*

—— 18 ——

The Sadness Pay

Just back from a weekend conference on solar at Asilomar. Never again would Alec ask himself to sit in a hot tub under the redwoods in the evening with the other naked, aging architects with whom he was supposed to discuss the intricacies and beauty of the photovoltaic cell.

Boom time in the belly culture: architects were plump and wet. He'd climbed into the hot tub after a couple of quick wines, had taken off his steamed-up glasses and scale suddenly vanished. Golems appeared. Architects were beasts: their heat-reddened torsos became hairy faces, their nipples the eyes of these.

Alec shut his own eyes against the vision, but once seen he couldn't stop seeing it: the faces of beasts, the slit of a bellybutton making the goatish nose and the hair of a dripping pubis, its beard and mustache.

"Know what your problem is, Daddy?" Cecily asked by way of conversation. She was fifteen, was bent over dialing the radio receiver on the stereo in the living room. He was lying in his chair in a lambent state, dreaming of going on a real vacation.

"You're just so negative," Cecily said. Then she turned away and went down the steps into the dining room.

And why not? Alec felt like shouting after her.

Before going, Cecily tuned to easy listening on *The Quiet Storm*—this to demonstrate what fools the grown-ups be. "Cecily!" he yelled. "Get back up here, would you? Would you get in here and change it or else choose a record? I can't stand this dreck." But she had gone on into the kitchen.

Cecily was dressed as a pile of laundry—wide-legged lowrider pants that she wore down on her hips, layers of shirts, her face dusted with what looked like particles of silver. Roughly cut and sticking out from her head like straw, she styled her hair with little pieces of metal junk and plastic. That her hair was bleached the golden white of wheat drying in the sunshine was what Alec tried to remember from hour to hour and day to day, but the sight of this strangely luminous girl still often came as something of a shock to him. Her hair was dark blond naturally, or had been until she ruined it—who knew what color it might be when it grew out? The white part made the growing-out roots look black. It looks fake, he pointed out. It's *supposed* to look fake, Daddy, she told him, *fake* is the whole idea.

Cecily believed he was negative because he'd just had the temerity to criticize her Social Living teacher, an icon in Berkeley, popular, as Cecily said, as well as famous. Social Living, which was required for graduation, encouraged high school sophomores who lacked all life experience to counsel one another on sex and self-esteem and heroin and venereal disease and all other intensely private matters in a very public classroom in a way that sounded to Alec way too much like a twelve-step program gone non-anonymous.

"Get me something, will you?" he called down to her. "Bring me some crackers and some cheese." Gina hated their shouting from room to room, but he was tired and Gina wasn't home.

"Bring that chunk of Gorgonzola," he yelled.

"Threw it out," she yelled back up. "Smelled like toe gunk."

Alec's front teeth braced edge to edge. Why wasn't Gina ever around? Why didn't she take the time to teach Cecily not to yell out "Toe gunk!" and "Crud!" and "That sucks!" The children of Berkeley were encouraged to be this raucous, particularly the girls. The mothers were determined that no one was to going rob this generation of girls of self-confidence. Cecily was honest and she was direct. Still, he told her, she was going to turn out like that loud planner down the hill if she didn't learn to modulate. Now Basta! was one noisy dame. A voice like that could pop fillings out of molars.

MacArthur Park was melting in the dark and someone left the cake out in the rain and Alec honestly could not stand it. He heaved himself up off the chaise and went to tune the radio to the last Bay Area jazz station, the other recently bought up and replaced by Christian programming. His house had survived the earthquake of 1989, the wildfire of 1991, but now felt poised on the brink of some new disaster that might be precipitated by another coming of the Jesus Christers.

He went down to poke through the liquor cabinet in the dining room, finding the sticky half-empty bottles of peculiar drinks his wife passionately loved for some short while. Gina spent one summer drinking bright syrupy green crème de menthe poured over chips of ice, making everyone try it, insisting it tasted exactly like mint ice cream, when it actually tasted more like alcoholic toothpaste. She went through a period of making a great peach-tinted martini she and Veronique devised. Alec and Ravi both liked the martini phase, in which they eagerly participated. That phase had a certain sort of Kennedy-era elegance. Now there was only an inch of gin, no vermouth, onions but no olives.

Alec needed a vacation. The only places he ever went, these days, were east to see his mother or to L.A. on business. Alec was hungry, thirsty, but what was it he wanted? "To Exit Program," he said aloud, "Press Here Now."

"What's wrong with now?" Cecily asked as she came in.

"I don't know," he said. "The house is cold. The fire seems to have gone out." He looked at the fireplace that opened from the living room into the dining room. The firebox was immaculate.

"Daddy," she whispered. "There wasn't one." She opened her own eyes wide to register his surprise.

Cecily had a way of pressing her pale lips together at the center in a gesture much like Gina's when she used to smoke cigarettes. Cecily's cheeks sparkled, her lips were shiny. She turned. He followed her upstairs back to his chaise. Even these few steps separating the levels were a physical effort at times like these. Pick your feet up, Gina told him. You're slouching, Alec, lumbering. Hey Dad! Peter told him, you got to pick up the pace. Cecily just looked at him, just raised her no-eyebrows.

She'd brought a platter of crackers and cheese, paté, a little pot of mustard, both red and green grapes. She gestured for him to sit, then showed him how to move his feet, all wordlessly like a little bossy wife. The cheese was two very orange, very thin slices of American, each one still in cellophane. He unwrapped one, sniffed it, got nothing. It wasn't actually a slice, he noticed, but a thin molded slab of "cheese food," something formed by being poured wet onto the sheet of plastic that was then heat crimped at two edges. This was low-fat, undoubtedly. Cecily probably bought it. He put it back. It was amazing to Alec that in the 1990s you could stumble onto Burt Bacharach on the radio, that—in the city of Berkeley—food as wretched as this could be sold legally.

"So how was my day, by the way?" she asked.

"So how was your day, Lee-lee?"

"Okay," she said. They waited in a companionable silence.

"Oh, I don't know, not much," he added after a little while, answering the question she hadn't asked.

She was down at the end of the chaise, bent over concentrating as she spread paté on a cracker for him. He hoped she wouldn't start on how geese were imprisoned and force-fed to fatten for foie gras. Cecily's fingernails were metallic blue. He loved her more than life itself.

This was his sturdy, menschly kid, yet even she exhibited elements of the Berkeley wick-wack. He'd been working in his study off the dining room the weekend before when the house had rapidly darkened. Through the skylight above his worktable Alec watched the towering front of a thunderstorm come in, its blackness then breaking. The sky became electric, the black clouds spilled white out blindingly. His papers lifted. He could smell ozone in the wind that was moving swiftly from room to room.

Alec went upstairs to close the window that must have blown open only to find Cecily at the end of the bedroom hallway. She stood like a figurehead at the prow of the house before two flung-back windows, her face wet, her plastered hair looking white and sculpted. The storm was so loud she didn't hear him coming. She was talking to herself, breathing in a measured way, saying as he approached, You are a good person. Even now, in remembering, Alec's cheekbones ached with grim love, a sensation so close to sorrow that it prickled across his face like hot sand flicked.

"It is always a matter of life and death," he said now as then, "as I had forgotten."

Alec could discover himself so easily in her: she was so present one moment, so alive and intelligent, then gone, hollowed out by this adolescent vacancy defined by nothing so much as appetite. He'd been like that: a hidden, twisted, day-blind thing, something hand-sized and rivalrous, set loose in his father's house in order to ruin it. By day he excelled, was president of everything, but when the sunset came he went back up to haunt and study. His room in Queens was miniature, only large enough for a little desk and his single bed, and seemed to easily fill with the stink of him. He kept the shade pulled down. He ate candy bars. He hunched there brooding over what he thought of as his privacy.

Alec studied, got honors, won scholarships that stood for money, but all this value was shoveled into the bottomless hole of his negative quantities. He was a piece of night—long columns could be added of his pus and shame. Goodness subtracted, hatred took up residence. Queens was still in love with the war in

Vietnam. His father vacillated, but he was a good liberal then and finally could not support it. Alec might have stabbed his father in the heart had he enlisted instead of going to college. He told his father he was considering it.

Alec had always known that fighting a war would provide his soul with the good of a palpable enemy. Alec wasn't drafted, did not enlist. Instead he rebelled against his father by refusing to apply to Yale, saying he didn't get their Yaley jokes. Being a town boy from the ghetto on Oak Street in New Haven who graduated Yale was Alec's father's proudest achievement. Alec hurt him terribly in choosing Columbia where, as he told his father, more of the boys spoke Jewish.

Alec studied; the antiwar movement swept him in. He marched, he hated: the boys who had the girls he wanted, the girls who were cold to him.

His daughter was now here, now not. She was a good person, but her physical self was crowding him. "Sweetie-hurt," he told her, saying it in the way of Veronique the French. "This is my own area. Do you think you could find another distinct three-dimensional space that you could stake out and solemnly occupy?" It was what everyone needed, Gina was always saying, his or her own private space, everyone working—he guessed—toward independent status as a city-state.

Cecily moved off—she sometimes seemed so slumped it looked like she'd lost skeletal integrity. She now sat cross-legged and so close to him on the floor that he could hear all the different parts of her eating, sucks, licks, cracker crunches, small interior smackings. The view of the sunset through the treetops was gorgeous but did not distract him from his irritation. He was going to have to ask the Peeches to window their redwoods. He was going to have to ask Cecily to chew less noisily.

"Do you know what today is?" he asked.

"Hitler's birthday?" she asked. She didn't miss a beat. It was the rhythm of the TV laugh track, he guessed, that conditioned children to cynically quip like this.

"This, Cecily, is November nineteenth," Alec said. "The first day of the Arctic night."

Cecily was intently spreading mustard on a cracker. With the low-fat cheese food gone, she was eating the rest of the crackers as small mustard sandwiches. She was nothing but appetite—she could eat twelve of these sandwiches. She could eat thirty or ninety.

He breathed in, breathed out, began again. "When the sun goes down today in Barrow, Alaska, the people won't see it come up again for almost two months, not until the seventeenth of January."

"I know," Cecily said. "We had a unit on that in science."

You do not *know*, Alec wanted to yell at her. "Cecily," he told her quietly. "You did not have a *unit* on Sunset Physics. No one has had the opportunity to take that unit yet. That's the class they keep *canceling* at Lawrence Hall because not enough people are interested." His choked voice sounded almost breathless.

For longer than a year now he had himself been trying to take the class in sunsets that was offered in the community science lab not ten minutes away, set on a ridge at the top of the hills. The lab was close, the class scheduled in the evening on a weeknight, slotted to meet a quarter hour later each week in the springtime, fifteen minutes earlier each week in the fall, so the moment of the sunset across the bay could be noted, tracked, jotted on the special maps they'd make as its transit moved north or south.

The registrar sent him the syllabus; he bought the books it mentioned. "Sunset Physics" had been offered three times so far. Each time Alec enrolled; each time it was canceled. He did irrationally blame his wife's generation for this—she was nearly a decade younger. Gina herself couldn't find time to go with him. It was Gina's women friends who were all busy slamming their Volvos and SUVs up and down the hills, going from one important place to the next important place, all the while yakking on their portables.

Lawrence Hall was going to arrange to offer it one more time; this time it would be taught by an eminence. Alec was collecting data on sunsets in order to have something to share with others in the class, people who would be similarly interested.

In Norway, for instance, Alec had learned, the liberal and oil-rich government paid its northernmost citizens a certain stipend during the winter months. Alec wasn't going to waste his breath telling Cecily this. She was at an age when she was just too self-involved to understand the cracked beauty of something called Sadness Pay. Of his two children it would be Peter, Alec knew, Peter, the smaller and somehow more broken one, who'd be the one to get it.

— 19 —

Night Falls in Barrow

It was when Cecily was still a toddler, when they were still down on Oxford Street, that Alec began to understand that the societal net that confined a contemporary marriage had weakened its hold on them, as on all of the members of this, their little tribe.

It was during the first El Niño, the first winter of awesome climatic change. A marriage was so easily damaged, he saw, it hit any sort of bump—an illness or mild good fortune, some small fame visited on only one of them—and the spell of love was broken. There were no rabbis any longer or witch doctors, no leaders of whatever community they might claim. There were only therapists who offered words that you paid money for, words that weren't holy enough somehow to ever really render anything whole again.

Not that the economy of the second family wasn't good for his business. A man who was a father again at fifty-five or sixty could afford the good big house to put the new babies in. And there was this swarm of the blond divorcees, growing young on protein drinks and exercise, who also needed the new and perfect house to which they had always been entitled.

Now the sun had nearly set. "Point being," he said to Cecily, "it's almost winter."

"I know," she said. "And it was seventy-eight on the savings and loan when the bus went by and I was completely sweated. The maniac who is our substitute gym teacher made us run laps with the football team to be like, you know, equal? What an . . ." Her voice dropped off, but he believed she said *asshole*. Alec couldn't swear to it. He was conveniently losing hearing there in the high range, right where women hector and babies cry.

"So these huge black jocks run right up behind us going, 'Hey, mama, give me *bawd*-dee.' Then one of them goes, in a little high voice, 'Hey baby, how come such a fine young Negress as you gots such a flat little white girl's ass?' And the third one says, 'She not *white*, she too *fine* to be white. She must be *Por-tow Rican!*' Which *is*, of course, harassment. Which, of course, the dumbass teacher doesn't do a thing about."

Cecily looked at him, must have read his skepticism, opened her hand, flattening it against her chest, and told him solemnly, "I swear to God," she told him, "they said these things to *me*." She had filaments of mustard at the corners of her mouth.

"Cecily, they were teasing."

"What about *my* feelings—what if I felt threatened?"

Threatened? Alec thought. This kid of his could easily flatten any three black jocks.

"We can always take a look at College Prep?" he said. Alec offered this about once a week after some new horror story about her school—she was proud of these stories. Her job was to tell the stories, his to be horrified.

"No thanks, Daddy, really," Cecily said. "Berkeley High may be a shithole, but it's *my* shithole."

"Cecily."

"Sorry."

"Well, really—where is your mother, by the way?"

"Maybe she went after Peter. Maybe he had cello."

"Did she leave a note?"

She lifted her shoulders and let them drop to show it would be impossible for her to be less concerned.

His irritation welled up again. "You know, it's all catch-as-catch-can around here, no one's ever knowing where anyone is? Isn't there some special place your mother leaves a note in order to tell you where she's gone and when it is that she'll likely be home? Did she get something out for dinner?" His voice, he heard, was peevish.

Cecily glinted at him, her irises the same hard hazel as his that Gina defined as smoky topaz.

"I wouldn't know, Daddy," she told him. "If there is some special place, I guess it's so incredibly *special* I just haven't found it yet."

He ran the fingers of both hands back through his hair, then pressed the fingers of either hand hard on his closed and weary eyes. He pushed on the eyelids, his fingertips rounding the solid smooth of the orbs. He pressed until he began to see the view out the window in reverse: black sun burning in a less dark sky, its setting against the glowing white hills of Marin, the Golden Gate Bridge, a lacework etched.

Alec pressed harder, pressed until his eyeballs ached. How were they going to get through Cecily's adolescence, he wondered, without his smacking her?

His father taught Alec never to hit his sister. He was never to strike a child or any person who was physically weaker. He had smacked Timmy, Gina's doped-up painter friend back during the first year of storms when it rained every day of January, every day of February, then the mudslides came. Alec might have killed him. Instead he punched him in the face, then threw him into the trash cans. He remembered this, that he had practiced a godlike restraint.

He was like God too in his forgiveness. He often came back to how good a man he was, at the lack of effort it took to lift Timmy and throw him, to the huge and rattling, triumphant sound of a body's smashing trash cans, the great crash of metal and percussion, Alec's New World Symphony.

20

Shmutz

ALTHOUGH IT WAS soul murder to build in the hills of defor-
ested Los Angeles County, Alec and Carlo kept doing it. It
was in L.A. that the intellectual life of the American century could
be seen to be subliming. Subliming is the process by which a solid
becomes a gas without its passing back through the liquid state—
this is the way plastics naturally break down. Plastics rotting is
what Alec held responsible for the sticky black film that seemed to
coat nearly everything.

He and Carlo traveled to L.A. together, Carlo serving as inter-
preter and guide on what felt like a safari. Alec rode shotgun in the
rental car; Carlo drove. Alec could not drive, because, as Carlo
said, he took it all too seriously. Alec could so easily imagine driving down Sunset and becoming suddenly one of them, the Jews of
the Entertainment Industry who have lost their bearings: himself
getting drunk, himself picking up a prostitute, a girl who was still
technically a child, himself having sex with a girl who turned out to
be Cecily's age.

"Christ Jesus," he said. "Even the respectable women dress like
whores here."

"Alec," Carlo said, "these women *are* whores. What's more, a few aren't exactly women."

He and Carlo were driving down Santa Monica Boulevard past a neon-lit sexual paraphernalia shop called La Sex Boîte. Dick-shaped objects are grandly displayed on satin pillows, these set into Claes Oldenburg–scaled candy papers. The building was elegant and new, done in L.A. vernacular—a duck, according to Venturi's lexicon. The shop's roof tipped upward like the left-open lid of a chocolate box, as if God himself had succumbed to retail.

"Did you know that Hebrew has no name for the genitals?" Alec asked.

"Really?"

"No words for the unmentionables, polite or impolite, none scientific that are not borrowed." Alec was watching whores on the sidewalk and was speaking wistfully. "No cunt," he said. "No cock."

"Putz?" Carlo offered.

"Yiddish," Alec said. "Like shmuck."

"Pity," Carlo said.

Carlo loved the spectacle of Los Angeles and entertainment entertained him. After his hidebound upbringing in Surrey he loved too being taken as an exotic. One of their clients spent seven months calling Carlo "Carlos," thinking Carlo was some weird kind of Mexican, one who was intelligent.

Carlo's mother had been sent out of Italy to England at the beginning of the war to finish her education. She always phoned her son in Berkeley early on his birthday to lovingly describe to him, in her soft Italian, the way the snow covered England on the morning he was born. One Jewish uncle died in a camp, but the rest of her family had survived. Old men in L.A. loved Carlo when they found out he was Jewish. Alec's father had been like that, loving nothing more than finding a semisecret Jew hidden high up in famous places. *They Too Were Jews* was one of the books Alec was given when he was a little boy.

The night before he and Carlo flew down, Alec dreamed a dream so clearly anti-Semitic he was ashamed to have been the one to dream it. He was in a Hollywood peopled by loud, thick-browed Jews out of Nazi propaganda, Jews with big noses and Groucho glasses, spitting on the glass at Cantor's deli on Fairfax: "I was here before the whole line was here—waddamI? Invisible?"

Then the dream transfigured, became the hard, hot glittering streets of yet another stern reality—crass hipsters, old men dressed like geriatric gangsters—these were their rich clients, Alec guessed, producers and the sons of producers, decked out in the stereotypical way the *goyim* could so easily caricature, tight jeans riding below their bellies, yellow cashmere sweaters worn without undershirts. They had deep leathery tans; the daughters of these had noses and chins and tits all paid for by their fathers and made of synthetics. These Jews of Industry wandered aimlessly in this place that was so recently a desert, doing no philanthropy, marrying blonde after blonde. The serial blondes came by bus from small towns in the Midwest, but where did they get Jews like these? Devoted to money only, Jews who found no time to read? They were rich beyond anyone's dreams of avarice, but not one of them had ever asked Carlo and Alec to make a place in his house for a library.

Half-sickened, he woke up. Hollywood was a geriatric asylum, just like the Jewish Home for the Aged in Queens, Alec realized. His father was in Heaven, and West L.A. was the locked floor in some Old Folks Home. It was the Hell on Earth he and his sister had just consigned their mother to.

21

At Home in the Proximate World

T HE DRIVEWAY, he saw, was full of them, the stylish cars of her stylish, dykish women: Volvos, Broncos, an old Suburban, a Range Rover, the new off-road Lincoln. He'd just read about a lawyer's first blond wife, married sixteen years then abandoned, who'd driven her four-wheeler uphill in the early morning light to the new and bigger house of her ex and his new blond wife and shot them both to death as they slept.

But then he read too much and knew too much about the wrong kind of things: that the family name was Ickes, that the license of the first blond's Jeep Cherokee read LODEMUP. He should have being reading Torah, should at least have turned, in his physics text, to the chapter on the properties of light. He needed to know less about the geography of entry and exit wounds and the lividity of bodies and more about colliding galaxies.

This was the time of year when night poured quickly into the canyon, and a new and liquid darkness spilled upward from the place carved by streams, filling the world to the top of trees on the still luminous hills. His house was, simply put, a jewel. The outer walls emanating a hot gassiness, the blue concrete looking warm in the way of new stars or neon. He stood at the end of the walkway. Her women were in the Water Room.

He'd once imagined that vaulted entry as a kind of small cathedral, a place free from real use of trade and commerce, lying between the house and the proximate world. Life was simpler once, down on Oxford Street, before he needed this kind of buffer. That was when Gina was home with Cecily, who was a soap-smelling baby already bathed when he came in, already dressed for bed in her fleecy Dr. Dentons. Gina used to stand on tiptoe to kiss him, to pull him to her so she could whisper: "Wanna? Want to help me get the baby right to bed?" Her breath moved the hairs in his ear. "Wanna skip dinner and come upstairs and mess around?" Her voice was huskier then. She would still lie down with him in the afternoon, would still stay in bed for a moment on a weekend morning.

He suddenly understood: this was an art tour of hers, the kind of thing she did that was most excruciating to him. Gina was wearing tight-cropped pants and a little gray silk top so short the curve of her belly showed. She was gesturing toward one of the resin pieces. She had so little modesty. Gina walked like a model, with the bones of her hips pushed out. Her dark hair was shaved up the back of her neck boyishly but with the bang left long. His urchin looked so styled now, so carefully tended.

Alec patted his own hair down. His thick hair was often messy. He worried his hair the way people smoke or bite their fingernails, pulling at it as he sat thinking at his drawing board—Carlo said he also made grunting sounds when he was most actively thinking. Alec discovered himself in the mirror, wide eyed, the tufts of graying hair sticking out owlishly. Who was this solitary one he had come upon, the one looking so nervously rearranged?

He rubbed his face hard to clear it of expression. Gina's friends simply exhausted him. He cleared his face of this: she was sensitive to criticism. She once overheard him trying to explain her work to someone at a party, stumblingly, incoherently comparing it to Duchamp's Ready-mades, saying it had elements lately of both autobiography and of interior decoration. She had come apart driving home recently, crying out, "Don't you fucking condescend to me, Alec. My work may not be *big* as a fucking house, but that doesn't mean it lacks moment!"

"Moment?" Alec asked quietly.

"Don't," she breathed almost inaudibly. "Don't criticize my word choice."

"All right," he told her. He said this very carefully, knowing it was dangerous at times like this to say much of anything. He once said the wrong thing driving home from a party and she'd lurched out with bunched fists, striking the windshield with such force she shattered it. This was back when he still had the little blue Volkswagen and he knew that any fight with her would always be fueled by the secret rage her parents' leaving caused. She learned from that, would never be left again, he knew: it would always be Gina who did the leaving.

It was an accident, they told one another: she'd caught the glass with the hard line of diamonds in her wedding band. They did, however, become more tentative then, knowing how easy it was to find themselves sitting behind a wall of cracked glass lit by the red of brake lights, like a spiderweb hung with drops of terrible rain.

Gina was as socially adept as he was awkward. She didn't talk so much as she did what he thought of as *wording*, an accelerated intellectualized babble about artistic theory and its practice that caught the listener up in a lurching and chaotic logic. People stared at her; he couldn't bear the thought that they were merely being tolerant of her. He honestly didn't know if she was really good or not, honestly didn't want to know how she might rank in the larger scheme of things.

Alec began to trudge his slow way in out of the darkness, stopped where the walkway divided, running by the side of the house to either the kitchen or the carport. He kept extra presents in the carport, things he bought sometimes, imagining the occasion for these gifts would eventually offer itself to him. He needed to go into his house, but his wife was having a party. The language-making part of his brain seemed to have shut down. This was word blindness. It happened at work on the phone sometimes when he was talking to clients. It may have been that he was being short-circuited by the waves of cold fury he sometimes felt. The richer his clients were, the cheaper they seemed; the more demanding they became, the more he hated them.

Words swarmed, became as dense as thickets. Everyone he knew was suddenly a lawyer or had a lawyer very prominently on his board or payroll. Lawyers generated documents. Why didn't everyone quit this and go back to writing in longhand, he asked Carlo that morning. He thought they should retreat, go back before typewriters, back before carbon paper.

He stood for a moment in his carport.

Longhand, Alec thought, and the word was like the name of God, Blessed Be He King of the Universe. The word rose, worked its magic. Alec's mind suddenly cleared and began to fill with great stretching hums and clicks of emptiness, like sonar or whale song.

—— 22 ——

No Pause

S HE HAD PARTIES to which she invited women only, then wondered why Alec didn't want to be at them. He wouldn't go in;
he'd go instead to sit in the Fiat in the carport, where he kept a
long yellow tablet. He was self-sufficient. He had several of his lay
physics texts there, also the mittens Betsy recently sent, as well as a
box of Triscuits.

He would study physics. He loved the old ways of science, of
the dusty model his sixth-grade teacher had in P.S. 135, his book
Our Friend the Atom. Alec was current up to the discoveries of Isaac
Newton, who both believed and did not believe in gravity at the
same moment and with equal fervency.

Like Newton, Alec found the new discoveries logical but also
baffling: apprehension of the quantum, he knew, would forever lie
beyond him. Even the story of relativity—about the spaceship and
twins aging at a different rate and the baseball being thrown from
the train—seemed to be what Alec had to learn, then forget, and so
need to learn all over again.

People who really *got* higher math, who were able to walk inside
the mind of it and live and breathe and really participate were simply

of a different sort than he. This became abundantly clear to Alec when he was at Jamaica High. Alec studied, learned what he needed to get good grades, knew what he needed for engineering, but understood nothing in the muscles of his heart past solid geometry.

He understood gravity, understood the properties of light, *believed* it when light turned out to be both particle and wave. Light had always had this thingness for him, so it seemed logical that it proved to be as material as air or water.

In matters of the quantum, however, Alec had the sense that the truth being set down now was subject to infinite revision, that the Unified Theory would forever recede, that it was the illusionary point where the parallel train tracks met on the horizon: *il n'existe pas* except in the mind of God, who also did not exist, except in the mind of man.

Jerry Bloom tried to explain it, speaking as slowly and as patiently as he did to the undergraduates he taught. The two sat out on the deck at the Blooms' smoking Cuban cigars Jerry brought from Germany, and the gorgeous concepts of physics were placed before Alec: that Time was as a river rushing one way only, that Time went only onward toward the end of Time, that this happened at the edge of the Black Hole where Light disappeared and Time was anointed with the density of matter. Time there became like something solid, could be changed therefore, could also be transported. It might flow backward or move sideways or become gaseous and disperse from its own center, flowing every which way and all at once. Conversely, Matter at the Event Horizon—and Light was part of this—was swept in and began to flow timewise, away from us forever.

Alec could make himself believe only in the thingness of the physical world, the one he could see and touch and feel. He believed in the most simple machines that mankind made and used to act upon the objects the world held. Society was too abstract; it was an invention women had devised, an elaborate town the mothers made so they could yak and raise their babies.

Her women had invaded his house. They were too complex for

him. He read to escape from them. Reading, learning, reminded him of Saturday mornings studying at *shul.* He copied passages from books, hoping that the physical act of spelling out the words and placing them in sentences next to one another would help him to better understand them. He took paragraphs he copied by hand to the office with him, typed them up on his computer, sent these passages around to friends by e-mail.

Alec was reading physics, was also taking notes for an article he might one day write. It might be called "Frank Lloyd Wright: Materials for the American Century." His pleasure came from copying out Wright's own sentences, letting the other man's thoughts run down the muscles of his arm and into those of his moving hand. Monks had done this work before the advent of the printing press. Alec wrote neatly with a good fountain pen.

Wright knew the intrinsic beauty of materials, loved the strength of concrete and its marriage to galvanized steel. Wright called concrete Aggregate, imagined its becoming the man-made marble of the Machine Age cheaply produced at the site, made lovely by the work of the hands of a gifted artisan. Wright was a visionary, a futurist, an optimist despite his personal hardships.

Wright was just Alec's age—not quite fifty—when his hope all but ran out. These were the wilderness years during which Taliesen burned, he divorced, then went bankrupt. Then he was brought up on federal charges for crossing states lines with "an immorality of purpose," meaning he traveled from one state to another with a woman while each was still technically married to someone else.

After the Mann Act charges, Wright's commissions all but stopped. It was then he began to abase himself and to misuse his talent by taking any job offered him. A lesser man might have been destroyed, but Wright was too arrogant.

Wright kept working well into his nineties. When his world flew apart when he was nearly fifty, he still had four decades of his best work ahead of him: Taliesin West, Fallingwater, the Guggenheim Museum, the work of another entire lifetime. At seventy-two, Wright proclaimed that genius had become so easy he could shake a design out of the cuff of his shirtsleeve. He had at that point twenty more years of plans to give unto the world.

Alec was sneaking in the back way, coming into the house through the service porch and pantry to avoid her party. He found Veronique sitting on a high stool talking on the phone in the kitchen.

Veronique pointed, wagged two fingers at him meaningfully, jabbed the air hard, pointing again. She was pointing behind him at her leather bag on the floor—he brought her this. She dug in her bag, took out a cigarette, then began to gesture again. What? he mouthed.

The noise of Gina's women was behind the door to the dining room.

Veronique pointed again. He brought her the ten-inch torch Gina used to light the pilotless stove. All this happened as she sat upright in her imperial way arguing vehemently in French with one of her children.

The mail lay unsorted on the counter. On top was the newsletter from Peter's Boy Scout troop, mailed from Piedmont. Piedmont is its own municipality, with its own police and fire, entirely surrounded by the city of Oakland.

Peter belonged to scouts in Piedmont because the city of Berkeley, in a moment of typical righteousness, had thrown scouting out of its schools. Berkeley was anti-BSA because it was paramilitary, also in reaction to the Scouts' recently voted policy of being pro-God and antigay. Peter went to scouting in Piedmont to learn to sail and ski, to learn the names of trees and birds, to become a more American boy than his father had ever been.

The unsigned newsletter had been written from on high in that passive Founding Father's broad-voweled, bowed-tied kind of voice. Where did they get these people? Alec tried to read it through but kept coming back to Item Six. Item Six had been slipped in between Five, which concerned the credits earned working the Christmas tree lot, and Seven, proposing a trip to Squaw Valley during Ski Week. Item Six read in its entirety:

Please Note: There is to be NO PAUSE
between the words "one nation" and
"under God" when the troops are
reciting the Pledge.

Alec looked up, stared all those years back toward Queens, to the auditorium of P.S. 135 where, during the 1950s, he and all the other Boy Scouts of America paused to breathe right where they obviously shouldn't have. They didn't know any better. They were still so earnestly American, then, being the sons and grandsons of immigrants.

Now in his own immaculate kitchen, Alec tested himself by pledging: One Nation (one breath is taken). Under God (another breath is taken, the breath used to fuel the sincerity of the words that are to follow it.) It seemed impossible not to breathe like this. But was *Under God* always in there? Did Alec remember something about that being added by Joseph McCarthy so the Scouts wouldn't fall to godless communism? Wasn't Under God the opposite of Jeffersonian democracy somehow? How had people let this happen?

Alec pledged again, taking out the Under God. *One Nation* (one breath). *Indivisible* (all Scouts were to breathe correctly there, weren't they?) *With liberty and justice for all.*

"I knew theeese," Veronique said disdainfully. She'd come to stand by him and was reading what he was reading, smelling of smoke and perfume. "We shouldn't ave let our keeeed do this."

The smokiness of her was intoxicating. No one in Berkeley smoked any longer and nobody drank aside from Veronique Chakravarty and Chakravarthi Chakravarty and the rest of the French and East Indians and the upscale Japanese and the wealthy Chinese fleeing Hong Kong and the Moroccans and Brazilians whose children went to the French bilingual school with Peter, those citizens who imagined they inhabited not just Berkeley but the larger and more interesting world.

"We don't ave theeese in France," she said. "Oh, we ave plenty of fascist organization, but we do not ave *theees* one. The French believe only in style." She began to whisper. "The woman may all be beautiful, Ah-lik, but they don't brush their teeth. My mother? *Jamais!* Which is why my keeeed ate to *go* there."

Alec filled a big kettle from the InstaHot, put it on the stove, then leaned over to watch himself touch the gas jets of the burner with the long flame from the torch. "Where's Ravi?" he asked. The party became suddenly loud in the other room, then the laughter died away.

"India," she said. "That man is *always* in India, where I imagine *he* as a mistress. Thees does not shock me. I ate the French but at least they are not prudes and Calvinists like everyone in theees place." Veronique stared off. She was watching herself in the night-blackened window, smoking dramatically, being sophisticated and liberal-minded.

Alec poured the boiling water over the teabag in the mug, then opened the cupboard and got himself several thin ginger cookies. He came back to the stove and began to thoughtfully dunk his teabag up and down, watching the amberish blush beginning to bloom and undulate.

"Want one?" he asked. He showed her the round of one brown cookie.

As her nostrils flared, Alec remembered her saying the French do not snack or graze. "A mistress eees what *you* need, Ah-lik," Veronique told him. She was staring at him diagnostically. "Your wife appens to agree with me." Alec, dunking, said nothing—what was there to say?

"But ooo?" she asked. She was back on her stool flipping through the French school directory. "There ees theees one!" she said. She thumped the page with her smoking hand. She was wearing a short black skirt. The line of her thigh muscle was etched as a deeper shadow in the darkness of her hose. She walked her dogs uphill and far into Tilden Park each day, rain or shine. The mothers in Queens didn't have legs like this, didn't sit on a high stool in her friend's kitchen with the school directory picking out a mistress for her friend's husband.

"Or theees one, theees!" she said. "Theeese one as a glorious voice, a voice for the theater, really. Gladden? Blaudette, what eees the name of er? Divorced, she took er old one back. She as a pompous one—French, I've occluded it. Very chi-chi. I ate er, actually. Never mind, Ah-lik, I know this woman and she is one pure snob. She thinks Ravi is a black man and that all Indian woman are the servant of someone. Also, she doesn't wash—I mean thees. She as good style but her neck is dirty here." Veronique reached out, lightly touched the naked skin of Alec's neck right above his shirt collar with the flat of her fingernails. His heart kicked as if he suffered an electrical shock.

"No, never mind!" she was back turning pages. "*Bon chic, bon genre*, but not for you. And, oh: she's an artist, like Gee-na, only worse!"

Veronique looked at Alec. Her eyes, marked all around with black smear, widened as she heard herself. "Oh," she said. "*That's* a good one." Then she lowered her head and asked him: "Please, Alec, don't ever tell Gina I said that thing." Then she was off again, quickly paging through.

"But she does! Lauden? Blander? What *eees* the name of er? She paints theees orrible ugly thing, Tahiti landscape or she might do That Little Boy Sitting Like a Black Beggar in the Corner. So Victor Ugo!" She got up then and went to run her cigarette under the water in the faucet, shoved the butt down through the rubber lips of the garbage disposal.

He had been standing very close to her, smelling the twining way of the smoke and perfume held in perfect balance. The party erupted into laughter again.

He removed his teabag, put it in the sink. Alec took his tea and cookies, and in as polite a manner as possible he moved away from Veronique to sit at the kitchen table. He felt overheated suddenly and reached up to feel his own forehead. Might he be getting sick?

"Talk about ugly!' Veronique was saying. "I went at their ouse but I couldn't eat there. Cheesus! So Goya. *Je déteste Goya! Je déteste Utrillo!* You *ave* to admit it, Ah-lik—Utrillo is the most Joan Collins of painters." She poured herself more wine, lit another cigarette and came to join him at the table. "And who is that other one I hate? That Spaniard." She pronounced it *Spin-yard.* "El Greco!" she said. "I hate El Greco!"

Veronique came to sit right next to him. She'd brought the directory. Her eyes held his for one long moment. "Or do you even want a French?" she asked.

His already-hot face flushed. Alec was dumbfounded by this lawlessness. Women had their own system of mores that men had only a glimmer of, were their own tribe with rules and laws they kept secret. Was Veronique's offering herself to him to free Gina from the clammy grip of his possessiveness?

But, no, Alec misunderstood. Veronique was thumping the book again. "Oh, theees one! She as nice airs, blond, but she does not *brush* them. French, good style, but perhaps too adolescent." She raised her eyes to appraise him. "She as a good shape when she is walking away, but when you look at er face? Holy Jesus!"

Veronique then leaned in and began to whisper. "Er usband is a Jewish, quiet, somewhat dour like you, but not so andsome. But she divorced im, so she may be anti-Semite, most French hare. Or rather they do not believe there is such a *thing* as a Jewish— One Jew? *Il n'existe pas!* A French never *eard* of it." She blinked to show him the disappearance of a whole great lot of them.

She took his hot hand with her two colder ones. "Alec, aren't you feeling well?"

He shook his head. He could no longer follow her: he spoke French, but he did not *spik* this. He wanted to go out, then come in again. He wanted, for the love of Ravi, for Veronique to please *vous* him.

23

Item Ten: Where's the Butter?

Any of a class of naturally occurring, extremely complex combinations of amino acids, which are essential constituents of all living cells, both animal and vegetable, and also of the diet of the animal organism.

ALEC MOVED AWAY from Veronique, got up from the table, went to stand before the fridge. Good, it was still there. He'd written it out in his careful architect's hand, printing it neatly on a scrap of thick vellum and underlining the words *essential*, *diet*, and *animal organism*, then stuck it to the face of the Sub-Zero with a highly realistic chocolate-chip-cookie–shaped refrigerator magnet. This, he thought, was the kind of basic information people should send around on the Internet instead of all that porno. It was the definition of protein.

Alec wrote it out a couple of days before in response to yet another of Gina's white or nearly white dinners. She'd served a pale creamed soup called *potage de cresson*. Alec scrolled through, looking for substantial pieces.

"Is this the main?" he asked. He looked up, his voice hopeful.

Gina squinted, angled her small face at him. "Don't be churlish," she said to him.

He needn't have asked—of course it was the main. Gina served only cold white food these days because she needed to rush through dinner in order to get on to the more interesting parts of her life.

He'd had two ginger cookies, the cup of tea. He was under the influence of Veronique, who sometimes sat out on her deck and smoked marijuana. The scent of it drifted down along the same breeze that wafted through the chaparral, carrying the low jazz of Jerry Bloom's saxophone, the two together seeming to rope everyone into the same luxuriant memories. People once worked less, Alec thought. Music was sexier then.

"I guess it's just about dinnertime?" he said hopefully to Gina when he found her in the dining room. "So I guess they were just about going?" His cheeks were sunken, his face wan and thin. He was *becoming consular*. This is what Gina called it when Alec turned into an elective mute.

"You knew about this party." She narrowed her eyes as she accused him.

"No," he sniffed. "I actually did not."

"Why don't you get yourself something to eat?"

There were plates out on the dining room table, he saw, the little white ones from her grandmother's buffet china. Gina's women were careless. Her women would break them, probably.

"No, thank you," he said. "I have certain dietary restrictions," he added.

"That was your *faw-ther*, Alec." Her voice was crisp with impatience.

He leaned over so he could whisper right into her small and perfect ear. "Is there a toilet on this train?"

Gina stopped, raised her dark and guarded eyes to his. Her lips parted. The skin of her face seemed suddenly young and expectant. They had such a long history now, almost half their life times—did they still have a long and brilliant future?

For this moment at least they were still together, each staring into the same deep past, far beyond the current night that lay sequined and blinking below them on the flats spread out in illuminated grids.

They were together, walking again down the dirt lane in the Santa Cruz Mountains during the last days of summer. They had just moved up the hill from Oxford Street. They had their new baby; their marriage and lives had both been saved. Peter was such a stately child they joked he was like a little pope riding along in his Strollee, bestowing lazy blessings. Peter's calm as a baby did make him seem good and wise. Cecily was wild, her long blond hair flying as she ran ahead. She would run until she hit something. "Easy!" her father called out after her.

They'd come to the mountains to take his parents to ride the sight-seeing train. The lane was lined with poplars, their branches tossed with wind rush, leaves wild, turning at the top, a few of them already bright as mango. This gold against the evergreen was shocking to the eyes. Alec heard the rustle, felt his heart fill, happiness pumping like blood through all the various parts of him: nothing was wrong, nothing could ever go wrong again. He and his family had found safe haven, would go into the new house he'd built for them that was like a bunker. They would close the doors, never let a Timmy inside again.

They sat at tables to eat the picnic Gina prepared—the lunch was spoiled by Viv and Stuart's fussing about what they could and could not eat. His parents also had to excuse themselves frequently to go off to gossip and confer, then they left to go buy the tickets for the excursion. Alec and Gina stayed to pack the picnic up, to change the baby, wash Cecily's hands and face and comb her hair. They were struggling to make Cecily into the kind of child her grandparents might like, though Stu and Viv obviously no longer cared for little children.

Our treat, his parents came back saying. They offered the tickets, they themselves would not be riding. They wouldn't say why, then Stuart confided: they couldn't go on the short train ride since it lacked facilities.

Alec argued, reasoned; there was no getting them to budge. He'd send Gina and the kids and he'd stay behind with them, he said. No, Alec, we prefer that you not. What kind of parents were these, he wondered, who would talk to their own son with this kind of bland formality?

They were suddenly so old, were becoming frail before his eyes. He thought his heart might break. They needed to go bundle up, needed to go wait in the car. They'd cash the tickets in, Alec said, they'd all start home. Oh, no, Cecily would be disappointed. His parents somehow insinuated that a five-year-old's wanting a train ride after being promised a train ride demonstrated the degree to which she was already spoiled. His fury rose again. Alec and Gina took the tickets and the kids and went off just to spend the time away from them.

His parents waved and waved in their phony, joyless way as the train chuffed off into the redwoods. His father needed a toilet, Alec said, which might be natural enough, but his mother couldn't go because of her fear of trees.

Enjoy! his mother chirped as she waved goodbye. *Enjoy! Enjoy!*

24

Gorgeous Things

I F YOU'LL JUST relax for one single second and act like a human person, I'll pay you," Gina told him. "I'll pay you ten thousand dollars."

Alec looked down at the face of this, his bride, offering to pay him money to act like a human person. Her face was lean, its muscles active. Her eyes darkened with the same mix: her love, her loyalty to him, her loss of that single chance, the one moment she might have broken free of him, her resentment too at being forgiven.

He turned away from her. *"Qu'est-ce que c'est?"* he asked Cecily, who stood at the door to the study. "Ear of human?" Alec poked a small fork into a slice of fresh mozzarella, lifted it with great delicacy.

"That is *so* not funny," his daughter told him.

"I am so funny," Alec told his daughter. "I am deeply, bitterly funny and probably as profound as Shakespeare."

"God, Daddy! It's Mama's *art* group! Why aren't you more supportive?"

Alec didn't bother to reply, *supportive* being one concept he'd long since lost interest in.

Through the open door of his study he saw a little girl sitting on the piano stool that had been moved in there and raised. She sat at his library table coloring with crayons.

"What's this?" Alec asked.

"It's Maggie," Cecily said, going in ahead of him. "I'm baby-sitting."

"Not in my study, you aren't."

"Uh-huhh," she said. "Ask Mama. Mama *told* us to come in here."

Gina, in the living room, called for Cecily to come help someone find her coat.

"Don't even think about leaving me with this."

"Daddy, she's just a little girl."

Her mother called again. Cecily stomped off, saying, "See? See how you and Mama both keep giving me simultaneous jobs?" She was gesturing as she went, her beringèd fingers spasming as if she was giving gang signs or being electrocuted.

"Get back here! Cecily! I won't be stuck with this," Alec said. He may have been bellowing. This may have been why, when he turned, the little girl's eyes had begun to brim with tears. Each of her small fat hands now gripped a number of crayons.

"You need your mommy?" he said. She nodded. "Let's go find her."

"The hair of my blonde is as cow's spittle threading the wind." He whispered this fondly into the little girl's hair, which smelled like baby shampoo. This was a piece of fond nonsense he used to whisper to his blond babies. His face had gone gruff with love; he held her tightly to himself and did expect some small gratitude for this act of comfort. The little girl stiffened as he picked her up, and she now tried to twist away from him.

She was three or four, somewhere in there. He'd just heard the name but had already forgotten it.

He started in softly singing the ABCs—the juvenility of this seemed to offend her. Her whole body was tense, her face suspicious. They went looking, moved through the crowd in the dining room, went up the steps into the living room, out to look in the entry.

Her face was bright and sweaty. He had bellowed. He was babbling, random, a person who *made no sense*, as Cecily liked to tell him. Alec was too tall, his voice too low, was a man among women, completely out of scale with the rest of the population. She felt lost, was trying not to cry, but her nose and eyes were running and her cheeks were slick. Alec patted her. Her hands smelled like sugar, were sticky as dampened jellybeans. He smoothed the blond curls back from her hot face. Her mouth had gone boxlike— her eyes began to glitter like she was revving up to scream or to bite him.

"She's here somewhere," Alec said. "What's your mommy's name?"

She stopped crying, took her hooked fingers from her mouth and said with an eerily perfect pronunciation: "Anna Bell-Shay."

"Anna?" Alec asked. His mouth went wide. He moved his jaw around. "Anna?" he said again. She never came to parties.

His house was currently peopled by fashionable women dressed either in black or in the New Black which was gray, as Betsy had just explained to him on the telephone, gray being fashion's long overdue rebellion, as she said, against black's hegemony. He needed Betsy to explain these things to him, to tell him why women all had the same haircut and liked to dress alike and crowd into rooms like this one. They were all so animate. The haircut they all had was the same short sleek cap Gina and Veronique now wore. It was either that hairdo or the other one, he noticed, the one with the big and curly.

In the hall that led to the entry, he found the one who looked like a little Betsy: Something Hoberman, he thought. "Hey, Alec," she said. "*L'chaim.*"

"*Mazel tov,*" he said back at her. This was Jewish as high sign, as hand jive, the last traces of the language in which neither had ever had fluency. Still, they were of the same people, still recognized one another in that racial way and so still spoke wistfully across the ever-widening crevice of what would by the next generation be completely lost.

"One mother seems to be missing," he said. What was this one's name? Something invented, something end-of-the-alphabetish, maybe? Something starting with an *S* or *T*?

"Anna?" the woman asked. "She was down in Gina's studio a minute ago. Maggie, want me to take you to get her?"

"I'll take her," Alec quickly said.

So what was this woman's name? He knew so much else about this woman, that she did kick-boxing, that her new first name was something really arch or stupid; he even remembered where the name came from, deriving from the mispronunciation of her real one by the much younger Japanese lover with hair to his waist. This aging boy was conspicuous in his beauty, he could be seen sitting out at almost any time of the day or evening drinking coffee at the tables by the dumpster in front of the French Hotel. How did these people support themselves? His hair was turning white so rapidly it sometimes seemed to Alec like time-lapse photography.

"This is such a great house," she said.

"Thanks." Alec smiled his tightest smile.

She was wearing thin-legged black cotton pants; her hair was a mess of shiny curls. She was chewing gum, not something Alec really admired in a girl. She scuffed her flat-bottomed Chinese shoe off, rested one socked foot against the other knee so she stood storklike—it was the flat of this white foot that she moved up and down seductively.

"You and Gina have such beautiful things," she said. Her eyes flashed now with some dark humor only she could see, the lids so shiny they might have just been licked. "All these gorgeous things," she said. She said it *goyjusss*, which is how he first knew he was being led along.

"Whenever I come here," she said, "I always wish I'd remember to bring a bigger purse." She winked, her tone was layered and confidential.

Alec started, squinted. His face turned bright. He smiled the cold, shocked smile of the prideful. He was *such* an asshole, something she clearly knew.

The girl whimpered. Alec remembered Anna, who had always liked him. He went to find her, suddenly knowing she might save him.

25

Hue, Saturation, Brilliance

Tⁿ HEY MET ON the stairs leading down into the old studio that
occupied the entire downstairs space. Gina had recently set it
up as a gallery space. She was having these monthly gatherings at
which she showed her own work, that of others too.

Anna was coming up the stairs as they were going down. The
baby lunged out and Anna took her, as Alec tried to formulate an
apology. He was still stung, felt graceless, charmless, large-faced as
a golfer. He suffered from the sin of pride; he probably needed to
apologize for whole realms of nebulous crimes, for the fact that
while deeply married he had once presumed to kiss this woman,
the one who stood now before him. She was shushing her daughter, who sounded desolate. Anna was looking at Alec, however, her
eyes seemed slightly amused.

She was very pretty in the naked-faced way of blond women
who wear little makeup. She was tall and had on a long dark green
sweater; around her neck were a silken scarf in a darker shade of
the same deep green and several strands of malachite spaced with
long, slender beads of gold.

Light fell on these and upon her hair, which was kinked out in wiry curls. There were new track lights in the stairwell that led into the gallery. Gina had hired a lighting engineer so her pieces could be shown in the way she liked—this lighting was shapely and subtle and cool. Anna stood in the glow of one of these spots—it made her hair look so golden it almost seemed metallic. She lifted her eyes to him, touched her lips with the tip of her tongue, as if she too might be remembering. Her eyes were pale green, this same color smudged at the edges of her lower lashes. "Maggie, please stop now, you're okay, you're fine. You're scaring Cecily's daddy."

"My fault," Alec told her, shrugged, lifted his shoulders, twisted his mouth in a way he hoped was rueful.

"Oh, no," Anna said. "It's us, we're just cross, aren't we, Maggie? It's just that time of evening. I'm sorry, Alec—we're both just generally wrecked these days. We just don't bounce back the way we used to."

"Sorry," he also said, one more time.

Anna passed him, went on up the stairs. She was very close to him but for only an instant; his arms felt suddenly empty.

He turned to watch the movement of her hips beneath the draped material of her sweater. Her skirts, in several layers, were see-through, curtained liquidly around the articulation of the knees that moved on ahead of him. He witnessed the faint backs of her upper thighs, backs of knees, calves and ankles. Her legs were long and pale and naked beneath the fabric—she wore no hose. Her shoes were ordinary shoes. There had never been a place of more ugly-on-purpose shoes, he thought, than those on the feet of otherwise beautiful women in Berkeley at the end of the twentieth century. Shoes no longer made sense to him, now that women wore Fuck Me lumberjacking boots with all their most dainty outfits. He honestly didn't get it. Was it Fuck Me, or actually more Fuck You?

Alec followed her as she made her way back into the study. Gina was in there along with several other of her women.

"Cecily bit me in the bank line once," Alec mentioned.

"She did not." Gina was gathering dishes off the top of Alec's desk. "That's my story, Alec," she said. "And, anyway, it was Peter."

"Jock used to do that," one of the other women said. "Expropriate my stories." This one was sitting in the red leather chair where Gina's father read himself to death.

Rather, this other woman wasn't properly sitting in the chair but was crouched squatting on her bare feet, huddled back into the chair with her bottom poised on one arm of it. She was wrapped up around herself, dressed in a white silk sari, wearing a necklace of what looked like eucalyptus pods. She had elaborate henna tattoos on either hand.

She was smoking, pulling hard on one of the long white plastic As-If cigarettes that had no kick to them and weren't therefore one bit worth it. She knocked the imaginary ashes off into the palm of her cupped hand.

"Expropriation," this woman drawled dramatically, "being only one of the many reasons I divorced him."

"Community property," Anna said. Anna was talking, Alec noticed, to him alone in that she was all but whispering.

She and Alec both turned to watch as this vision got up off the chair and followed Gina from the room, trailing the scent of Sen-Sen.

"She just got back from Tangiers," Anna said.

"Where she obviously left some luggage," he said.

Her humorous eyes sought his. Her mouth was very wide. He knew so much about this mouth, the soft give of her lips, the slight pressure of her teeth and tongue.

She put her little girl down in the leather chair, went to the table and began picking up crayons, putting them carefully back into the crayon box. Her fingers were long and pale. She wasn't wearing a wedding ring. He folded his arms across his chest, leaned against the wall. He watched her fingers, their care, imagining she might take the same care with him. Then, as if hearing him think this, she raised her eyes to his.

She stood over the library table; he was across from her. Other people were in the study; they suddenly no longer mattered.

"Cecily was supposed to be minding her, but then went to do something. Loss is what set her off."

"Loss. Abandonment," Anna said. "Those are the tough ones."

"It's Cecily's age," Alec told. "She's impossible."

"Maggie too," she said. "She's almost four. It's the worst, but then isn't every age just the worst?"

"Cecily's fifteen. Fifteen's volatile."

"We know something about volatile, don't we, Maggie?"

The little girl, sucking the first three fingers of her hand, shook her head, took them out to be able to say "No" with her great precision. This child spoke the opposite of baby talk.

"It really is just impossible to ever tell if you're winning or losing." Her face was thoughtful, maybe more careworn than when last he saw her. She was getting divorced, but Charlie was no great loss. Still he hoped for her sake it was Anna who'd been the one to initiate.

Her face was sober, but her eyes did blaze out. He felt almost burned by them. The color was the early green of apple trees. He saw her swallowing, saw the muscles of her long white neck as they moved. In any social gathering over the long, nonintimate past in which they'd sat at dinner kitty-corner across the table, things had passed unspoken. She would glance at him sometimes and her face would seem amused. He knew her in the material way, knew how she felt as her body relaxed against him. It was from the time he held her in his arms. She was tall, shy, didn't like most people much—he could see it in the way she held her mouth in a kind of patient but humorous scorn.

That one evening on the back wall outside the party, she had relaxed so completely. He'd held her gently and for a moment longer than he would have had they both not been slightly drunk.

He remembered her thighs lying along the length of his own thighs, the slight press of their bodies meeting, the almost imperceptible weight of her as she gave herself up to him, a relinquishment so sexy he had always remembered it, holding the memory in a place so deep within himself he hadn't thought of it in years.

26

An Accurate Measure
of the True Extent of the
Entire Universe

PEOPLE CAME TO Gina's parties who were frankly important to her career. Though she prided herself on deferring to no one, these were people to whom she did defer. Was it this kind of nakedness then—that one might witness the degree of the other's vain ambition—that was the true intimacy of a marriage? It was knowing the depth of her ambition that most shamed him, he found.

There was one among the women on this night, an older woman with silvery hair, very elegantly dressed in a suit and high heels, who had something Gina wanted. She held it out to Gina—was it fame or money or another kind of magic? Alec's own stomach had begun to ache for Gina, for the way such a person mattered and for the way it all seemed so immaterial, so much a matter of illusion.

Her name was Dolora Conningham, and Alec was going to run her down the hill and drop her at her hotel on his way to pick Peter up from soccer. Gina insisted. This was no trouble for Alec at all, Gina said.

A few people were still leaving. Everyone had been leaving for such a good long while. Time was suddenly as huge as the universe and the universe was large as it was old. The extent was being continually rediscovered, continually expanded, realigned in the human imagination to picture what might be either proved or somehow witnessed. But the realms of heaven held steady for this moment, were, for this brief time, as perfectly understood as they had been in the time of Dante. It was because Anna was still there with him.

Anna's car was blocked in high up the drive—she couldn't get it out until the others moved.

Someone had turned on the television, tuned to the *NewsHour* on Channel 9. Had someone died? Alec wondered. Had we just bombed someone again?

"Why is that puppet talking out a radio?" Maggie asked. She and Cecily were sitting together in Gina's father's reading chair.

"It isn't a puppet, Maggie. It's actually a regular man who's just disabled."

Alec turned and saw what they were seeing: Stephen Hawking being interviewed on public television, his huge head lolling to one side of his doll's body, his mouth a toothy grimace, shiny bangs hanging down into brilliant eyes.

"Isn't it amazing that he's still alive?" Anna said.

"Is this *nine*?" her little girl asked. "Where's Mr. Rogers, Mommy? Is this the Children's Television Workshop?"

"Mr. Rogers will be back tomorrow, Sweetie," her mother said. Anna turned to Alec. "We depend on Mr. Rogers always being *the same*." She began to sing softly then: "Won't you be my, won't you be my? won't you be my?"

"Neighbor?" Alec asked.

She broke off, her eyes bright in the flush that was spilling up her throat and onto her cheeks.

"I want Mr. Rogers," her daughter said. "I want Big Bird back."

"Okay, Honey. We *are* going, we'll be going in just a minute."

Anna was on the floor picking up the small bright crackers that had spilled out of a Baggie onto the museum-gray carpet of Alec's study. She sat back on her heels, pushed her splayed fingers back through her kinky hair. She looked around. "What else?" she asked.

"Help her," Gina ordered. Alec was already down, trained, uxorious, dutiful as always, doing what he could to help the women who were always off unto themselves and secretly sufficient and who could therefore be actually reached or touched or moved. A man could fuck a woman and not have it change her in any way— she might not even notice him. He'd brought Anna's things, her big purse, her daughter's backpack. She seemed intent on picking up all of the crumbs of the crushed Goldfish.

"Leave it," he mentioned. "I'll get the shop vac out."

The patched-together phrases of Stephen Hawking's electronically synthesized voice had the same plain middle-American accent as the one on Gina's first answering machine, a model equipped with its own phone. *"You have a telephone call, you have a telephone call,"* it said instead of ringing. *"You have a telephone call, you have a telephone call, you have a telephone . . ."* it would insist until the machine clicked in to answer it, all of which drove Alec insane.

The phone was cheap plastic—Gina had bought it for herself at Costco. It destructed easily when Alec broke it apart with a hammer at the shop bench in the carport. He smashed it impulsively one day after it had sounded off one too many times.

Alec smashed it, then put the pieces into Cliff Peech's patented FanciCan, embarrassed that she would see the broken phone in their own trash. He felt so unglued, so deranged by the time he threw the phone away, he half-expected Gina, who knew everything about him, to already *know* he'd smashed her telephone and call right then and confront him. He half-imagined that its pieces would ring from the trash can, so stood by its side for a while with his head cocked to listen, then drove to San Francisco to buy her a better one. He got a beautiful MOMA phone made in Italy of titanium.

That Stephen Hawking had been given computer speech that lacked his native accent made Alec more than a little sad. He mentioned this to Anna, then told her the abbreviated story of how Gina got the MOMA phone. They were still sitting on the floor very close to one another. He could speak to her; no one else could hear him. He asked if she wondered if Hawking could even recognize these utterances as coming from himself.

"Echolocation," she whispered. "Like bats have."

It was part of another conversation they had, this was from years before. With her he seemed to have continuity. She was drawn to him, Alec was certain of it. He knew from the way each of them stayed close to one another on the floor, in close proximity but without actually touching. Their eyes held one another's, they looked at one another for too long, their needs became naked, he felt his heart race, heard his own blood rushing.

Alec was becoming transparent to himself: he understood the mechanics of his body; one of his knees first popped then clicked as he knelt beside her. He was very close to her, could smell the heat of her sweater, the bright color of her hair, the faint traces of her botanical fragrances, lemon and maybe sandalwood.

"*What he actually is,*" a bossy voice was saying, "*is specially abled.*" It was a bullhorn voice. Holy Jesus! It was Basta! The real live Basta! And she was in Alec's house! How had this happened? That the planner from down the hill—the one who stormed into the Loud Library on Hopkins Street on a Saturday morning, who came to yell at the Loud Librarians who then yelled back at her— was now *in his house*, right here at Gina's art thing?

"*And what you are,*" she was braying at Cecily and Maggie, "*is temporarily abled.*"

"The fuck," Alec said out loud. "What they are is children."

"Know what I was thinking?" Cecily asked, but the planner went right on.

"No, *what!*" Alec yelled, though he was technically not part of that other conversation.

"*People in wheelchairs,*" Basta! yelled, "*are just like the rest of us.*"

"Actually, Sweetie? Honey?" Anna was speaking to her daughter—calmly, but somewhat insistently. "There are all kinds of people with all kinds of disabilities, some old or young, some very brave—most of us do have something or another or we probably will if we live long enough. Some of us, for instance, need to go home right now and take a good long nap." Anna had veered off somewhere, had subtly changed direction, Alec noticed, and was now talking to him again. "And some people are smaller than they used to be," she was saying. "Hawking, for instance, has become very small while his mind keeps growing. His mind is now so large it can almost encompass the whole huge idea of their being a real *size* to the universe."

"And some of us," Alec added, "have lost our voice box due to an advanced case of ALS and now talk like a puppet out a radio."

"Daddy!" Cecily said.

Anna's face was alive. She thought he was funny. Basta! clearly did not. Basta! was lecturing again. Why wouldn't she go home?

"Wanna blow this joint?" he said to Anna.

"Wanna go sit outside and smoke?" This was probably the sexiest thing a woman had ever said to him.

"Was Hawking ever not sick?" she asked. She was watching the TV, sitting back on her heels. She turned to him. "Did you hear he left his wife to run off with his nurse?"

"To run off?" Alec asked.

Each looked at the other, then carefully away. They were unruly; it had all gone slightly out of their control. Over the open Baggie their fingers touched. They lifted their wet eyes to acknowledge this. Other people spoke, moved. He glanced at his wife and daughter—his family was so far away back in the other country, the name of which was Duty.

The air of the room expanded. Light shimmered strangely, all things turning luminous. This was the Power of Nothing, Alec understood; this is what balanced the weight of the known

Universe. He felt the urgent need to tell her this: physicists at Stanford had just created two tiny specks of matter—an electron and its antimatter counterpart—by colliding two beams of light in a vacuum.

It was into this vacuum that he and Anna were clearly moving. It seemed destined, written. They were going without any evidence of will.

She dropped her eyes, pressed her lips together, began to say something, then stopped. She had the slightest suggestion of a stammer, he only now remembered. Her face carried a high flush. All this was attractive, that he would be the one to know how to step back, give her time and room in which she might feel free to say anything.

He was awake, alive. The world was immediate and dangerous. He was animal, pure and consciousless. He had tightened along his seam and scrotum—cock, balls, ass—this was where he'd begun to think. Light changed, time shifted, particles had been created. Whatever the other said mattered greatly, all words becoming now both reckless and significant.

She could say anything she wanted, they could take all kinds of time. They were in that furthest and most roomy place, where there was only dark above them and the galaxies were colliding and the stars were brand new and therefore bluish and the shape of the heavens looked so different now.

27

Social Living

THE LAST FEW were in the Water Room, where a big piece of Gina's hung. It was resin; it dated from when she began to hide all meaning behind several levels of abstraction. The piece was large, geological, and it lay almost flat against the concrete, as if it was something the wall itself was in the process of exfoliating.

Alec wanted to speak of his own work to Anna, to tell her he'd made his house in a place as arid as the Holy Lands, then ran a stream through it. The stream, he'd tell her, demonstrated the On-rushingness of Time, how it pooled at the bottom of the Universe somewhere, then was pumped back up the incline to flow downhill again. There were rivers within rivers in any stream, he might have said, currents that ran faster in the center or slowed at the edge. Time was speeding up, time was sweeping by them.

She was dressed in what his mother would have admired as a good winter coat, gray kid gloves. She held her daughter to her chest, chin resting on her curls, hands cradling her bottom. Anna was rocking slightly and Maggie's mouth was open, her eyes nearly closed. He stood next to them holding their bags, dutifully as a husband.

Gina became anxious at moments of departure, and in this he could always see the girl she was in the halls at Cal, loud, raucous, telling stories with extreme animation, as if the pull of this mass of energy would serve to keep people close to her. Her need was age-old, beyond remedy, the hole dug by her parents' dying so deep nothing would ever fill it. Dolora mattered too much; it hurt Alec now to witness it. This woman, whoever she was and whatever she had to offer, didn't have enough. His eyes stung; he wanted suddenly very much to escape this zone of heartbreak.

But Gina was telling a story. This was a Berkeley story about the ways of parents and their children, about Cecily's friend Gretel's getting her nose pierced on Telegraph. And Cecily's father can only imagine the worst case, in which the person doing the piercing has AIDS and has decided to use a kit he's dug out of a trash can in the park, and this piercer's name is Jawn, J-A-W-N, and he's a really nice, really caring person, and Alec yells, Hold it right there, this is already much more information than I can possibly use, but Cecily goes right on to describe their *relationship* with Jawn, and Alec begins huffing and snorting and Gretel, who's a child of divorce and can't bear conflict as she holds herself responsible for the cracks she finds in everything, is cowering in a corner and Cecily steps right up to defend herself and all young womanhood, yelling at her father, Why exactly would we be so stupid, Daddy, as to go out of our way to go get AIDS? And *Oh my god!* you'd have to like go so out of your way to go find a *junkie* if you'd think about it for even two seconds and what are we like *idiots* to you? And it's obvious you don't respect us and how is that supposed to make us feel? And, anyways, Jawn's like this incredibly artistic person you'd probably like if you got to know him and Alec says, I sincerely doubt that.

Alec turned to Anna, their eyes caught helplessly. Life was too thick to solve—how might they extricate? Water in the creek was almost soundless as it slipped over the rounded stones in the streambed. Blameless, blameless: these things happened, were no one's fault. He simply couldn't take his eyes from her.

Alec reached out, stopped himself, touched his fingertips instead to the cold glass of the window. Gina was going on.

And anyways we already walked in the AIDS Walk and made money for the cure and our Social Living teacher knows so much about teenagers and AIDS and shit she was in *People* magazine and she wrote this book and shit and why can't Daddy like respect this? And Alec shouts, That will be about enough of that! I won't stand for it! She was not in *People* magazine! And Cecily says she was like *so totally* in *People* magazine, wasn't she Gretel? But Gretel won't answer because Alec's bellowing, and Gretel's terrified and Alec's yelling, When is it that high school teachers began to actively participate in the Culture of Glamour Trash and whatever happened to adults acting adult for a goddamned change?

The women laugh together, aside from Anna, whose eyes burn on the side of his face, and Dolora, who was looking around the room like she was seeing but was not listening.

Maggie had fallen asleep.

He walked them out to her passenger van, an older Suburban parked behind the line of shrubs up behind the carport. He wanted to say something to Anna about his wife's doggedness, how it was this same determination that always kept her going, but to praise Gina in this moment would sound like exactly what it was: a piece of hollow hypocrisy, also self-serving, intended, really, to show Anna what a good husband he really was despite what they were now about to do.

He'd first kissed her in all innocence. He'd meant only to thank her for her thoughtfulness, to show how much he enjoyed the pleasure of her company. It began as a ritual Berkeley kiss. Women in this town always kissed one another on the mouth like this, as did parents their children, as did certain men whose relationship was really no one's business. Okay, there was sex in it. She'd shivered, was cold, as was he. They were hairless mammals; they'd left their coats inside. They held one another for a moment, the time somehow extended.

A storm had been moving ashore that night; branches high

above them rattled and sent acorns and tassels of eucalyptus
flowers showering down on them. The moon slipped from behind
a cloud as with intention. He held her, closed his eyes; she relaxed
against him.

Now they were walking out to her car, their faces grim. Alec
put the bags down, then took the sleeping child from her. Anna
went around, opened the door for him. He put Maggie into the car
seat and strapped her in. They were each so well practiced at the
mechanics of parenthood they had no need to speak of it. Anna un-
locked her own door, climbed up behind the steering wheel, rolled
the window down. In the car seat next to her, Maggie had not
awakened.

Alec came back to the driver's side, opened the door to the second seat, picked up the sack, then the backpack, stashed them both
in. He carefully shut the door, closing it solidly. He dusted his hands
off somewhat elaborately. There was nothing now to keep her.

Hers was an old-fashioned van such as the ones nuns drove in
Queens when Jews were Jews and nuns were nuns who prayed in
Latin and were still habited and empty-bodied and so held off at a
safe remove from the embarrassment of any needs that might seem
base or animal, also from the language needed to speak of these
kinds of things. Alec faltered; words were failing him.

Anna sat on the high bench, staring ahead. "Can I call you?" he
asked through her open window. "Can I see you for coffee?"

"Coffee?" Anna asked. She seemed to think about this in
a weighty way, as if assessing how much harm each of their lives
was going to be able to accommodate. There would, of course, be
damage.

Anna was looking straight ahead into the darkness of the
shrubs. Her gloved hands lay high on the steering wheel, one holding the car key, silver, pointing straight up. She had excellent posture. She turned, opened her mouth as if to speak yet said nothing.

She was going to refuse him—she was serious-minded, Gina's
friend, she needed to refuse him. There were responsibilities to be
borne, lives that made demands.

What mattered more than sex to the kinds of people they were was the bonds of friendship. Everyone's family was so far away, it was only by friendships this town was knit together; friends were what made these precincts a good place to raise their children. No one they knew went to *shul* or church—there was no other congregation. Friendships needed to endure; friends were all anyone had to depend upon.

And Alec already happened to know the true arc for people such as they, the well-mapped path of graphically delineated pain. He knew the pain that burned like bones on fire, knew it from what Gina had done to him.

But he also knew the slow throb of the pulse at the side of Anna's throat and the long whiteness of her body and the ways in which she fit his hands and that the pain they shared would be part of their hell and thrill. Pain would change them. Alec wanted it to change them, wanted it to make them people whose desire was finally greater than their will.

His eyes found hers; he saw her recklessness. There were no words for what rose in him. Her eyes widened as his face drew close to hers; they glittered as if struck by the cold night air.

Their need was now a force that would deform them. He leaned in, his mouth found her mouth. They were wind-charmed, lawless. The old physics did not apply and in this new realm she already belonged to him.

3.

Absolute True and Mathematical Time

This way, we can divide matter again and again, but we never obtain smaller pieces because we just create particles out of the energy involved in the process—the subatomic particles are thus destructible and indestructible at the same time.

FRITJOF CAPRA, *The Tao of Physics*

28

The Little Ice Age

SLEEP WAS THE high silvery breath at the bluest edge of heaven; anger ruined it. Anna was so angry now she popped awake, lay there alive and ticking.

Anger floated, might fix on anything. It could wipe out control, could make her feel actively dangerous. It ruined pleasure, all sense of peace. It throbbed through her like the heat of alcohol, and Anna could no longer drink even a single glass of wine without finding she had direct and lethal access to an anger that felt corrosive if not nuclear. Fury lay beneath the surface of everything the world was made of, like an inchoate form of the final remedy.

It was Saturday morning, the morning after Gina's salon, Alec's kissing her. She could hear Charlie downstairs in the foyer—he'd let himself in. Maggie heard him too and had come running from the back of the house, where she'd been watching cartoons.

Anna stood in the upstairs bathroom splashing water on her face and shoving at the odd shape her hair took on while she'd been sleeping. She would need to get it wet, then to poke and spritz and fluff it, to get it to dry again into its springy curls—hers wasn't hair

she could just go run a comb through. It was so kinky her brother
Davis called it the Pubic Dog when they were in high school. She'd
grown tall so early, had become so quickly conspicuous. Her adolescence was the one long painful public agony she recently believed she'd somehow made it through.

Now she was sweating and blushing again, shamed that Alec
kissed her. Gina was a friend of hers. Anna didn't respect people—
Charlie—who did these things. She had always believed she was
more strictly moral than Charlie was, that good behavior had been
completely inculcated by her upstanding mother.

Anna pulled her robe around her and started downstairs. She
brought her fingers to her lips, pressed, still feeling the hard push
of Alec's mouth on hers. The fact of Alec's living in a house with his
wife and children only a mile or so up the hill disturbed Anna so
much she'd taken a sleeping pill when she got home and had gone
straight to bed though it was only eight o'clock.

She slept hard and almost instantly, then awoke before dawn. It
was shocking that Alec's attention—she'd always known he was
slightly interested in her—was turning out to be something actual.
This kind of affair was always hopeless. Still, she seemed to think
of him when she should not think of him, and she couldn't seem to
stop herself from having the slim bright hope that registered like a
series of tiny fluttering heart attacks, that there might be some little piece of life ahead for the two of them.

"Are you decent?" Charlie called. She turned on the landing,
saw him there below. She smiled in the calm and superior way
she knew he hated, the small smile that he said made her look
contemptuous.

His looks were easy, unstudied. He'd always been particularly
attractive to her in the morning. Bed-warm, he smelled whole-
some, like milk or toast. His smell was a matter of his good physical
health and of his skin's chemistry, his good teeth, fine soaps, his ex-
pertly laundered shirts. He probably didn't actually believe his
family's wealth indicated God loved him more than He did some-

one else, but it did give Charlie a certain confidence that she'd never had, that the earth would stay beneath his feet as he walked along.

She came down, stood there, kissed him in the cool perfunctory way that was their courtesy—this was to teach Maggie to be kind and mannerly even in difficult circumstances. Anna and Charlie were very close in height. Their kisses were always companionable.

"Hey," Charlie laughed. "And what have you been up to?" Her face was still hot from thinking of Alec; something stirred in her.

She began to move away, but Charlie placed his hands around on her shoulder blades, held her so hard against himself that her breasts flattened. Then he kissed her as if he was actually interested in the answer. Her lips parted reflexively and there was the heat of his tongue against hers, softly textured as a gumdrop, as he searched for the truth of her.

Charlie clearly had just come from being in bed with someone else—his face, lips, mouth were all softly perfumed with the blunt fact of his nuzzling another woman's cunt. Anna was drawn in by this, also repelled. Why did Charlie always need to involve other people? And what an ass this man was to leave some poor girl before he was even done.

She turned her face away, stiffening, pushed at him. "All right," she said aloud. Charlie wasn't as smart as he was clever. He smiled now in his clever way, teasing her for her Puritan ancestry, his pushing her toward the secret knowledge of what he thought she was all about. He knew nothing, really.

Anna knew what Charlie thought. He thought she was moral, but for shallow reasons, that she'd been dulled down by having come from the middle classes. My wife derives from a long line of shopkeepers and Yankee spinsters, he liked to tell people, those kind and dotty sisters who crochet doilies and have perennial borders and keep house for their brothers who are deacons in the church. Anna's family, he added, has been in this country since 1644, reproducing by parthenogenesis.

And Anna would smile weakly, murderously, at him, at his twisting any slight particle of truth about her almost opaque history. Charlie made her ashamed of her own dear mother, who actually was devout and did, as a matter of fact, happen to embroider vestments for the altar guild of St. Nicholas Parish.

Maggie was there, carrying her father's parcel self-importantly. The two of them smiled at this over her, turned and went into the kitchen as comfortably as the married family they still legally were. She put water on for coffee. Maggie put the package down and went back to watching television in the sunroom off the kitchen, this room added to the back of the house in their last attempt to save their marriage. Charlie had, he said, a surprise for her.

She turned, narrowing her eyes at him. Charlie's lips were full, well sculpted. His mouth was wide and turned up naturally at the corners, so he often seemed amused. His brow was clean and, at forty-four, virtually unlined. Beneath the skin at his smooth temple a visible pulse beat slowly.

Charlie took out a set of two keys from his pants pocket and shook them, then put them on the table. Then he opened one end of the long thin cardboard box he'd had Maggie carry in for him, tipped it, and metal license plates clanged down onto the marble tabletop. The license plates read RAWTHUR.

"And what is that supposed to signify?"

Charlie was sitting at the pie table in the little alcove of the kitchen. He'd had the table made for her; it was inlaid with a slab of green veined marble that came from the quarry near her mother's place in East Eden. The windows were open and the lemon tree right outside was blooming, though these were the last few weeks of what was still technically winter. She had chosen this house for that lemon tree. It was one of the few things about the house she still recognized after all the renovations.

"You need a new one," he said. "I thought it might be tough for you to go look at cars, then close the deal."

"So you went out and bought me *a new car*?" she asked. "Doesn't that strike you as a little . . . ?" Anna stumbled, struggled to continue. She was breathless, furious. Anna believed she might, right then, begin to shout or stab him.

"A Toyota," he said. "A little sports car in a badass color." Charlie grinned his most asinine grin. "Hoping you might, you know, try to learn to live a little."

Anna turned back to the coffee beans. Her hands shook as she held the grinder. She pressed it until the motor screamed, then screamed even higher. Live a little? she thought. Not fucking likely.

"It's a stick?" she asked. She looked over at him warily. Charlie nodded; he was, by nature, just so pleased with himself.

She pushed at her hair, sighed hugely. "I don't think this is going to work out." Her voice had gone soft with fury, her enunciation of each word precise and schoolmarmish.

Charlie scratched his chin, moved his jaw around. He ran his fingers back through his streaky hair. How had she married a person with such small eyes. He was as blandly handsome as some TV doctor, also oddly almost as unrecognizable as one.

Later when she called George Beemus to rant about Charlie's unilaterally buying her a sports car with a stick shift when she had a small child in a car seat and was going to need to carpool, her lawyer listened for a while, then suggested that the Toyota might not actually carry that much symbolic value.

And this insulting license plate? Anna broke in to ask him.

Its cost merely made for an easy tabulation, George Beemus was saying. Anna got the new Toyota on her side of Schedule C, while Charlie kept the BMW, two years old but worth about the same. Didn't Anna recall? Charlie and Anna had agreed to buy one new car, then go ahead and try to sell the old Suburban in the want ads or at the Buggy Bank on Shattuck Avenue. George reminded Anna that he said he'd help arrange this for her. They needed to sell it before it blew a gasket or its brakes failed utterly.

Failed utterly. Anna did actually now remember this part of that conversation. It was Sheila Krasner who pronounced those words. Sheila Krasner was Charlie's lawyer. Anna remembered almost actively not listening to the two lawyers as they argued over which things of hers and Charlie's they were and were not going to be able to individually go on owning. They were in Sheila Krasner's Montgomery Street offices in San Francisco. Anna had been staring out the window.

She was staring out over the bay at a shifting superflock of two-or-three thousand birds. The birds flew as one thing that veered in, folded, fanned out in a great sweep like huge shakes of pepper, dashed through the middle distance of the blue sky over the water, birds as tightly clumped as the stars once were.

These were starlings, she knew, brought to the New World from England, here to multiply unchecked, here to dominate, to drive out the native species. Starlings are known as one of the requiem birds because they feast on garbage.

29

Many Simultaneously

Sheila Krasner was short, dark, brainy. She had the silky voice and large breasts of someone who slinked through USC: First in Class, Phi Beta Kappa, Sex Kitten, Law Review.

When angry, she answered the phone like this: *Krasner!* Anna made her angry. Sheila Krasner clearly took the state of Anna personally, feeling implicated, undoubtedly, as a fellow woman, in Anna's low achievement. Sheila Krasner was continually angered on Charlie's behalf over what she called Anna's underemployment. Sheila Krasner was small-boned, dainty, but had the ability to puff up in anger with the pseudo-ferociousness of certain toads and fish. She seemed to tower over Beemus, yelling down at the cringing man: "What are we going to have to do here, George? Go to court to force your client to retool?"

Retool? Anna thought. This was months and months after they settled the tool issue—could they really be back on tools again?

Anna had been thinking of more interesting things—the birds of America, whether or not crows actually do post sentries, as she once heard. If she knew more about birds and nature, she could write poems about birds and nature.

Anna looked at Charlie, who wouldn't lift his eyes to her. This was because he was a poor excuse for a human being.

"Your client is *educated*, after all," Krasner yelled at Beemus. "Are you trying to stipulate that being a poet is a *form of disability?*"

Beemus started, then began again, begging to be allowed, please, to merely finish this one sentence. He was patient with Sheila Krasner, explaining over and over again that Anna, as a person trained in literature, had simply acquired very little in the way of marketable skills. "My client," George Beemus said, "can barely use a computer. She doesn't even type particularly well."

"*Which*," Krasner shouted, "doesn't happen to be *my client's problem!*"

Anna thought about what she knew about various kinds of birds; how pigeons, for instance, eat gravel, and these little rocks moving in the gullet act as millstones aiding in the process of digestion, then are eliminated as waste is passed. This is one of the miracles of a bird's design that makes them light enough to fly. It had always been remarkable to Anna that, with so much bird life, you saw so few dead ones lying around. Where, exactly, did all the dead birds go?

Anna thought about her own skills. She was an excellent laundress. She did do the wash just as her mother taught her. Cooking took some degree of attentiveness while, to accomplish the laundry, Anna only needed to rouse herself every now and again and drift off down to the laundry room in the basement where some wash was always waiting. She then moved one small, well-sorted pile from washer to dryer to the growing stack of still-half-damp things she probably would not get around to ironing. When these dried out, as they inevitably did, she put them back through the wash again.

These meetings were endless, with the same issues endlessly revisited and rehashed. This happened for one reason only: billable hours were adding up. Charlie's parents were rich, as all parties were aware, and cost was not an object of anyone's concern since his parents, one way or another, would end up paying for all of this.

Anna prayed for a solemnity of purpose, prayed to the God of her mother for the ability to pay attention. It was a prayer Margaret taught her. Originally in Latin, it came from the fourteenth century:

> *God be in my mind and in my understanding.*
> *God be in my eyes and in my seeing.*
> *God be in my ears and in my hearing.*
> *God be in my heart and in my knowing.*

Anna prayed to be attentive—attentiveness was bestowed on her. She began, however, to notice all the wrong things, that the Krasner-Beemus relationship was like one variety of bad marriage in which the couple must actively involve everyone around them in their constant arguments. Sheila made fun of George, who was plump and a little dopey. George, obligingly, became plumper and dopier, Krasner more brittle, more shrill.

Nearly everything Krasner said came with a little barb. "Right. Now, if we can now please turn to some *important* matters," she would say after George had gone on with some degree of eloquence. He seemed so helpless at times, Anna had to resist the urge to fire him. She wanted to fire him and hire Krasner, who was a monster but would probably win every little battle and then the war.

A divorce was agony. The worst of everyone was revealed. How could people specialize in a part of the law that showed everyone to be base, selfish, morally lazy, and less than honest? People, Anna thought, should simply set all this stuff on fire and go off on their separate ways.

Yes, but what I actually need from your client, George, Sheila Krasner would say, then she would begin to list so many items that Anna's attention began to drift. What interested Anna was Krasner's habit of *always* getting the jab in. She was reflexively offensive, Anna saw. It was a work technique, a skill that came like intuition, as when one needed to gauge the proper sheen and loft and stiffness of the beaten egg whites when making a soufflé. Krasner used this, her beauty too, to keep George on the defensive. Really? Krasner might add scornfully, or she'd say, All right, yes, yes, I see, but can we just speak frankly now? as if they hadn't been. But to put it bluntly, George, she might say apropos of nothing.

The language of the items being listed was so ponderous: Schedules for Renewed Mediation Concerning Spousal Support, Proposed Terms of Pension Buyout, Hours of Child Visitation Adjusted for Proposed Nursery School Vacations (Actual Dates TK). Projected Tuition Costs for Pre-Kindergarten (With Two-Day-a-Week Aftercare). Who knew getting divorced would be so tedious and boring?

Krasner had been reading just such a list one day, item by wearying item, when she suddenly looked at Anna with eyes alive and deadly. "Ms. Bell-Shay," she said, "Clorox is hiring."

— 30 —

Failing Utterly

ANNA WAS READING from the morning paper she'd laid out on the counter while waiting for the kettle to boil. "I see," she said to George Beemus, though she wasn't paying much attention to Beemus. He'd phoned so early she hadn't yet had time to make a pot of tea.

This call was about the title to the house. The house and its ownership were the Big Ticket Items, the last major things at issue. Though Anna lacked the means with which to buy his interest out, Charlie probably was going to turn out to be too decent to force Maggie and Anna to move. The divorce was a sniping petty battle of tiny selfishnesses. Lately they'd been attacking Anna's competence in household management as if this had something to do with what she was going to get in spousal support, though George assured her it did not and would not—this was just a ploy. It was a ploy and Anna felt aloof from it, hardly believing it concerned her. It was more of the same—hour after hour of costly foolishness.

She was reading an article in the morning paper: HARD-DRINKING MANSERVANT ENRICHED BY HEIRESS'S SUSPICIOUS DEATH.

She had the phone cradled under her chin as she warmed the pot with a rinse of boiling water, then spooned black tea leaves into its bottom. "I think so," she told George, but she was thinking about Alec and wasn't listening closely to what George was saying. "I'll have to look that up and call you." She was actually thinking of Walt Whitman's proclaiming "I am a poet of the body, I am a poet of the soul." This was the kind of poet Anna had always aspired to be. She was thinking of the line of Whitman's that went "Urge, urge, urge."

Civilization was only the thinnest overlay, she thought, the gauzy clothes that only slightly hid the nakedness of everyone's self-deception. Anna's desire for Alec was selfish: he was another woman's husband. Still, her eyes narrowed when she thought of him, her face shut down into something tight and small.

Anna was trying to pay attention to George Beemus, who might be saying something important. She should be taking mental notes. She was making tea, while reading:

The ponytailed butler, who is said to be only semi-literate, seemed an unimposing man in an ill-fitting suit as he watched from a corner of the courtroom while highly paid lawyers argued abstruse points of law. It is being asserted that not only is Mr. Lafferty a binge-drinking alcoholic, he also takes three sleeping medications, seven anti-depressants, three anti-psychotics and six anti-anxiety medicines, many simultaneously.

"Ha!" she yelled right into the mouthpiece.

While reading, she'd accidentally poured hot water to the side of the teapot instead of directly into it, and this was flooding the countertop. Anna mopped the water off the first few pages of the draft of the proposed settlement agreement, then wiped some other counters with the same wet tea towel. She was still talking to Beemus on the phone; she was thinking of Alec again.

She cleaned up, went back to reading, kept coming again to the addictive patterns of Mr. Lafferty. She wanted to call Alec when she got off and read him this aloud. She looked at the clock to see if he was in his office. She could leave it on his voice mail so she wouldn't have to speak to him. She'd read the entire article, then ask, *"Many simultaneously?"*

It was six days now since Alec kissed her, a moment's impulsivity he'd clearly regretted. He would have gone back into the house, settled in with Gina at the kitchen table, poured them each a glass of wine and asked, So what's up with Anna? Then Gina would have outlined some of the nastier parts of the Bell-Shay divorce; he'd then confess to the kiss part and his own culpability in that, and then they'd work it around to the place where they each were both pitying of her and forgiving.

Anna was now the woman all of the other women of Berkeley feared, the man-hungry divorcee looking for her next meal. Such women showed up alone at parties, talked too much, drank too much. Their language was always a little off, like they'd been raised speaking English but in a foreign country. They acted verbally prim, swearing not at all, or they swore liberally and oddly. They dyed their hair, became massage therapists, took tap dance lessons, picked up younger men while shopping for groceries at the Berkeley Bowl, then told everyone all about the weird kinds of sex they had. These women were as charged and free as ions and they evinced the same kind of atomic instability, and becoming one of these lay simply beneath Anna's intrinsic dignity.

Anna didn't even necessarily much want Gina's husband; she was sick of men and they were time consuming. She didn't want Alec to love her as much as she wanted him to come over to her house and fuck her violently once on the cold marble of the tabletop, one time only, then she'd send him home to his wife and children where all good men belonged. Alec was a good man. Anna didn't care for the other kind.

"Sure," she said to Beemus. "All right. I know. Sure. I've made a mental note of it. But I really have to go now, George, and get Maggie up and get her dressed for school."

George Beemus called Anna so often she knew he was either in love with her or he had no other clients—all these billable minutes did add up. He was exactly the type of man who always fell for her, drawn as Charlie had been by the trick of her anatomy, her coloring, the patient look her face took on. Men believed Anna would be kind, soft, maternal, as she may once have been. She was becoming more complicated now, more like her mother, who'd been through something similar and had turned out to be tough and flinty.

Beemus's call concerned the substantial mortgage she and Charlie still shared. Their house was a plain two-story box built for a working man's family at the beginning of the century—it was evidently warmer in 1907, since the house was poorly insulated and lacked all heating except for a floor register that sat between the living and dining rooms.

It may have been warmer then, or Americans were simply more tolerant of cold or were more stoical or were equipped with better character then than now.

The turn of the century marked the end of what scientists called the Little Ice Age, the period of advanced glaciation that spanned the four hundred years from Copernicus to Shakespeare to Pasteur, Freud, Einstein and les Frères Lumières. The fact of there even being Ice Ages wasn't discovered until the 1850s, proved by the fossil record—by 1900, scientists could convincingly demonstrate that the world was warming, the ice caps shrinking.

Western science in 1900 was a product of the same thinking that had shaped the Industrial Revolution. Science needed to believe in material progress, to believe that nature too was working toward perfection, and that all of this was somehow united in God's creation, so the warming trend was interpreted at first as a sign of God's approval of the Western world.

Directly ahead, of course, lay the most deadly century in all of human history.

The mind of man was an amazing thing to witness, Anna

thought, and she wondered always at the evidence of its workings: its ardent love for peace and war, for both order and for chaos.

Their old house, she thought, was proof of it: they'd had it torn up so many times before, but it was only now, as their family flew apart, that they were getting around to installing central heating.

—— 31 ——

Physicists Confirm
the Power of Nothing

S HE DROPPED MAGGIE at nursery school and drove directly to
Virginia Cleaners on Shattuck. Anna needed to get there, park,
get out of the car and actually get the job done before her will
failed utterly. Anna now had to perform what Serene Hoberman
called the Activities of Daily Living while listening to the snide
voice of Sheila Krasner, which Anna had completely internalized.

Charlie's faults were so large they seemed to go unspoken, but
Anna's needed to be itemized. The quarreling over spousal support
had somehow recently been diverted into a peculiar reactionary
eddy where Anna's domestic shortcomings were all brought out
and were being enumerated: that Anna sometimes left clothes at
the dry cleaner's for so long she forgot what was there; that Anna
had, upon occasion, served Raisin Bran for dinner.

"Which is perfectly nutritious," she said, "with two percent and
a banana cut up over it." She stared at Charlie, who wouldn't raise
his little eyes to hers. "Charlie, do you realize this stupidity is cost-
ing each of us more than two hundred dollars an hour?"

Anna pulled into the driveway in front of Virginia and parked under the overhang. She was heartsick; it felt like a physical state that involved the working of her internal organs, her breathing, the walls of her chest and abdomen. Anna had begun to weep sometimes in just this sort of place, weeping with the desolation of arrival, crying over such small things, the claim check hopelessly lost or a parking stub she could not now lay hands on and the full day's rate she would now have to pay.

Just the week before, Anna had arrived at the toll booth on the Bay Bridge on her way to meet George at the actuary to have Charlie's pension evaluated only to find she was literally penniless at that moment, having left her bag at home. The kindly maternal woman in the booth who had the most fabulously cloisonnéd fingernails, each a different gold-leafed jewel, said to Anna, You got to pull yourself together, Baby. One long, curved fingernail then hooked and flashed, hypnotically, to illustrate to Anna how she was going to accomplish this particular miracle.

From childhood Anna had nurtured a small faith that some kind and beautiful stranger would be along soon to rescue her from misery. For an instant she believed this might be the angel, like the one on the TV program, come to show that Anna was delivered, that the world had proved to be good and whole. Then she noticed that the woman was indicating to Anna how it was that she was going to need to maneuver in order to turn the van around to drive back to Berkeley the way she'd come.

Anna didn't miss Charlie so much as she missed the girl he married, the one who still half-believed in angels.

The three dry cleaning ladies—one dark, one light, one in between—were all dressed in starched French blue smocks that matched the blue of the paper with which they wrapped the shirt boxes. Their patience with Anna was excruciating. She'd left so much there for so long she had to fight the urge to lie. She thought of telling them she'd been out of the country, but this was a Berkeley euphemism for time spent in a mental hospital.

The ladies offered not a single word of criticism. Instead they worked as a team to gather and retrieve from the computerized go-around, carefully checking that they weren't handing her anything of Charlie's. They found so many items, arranged in collated bunches, dresses and blouses and slacks, clothes so out of season and style, Anna'd forgotten she ever owned them.

"Hello," he said. He'd come up behind her, may have been standing there awhile.

"Oh, hi," she said, turning to see him, saying it casually. "Are you dropping off or picking up?"

"Neither, actually," he said. He took another step and so stood very close to her to say this, his low voice going lower so Anna seemed to be listening to him with all the hollows of her empty body. "Frankly, Anna," Alec said, "this place is so expensive it gives a whole new meaning to the expression being taken to the cleaners."

He'd said her name, pronounced in that voice of his—Alec had the voice of Gawd, as Veronique liked to say. It thundered softly; Anna heard it echoing around in her.

"Expensive?" she breathed.

"We use Bing Wong up the street."

"Which is cheaper but just as good?"

They were whispering so the dry-cleaning ladies wouldn't hear them and in order to give themselves a reason to stand very close to one another. "Well, of course Virginia would be the most expensive," she said, "which is undoubtedly why Charlie has always insisted on this place."

She took a breath, went on windbaggishly. "This is what Charlie wants written on his tombstone: I ONLY REGRET MY ECONOMIES." Anna said this lightly but felt an almost keening sorrow begin to bloom below her heart, that—when tested—she was turning out to have so little loyalty: to Gina, to the dry-cleaning ladies who'd been so kind, even to Charlie in so swiftly revealing his penchant for shallow excess.

"I was on my way to the busstop when I saw your van. I stopped in to see if I could talk you into that cup of coffee I still owe you."

"Oh, yes. Well, that." Her face was hot. "The matter of that coffee?" She had been struggling with the Four Principles of Confucianism. Anna had printed them on a Post-it recently, stuck this up on her bathroom mirror. "Shame" was one she came by easily; it brought blood rushing to her face even as they spoke.

"I don't think we really made a plan to go out to have coffee, did we?" she said. "I think we thought about coffee, then each of us thought better of it rather quickly."

Alec was so tall he had to bend forward so she could hear him. His face was open, so boyish and unguarded—she had to resist the urge to put her fingers out to touch his cheek in gratitude for the way he looked at her, without guile, with nothing but perfect eagerness. He had a great curly bang of dark hair that was going gray. His brows were dark, very shiny—the ridge of his forehead shadowed his brown eyes, which were deep set and tawny.

"So how's about lunch?" he asked—one side of his face hiked up, one side of his mouth, one cheek, one eyebrow, to indicate the two of them were implicated in this, were together as antic participants in sex, which was, after all, only one of life's most comic foolishnesses.

"Alec," she whispered, "lunch is *more* than coffee."

Anna said his name, though she had not intended to. He had said her name and she had said his name and each heard the tenderness with which the other spoke and his eyes filled slightly with what she imagined was a solemn gratitude and she was afflicted with a profound understanding of how lost they already were. Each was going to protest a little, mildly, then they would go ahead and do what they very much intended to do because each believed they were going to get away with it and neither of them believed in sin or God or hell. Their affair was risky, would be destructive, and each was drawn to this in it. Having pronounced one another's names in a dry-cleaning establishment, they now joined in some small way for a little while.

Behind them the three dry-cleaning ladies were all lined up like the witches in *Macbeth*, who had seen everything and already knew and would speak, if asked, to tell in the truest riddles the ruin that lay ahead for the two of them. Anyone who was not a fool could see that no good was going to come of it.

This was a slow time of morning when shut-ins and convalescents might turn on their favorite talk shows to get a sense of real life. These weird sisters had no need of that—real life came to them, displayed itself.

This strip of North Berkeley was their own show, and they knew the names of all the players and all their troubles and excitements. When Enrique Zambrano, the waterfront commissioner and building contractor, bludgeoned an elderly Cal professor and his wife with a hammer in a typically Berkeley argument over class and caste and kitchen renovation, the parties were Virginia customers. And the dry-cleaning ladies were there the day the Secret Service closed the street for three blocks and President and Mrs. Clinton rode in one of the two black limousines, the extra one a decoy to confuse some random angry person, the kind who'd suddenly one day shoot fourteen cats, then get in a truck with his shotgun and drive for the Capitol.

Northside belonged to these three chroniclers of its history, and they knew its rhythms of clothes and sheets and the protocols of divorcement. They also knew with complete certainty that what stood before them was not a legitimate couple, in that the clothes of these two had never been slipped together into the plastic shine of one of their wedding sheaths.

Anna wrote out a check. These checks still disturbingly had Charlie's name on them though he was now using a different account. She was going to need to muster the energy needed to get herself to the bank and do something about this one day soon.

Alec had already picked up the cleaning, had gone ahead to hold the door for her. "See you later," he told the ladies pleasantly. Face flaming, Anna couldn't look at them. She carried the flat packages out. Her linens were wrapped in azure paper, were tied with bright white string as carefully as presents.

He held the door as she passed by, then he followed her to the car. She opened the side door for him, stepped aside.

Alec was like a character out of an American tall tale, his legs so long he simply stepped up into the van and began to organize its interior spaces, putting toys and books and the shrink-wrapped juice boxes she bought by the gross from Veronique who bought them by the hand-truckload at Costco where Anna herself was too agoraphobic these days to ever go into the way back, taking the flat packages of folded laundry from her and stacking them neatly there. Everything about him spoke of ease, reminded her that he was a man for whom the solidly geometric presented no unsolvable problem. Alec could plan and neatly pack and he could successfully visualize and he was going to fuck her soon.

He was crouching in the second seat in order to rehang the cleaning in two well-balanced bunches. He stacked the blue paper packages on the bench, then sat down.

"All set?" he asked as he pulled the door shut after himself.

The other three Confucian Principles were these, Anna was now remembering: Sympathy, Courtesy, Knowing Right from Wrong. They were atheists, unbelievers. How honestly were the ancient wisdoms supposed to be made to apply to the lives of moderns?

It was the accident of Maggie's car seat that made him ride as he did, in back hidden by the long drape of cleaning. He was hidden, so their behavior was already somehow covert, defiant of snoops and the jealous enemies of love—the world was full of these and it was important to act against them. There was such joy that spilled out of one small defiance, as if in Alec's hiding they were being released by a blanket acknowledgment of their wrongdoing. Anna's transgressions had always been so intricate and private: she hadn't broken large rules as a teenager because she hadn't wanted to cause her mother any more heartache than the males of their household routinely did. She hadn't broken rules as a girl in her mother's house, hadn't broken rules as Charlie's wife, aside from spiritually deserting him.

Besides, they weren't currently interested in consequence. It was more plain than that: Anna was clean from her shower and she felt intoxicatingly desirable, she could smell the soap she used, he was tall and eager. She was made to feel beautiful when Alec looked at her. And Alec's wrist bones were showing out the white cuffs of his dress shirt—this sight moved her so. He was wearing a lovely tie, a nice suit, but he was clearly a man who had never enjoyed a shirt that really fit. Alec was too long-limbed, too wide across the shoulders, someone who really would have been better off having his shirts custom-made, as Charlie always did. This was one small thing that she might tell him after he fucked her, before she sent him home.

She'd already started the car. "Where to?" she asked, but she didn't listen to the answer. She wanted to get off Shattuck before someone they both knew came up to say hello. This was such a small town that running into someone she knew happened all day every day and was the main reason Anna largely stopped leaving the house after she and Charlie split up, so she didn't have to look into any more faces marked by curiosity or pity. Pity had always seemed to Anna to be one of the most hostile emotions.

He was so tall he nearly blocked her vision in the rearview mirror. He was leaning forward so she could feel his breath on the skin of her neck. "I'm not very good at this," she said. "At least not practiced yet. This is the way Charlie acted and I've spent a long time believing I was better than he was."

"Me too," Alec said. His mouth was right next to her ear; his fingertips were resting lightly on the skin of her neck just where it curved into her shoulder, resting as if they were helpless not to.

"So we aren't pretending this is justified, are we?" she asked. "Or that we just get to do what we're doing for high-minded reasons or that this is anything but the most base kind of selfishness?"

"Guess not," Alec said.

"That's good," she said. They rode quietly along so they could each think this over for another little while.

"Because nothing will ever be the same again, Alec, and you and I will never get to sit on a wall outside a party and flirt a little."

His low voice moved against the inside of her ear. "We're here, Anna, because neither of us seems to be able to help it." Then he said, "I'm sorry, I am really sorry." He was saying this now, she knew, so he would have it said later when it was harder to say and he might mean it more truly.

They drove for a block before she said: "If we're careful, she won't find out and she won't be hurt."

"I don't want anyone to be hurt."

"Neither do I," she said, which wasn't altogether true. Her voice had taken on a hard, new edge in getting divorced. This demonstrated the degree to which Anna was being changed by her life's events. She was a different person now, not necessarily one she liked very well or very much respected.

The past steamed by in the rearview mirror. She and Alec had no past, would have no future. There was nothing but this blurring *now*, the place the van drove into, the rushing now and now of the present moment, which is where everyone in Berkeley was always urging one another to go and try to live. Anna just wasn't usually very interested in a place like the present moment, being by nature so bookish and abstracted.

His fingers were in her hair, which was still damp from the shower—she felt twisted, nearly sick, with desire for him. "You're married," she said, "so we both know what's wrong with you, but I probably should mention that I sleep way too much and that things aren't turning out the way I planned and I'm not going to have the future I thought I wanted, which was to write a few good poems and have a long marriage with its ups and downs and maybe one more baby. And I'm now economically dependent on a man who's increasingly sarcastic on the subject, and the state I find myself in can't be very attractive or romantic. And sneaking around, while maybe sexy, has never struck me as particularly adult. So we really ought to think for a second about whether we're really the kinds of people we ought to get involved with, people who can't be responsible for one another and are about to lose every scrap of dignity."

"Anna," he said, "I don't think dignity is what either of us is looking for."

— 32 —

What the Music Sounds Like

H ER VAN SWEPT in under the new dangling blooms of wisteria, beneath the twisted root wood, roped and old, the bark grayed but leafing now, pale blooms hanging skeletonized, still green, still only tinted by the brush of the bluish white they would soon become. Anna bumped up the drive at the side of the house, having left the gate open for the workmen.

Her neighborhood was filled with these big houses built for families with many children, tradespeople who would never recognize these new inhabitants or understand their conflicts and the degree to which their lives became complicated by privilege: that it often took two professional salaries to pay the mortgage and that there was no parent home with the single perfect child who was being professionally raised. These young families seemed to be able to afford only the big house but not the kids to really fill them. The many square feet of these houses were dedicated, therefore, to the storage of hundreds of millions of things.

With the children in day care and all the more able-bodied souls off earning money, no one was home by day but the very

young and the very old and those who cared for them. It wasn't until sometime after Maggie was born that Anna became alert enough
to actually notice this.

She spoke to most of her neighbors only at times of natural or
man-made disaster. She hadn't spoken to many of her neighbors
since the days of the quake and then the wildfire. The earthquake
hit at five in the afternoon when those who were employed were
still in their offices. Anna and the old people in her neighborhood,
those with canes and walkers, and the new people in her neighborhood, mostly au pairs clutching babies, all came out into the middle of the street to confer. Several of these women held the big
wrenches they needed to turn the gas off with, but no one seemed
to honestly recognize a gas turnoff valve. Then one man came
striding through walking his Airedale very quickly downhill toward
the bay, as if nothing at all had happened, and he yelled at them
not to turn their gas off, that they'd never get it turned back on
again and they had listened because this made a kind of bossy and
masculine sense.

The only men she knew in her neighborhood were the ER doctor who lived next door to her—he worked nights—and Jody Ingersoll across the street. Jody Ingersoll was a retarded boy of more
than forty who lived at home with his aged parents. This sweet,
frail couple packed Jody's lunch and stood together by the front
gate to wave him off as the little yellow school bus drove up and
toodled its horn for him.

Simon Heller, her next door neighbor, had bought himself a
pressed-tin sign at the Ashby Flea Market and got one for Anna
too. These were from the Second World War, were given out to
the night workers in the shipyards in Richmond. Anna left hers in
the front window in order to bother Charlie, but she saw it now as
Alec might and it no longer seemed entirely funny. The sign read
DAY SLEEPER.

The backyard into which she drove Alec was in a block of back-
yards that blended together into one long half-wooded lot without

an alleyway, traversed by falling-down fences that ran with vines, the field marked with young redwoods that were draped by ivy and morning glory. These were easy fences to see over, easy for a child to climb had children been home to climb them. She pulled up and parked on the concrete pad in front of the garage to keep Alec safe from being seen. She had driven into the heart of the yard, a place where the trees on the lot seemed to be returning.

Anna went to the window of Charlie's studio to make certain he wasn't in there, then went to close the gate. Charlie had moved into a rental house on Marin two years before but hadn't found a place to move the equipment in his studio. The house on Marin was, ironically, one he and Anna used to laugh at—it had been re-modeled in a way that added a huge picture window diagonally to the structure that looked out over the bay, making the house re-semble a swiveling TV set done on a Claes Oldenburg scale.

Alec climbed out of the back and began bringing the cleaning in. The crocus along the stone path were finishing and now the daffodils stood up on the little mound that was Anna's rock garden, the yellows and paler yellows only beginning to show in slits out of the green lips and, yes, it all looked sexual. The thin tendrils of the sweet peas had started up the trellis beside the Japanese deck. This deck, with its one-person soaking tub, was added to the back of the house when they did the sunroom.

The trapdoor in the deck had been left open by the Hungarians who were working on the foundation. These men had been hired by Carlo Empy and it was he who came by to check the job every once in a while, though he wouldn't charge Anna for his time or for the plans he'd drawn. She had begun explaining all this to Alec, then realized she was undoubtedly boring him with what he al-ready knew. She rushed on, trying to get to the explanation of why her house was this shambles, with its piles of debris of old brick and dirt and mortar lying in mounds on tarps at various stations around the yard.

"Guy's a mensch," Alec said. He hung the cleaning on a

wooden towel hook, knelt to look into the hole, professionally interested, then straightened, dusting off his hands and pant legs. "I love him. I've actually known him longer now than he's known Julie."

"I love him too," Anna said. "I love all of them. Maggie calls them the Empties. She says their house is funner than this one. She'd like to go live with the Empties. Many days I would too." Anna said this, then instantly regretted the pathetic way it made her sound, never mind that it was untrue. She would never be part of a large and happy family, she knew this in her soul.

She opened the double doors to the sunroom she hadn't bothered to lock and went in ahead of him. They stood together in this place, stopping as if it might be somewhere, might become significant, looking around, as if they couldn't tell what sort of reverence might be expected of them. It did look as if grave robbers had just left. Maggie's pink nightie lay on the floor in a fluid heap, her snuggly blanket next to it, grayed and fraying. A half-filled glass of orange juice, the picture books and blankets and pillows that made the little den into which Maggie liked to crawl. She wasn't yet self-sufficient and needed all this because she had parents who divorced and a mother who, while home, was preoccupied. It was her sad fate that Maggie was going to be an only child.

The odd black shape that lay in the center of the carpet took form gradually, revealed itself to be the remote control broken open at the back, with its bright wires and batteries spilling out like electronic guts. Anna stooped to pick this, at least, up. "Did you know that some woman in Memphis put a bullet in her husband's head last week," she said. "It wasn't in the course of an argument. She shot him when he flipped the channel one too many times."

Alec smiled at her, his eyes alight with the two of them, with what they were doing. He still seemed to stoop a little from crouching forward in the van. "Nice house," he said.

"Well," she said, "I wasn't really expecting company—it looks lived in, I suppose." Anna looked around. "I really don't get it," she said. "How we are expected to manage all this stuff we're supposed to own. People never used to need to have this much, did they? Or if they did, labor was still cheap enough that you could hire someone else to do the maintenance and the actual physical handling? I mean this as a question of architecture, Alec. When did this happen? There just wasn't a need for all these closets, was there? And the garages and storage slots? Just one wardrobe per person where they might hang up their one or two changes? Did you know that Samuel Beckett refused to own any more clothes at one time than a single pair of work boots, two identical pairs of pants, one jacket and two black turtlenecks and that this is probably why he got so much writing done?"

Anna was going on, but so what? She lived alone with a three-and-a-half-year-old and on many days talked to no one aside from her lawyer, who was so boring she couldn't be bothered to actually listen. Besides, Alec was smiling encouragingly.

"But this isn't actually the way I had imagined I would raise my daughter," she said. "Alone in a messy house in an empty neighborhood?"

"It's a nice house," he said. "A little dark though."

And she followed his eyes as he looked around. He did seem to be seeing diagnostically, imagining it as it might have turned out had things gone well, had she married a better man, someone more like Alec, who had had, up until now, the ability to remain true to his wife and family. She imagined the milk-white gloss of new paint on woodwork. A patient man like Alec would take the time to prepare the surface, to apply the paint in calm and steady strokes. He would see that the right walls were taken out and the skylights added and closets made and the rooms opened to the light so the air Anna breathed would no longer feel so damp and contagious as it did some days.

In the dining room the newspaper lay open on the table. Anna put the linens down, then folded the paper in neat quarters and stacked it on the piano bench. She witnessed the eccentricity of her saving things, the layers and layers of books and papers placed in a way that seemed almost archeological, all lying atop one another, and the way this, her working mess, had spilled into every common room and so clearly allowed for no other adult person to ever live with her.

Beneath the paper on top of various other things was an art book opened to a painting of Turner's, *Slave Ship Zong, 1739— Slavers throw overboard the dead and dying—Typhoon coming on.* Anna put her hand on the color plate. The image was so powerful she felt almost hypnotized by it. She wanted to tell Alec this—I *know* something about this.

Turner's image of the ship had been almost entirely abstracted in its detail. Turner was embarrassed, she knew, by these abstractions, as if they were imprecise and done in daydreams. The abstractions now looked modern because they reflect the unknowable nature of the contemporary world.

Turner here had put in only the sketch of rigging, one dark and flailing limb, a short length of chain. A poem might go with this; it might tell the truth of those basic economics, that this country was built on the backs of slaves who were insured as cargo if they drowned but not if malaria killed them. So, feverish and dying, these slaves here were being tossed in chains into the water with J. M. W. Turner there as the only witness.

"I keep these things for scrap," she said to Alec. She was slightly embarrassed, largely defiant. She marked the book with a strip of paper napkin, then closed it. She put the Turner into a dark bookcase in a room so dim she needed the overhead on to read the spines at any time of day. "Did you know," she asked, "that the American doctor who saved General Tojo's life just died?"

He smiled, shook his head, "Missed that," he said.

"But you did know Tojo was the head of the Imperial forces during World War Two and that Tojo attempted hari-kari at the time of Japan's defeat and that an American surgeon saved him."

"Vaguely."

She needed to speak quickly, she believed, in order now to get it all in before the rapidness with which she could suddenly speak shut down, except what was the real urgency? "They flew this surgeon in from somewhere, hari-kari being designed to kill you now or later in either of two ways, by gravely damaging so many organs of the abdomen and bowel that you either quickly bleed to death or if you do survive you'll still die slowly of the collateral damage. So we saved him, did it so Tojo could be tried for war crimes. He lived, was tried, found guilty, was hanged. Now isn't this just a miracle of perversity, Alec? That we are the animal with such a complex morality that we invent both these surgeries, then the notion of the war criminal who is first saved then killed by it?"

She was speaking quickly and breathlessly, enunciating carefully. It was like the same clipped way she ate, Charlie said, cutting little bites on the plate, chewing thoroughly, only one of the many things—he yelled this during the only raging fight they had ever had—he specifically hated and had hated since their very first date.

She heard herself as Charlie might have, Anna speaking, talking, in this clipped way, Anna going on and on in the highly articulate drone of National Public Radio. Shut up, she thought. Stuttering corrected, a monster was created, one who went on at such intelligent length, largely managing to ignore herself just as she might ignore an actual radio set at KQED, 88.5 FM on the radio dial, tuned in there in another room and only occasionally overhearing herself to say something that was interesting. Shut up, she told herself again. She wanted to die or at least to go to sleep, which would get her racing mind to stop. She always needed to go through the house whenever Charlie left to teach or go out to the studio, turning off all the radios he'd turned on in all the various rooms. It took hours then to get any real silence back.

Alec was still holding the bundles of cleaning folded on his arms before him. "Oh, here," she said and led him through the living room and into the entry, taking the bundled clothes from his arms, dividing them in the way of plants left in their pots too long, working together to get them up on hangers on the coat hooks. She walked away quickly to pick up Maggie's cereal bowl and put it into the kitchen sink. She filled the kettle from the tap and put it on the stove, got the bag of Peet's beans out of the freezer. "Or do you even want coffee?" she called out to him. "Would you rather have tea?"

Her voice flew up, went into the imperial range that scraped along next to hysteria. This man person wasn't even a friend of hers; she didn't know even the most basic thing about him, such as how he took his coffee. When was it a person became just too old to learn this kind of thing?

"Oh, and I do have scones," Anna remembered. "Or are you even hungry?"

His coming to her lay in the realm of perception where sex really lies, below the range of reason and normal hearing, where the animals, blessed by muteness, live out their days always knowing exactly how to be the exact animal they were born to be.

Alec was simply there. It was suddenly elemental; they wanted one another and weren't going to talk anymore in order to try to justify; they would have this no matter who was injured. Anna wanted to be injured. She had known this for some time, believing that in pain she might begin to come alive.

He was there pressing against her from behind. "We can eat something later," he said. He spoke with his face in her hair, his mouth against her throat and neck, so she seemed to hear him as she heard herself, muffled by the density of muscle and bone.

She turned and saw that his face was solemn, as if he was struggling with strong emotion. His white shirt was very bright in the morning sun. The sight of him like this, she thought, is one thing I'll always own.

He was hard, and as she turned in his arms she was already wet. Anna raised her face and his mouth was there, his tongue softly heated, his lips engulfing. It was as she imagined: his hardness, the intensity of his concentration, that he kept his eyes open, his glasses on to see her, that he stared down with a hawkishness in his handsome face that looked like it could ax into her with what looked like cruelty but was really ardor. She had honestly never witnessed this before, Charlie having needs that were so simply met.

They kissed, were pressed together against the stove, and because Alec was a thoughtful man who was calm and organized, he reached behind her for the knob to turn the burner off. This moved her. She could give herself up to him because he so clearly knew what he was doing. Everything about him was known to her, yet gorgeously strange: his mouth on her neck and throat, his big hard fingers poking at the steel studs of her soft, much-washed jeans. Her arms crossing his and Anna adept and calm, pulling his belt out, already confidently knowing the two spaced buttons of his waistband and the easily working zipper of the pants that made a soft woolen sound as the fabric fell directly down. She would never have to pretend anything with him, to be shy or modest or interested when she wasn't interested.

This was all a part of a new rapture, the way her woman's clothes were peeled away and were so much more like skin than his and she would now become so sincerely naked. A man was never naked in the same way, never so vulnerable, still armed as he was with the hard muscles of his hairy legs and with his cock and with what that gave him of a warlike nature.

The skin of Alec's inner thighs was taut beneath her fingertips, his balls cool and heavy in her palm and fingers.

Her face was pinned there hard against his shoulder as his hands got at her. He smelled like tangerines and wood shavings, wore a beautiful suit of a dark fabric with muted colors flecked deeply into it. He had the ties and suits and needed only this. He needed Anna, for her to help him find shirts that fit, for her to lead him where she knew they had to go, to go lie down in the dark place that lay right next to death.

—— 33 ——

A Tee Shirt Named Desire

THEIR CLOTHES WERE as immaterial as each had known them to be and these clothes flew off as clothes do in such a circumstance, but each had the worry that the workmen might then come and that this was the Hungarian crew Alec himself employed, so they needed to get out of the view of the uncurtained door and windows in the foyer. The contractor was from Budapest. He took off his baseball cap when he came up to speak to her, and carefully stamped his feet before he came in to use the toilet because he was from a class society where all was held more rigidly in place. Alec had used Istvan Kirali and his men for so many years he now knew a few words of Hungarian.

They got halfway up the stairs, then collapsed on the landing, made helpless by ardor. Anna lay beneath him, half undressed in her half-wrecked, half-owned house that seemed glorious for once, or at least humorous, so alive was it made by the fact of him and of her and that each had a body and they still weren't too old to be loved and that each still had hands and mouth and ass and belly and eyes to witness as they were being swept off in this wordless rush of need.

Alec was talking, using his calm low voice to say, telling, asking, saying, and she was pressed hard beneath him lying against the carpeted steps and could hear only the determination in his voice but no words distinctly. She had never known a man who wasn't almost perfectly silent in bed, as if men believed women to be less animal than they were and so were ashamed to speak except in words of false and pretty sentiment, language that was what everyone thought women were meant to hear.

She was still in her bra and panties, jeans off, one sock gone. One of his hands was up inside her underpants, down and hooked up in, his two fingers carving into her. She moved against this hand. She moved, then cried out as he shoved in more and his big fingers moved and moved and there were the sharp edges of his nails and she twisted to get both more and less of it. He held her hips and waist with the other arm and she fell back in order to be able to watch him, and his face came toward hers with his mouth made grim by what he felt and she was heavy in his arms. There was no hurry—they could take the time they needed.

Alec wore pale blue boxer shorts and the old-fashioned ribbed white cotton undershirt; the material felt thin as it slipped beneath her fingers. His shoulders were very broad, well muscled, his dark skin smooth, immaculate. He worked her right to the point of coming, saw this in her face and took his hand away.

He had skill, was confident, and because of this she floated there right at the peak of it. She found his hardened penis, thick and blunted, the skin smooth and taut and velvety, so weighted it bobbed with the gravity of its own heat and blood. His skin was darker than that of her pale hand. She pushed his blue shorts down, used both hands to hold his balls. She rested her cheek against his thigh; the hair of his groin was perfumed by laundry soap.

She sat back, brought him forward to her, saw the deep and ruddy skin of the heart-shaped head of it. Her tongue touched the heat of the slitted hole, went in, stayed there. She moved back and was sitting on her heels; he was on the steps below, his ankles wrapped in his suit pants and pushed-down shorts. They had waited so long for this. He let his cock remain lying quietly in her mouth for a while, neither moving.

Neither moved. He throbbed—she looked up to watch him as he grimaced—he was ready, was nearly coming. She waited, was completely still while holding him, her mouth feeling its subtle twitch and pump.

"Where?" The word seemed suddenly torn from him.

It was part of the same conversation they had been having off and on for years, since before Maggie was born, since the time Alec first kissed her in the backyard of the party when Anna had gone to sit outside because she was so furious with Charlie she believed she might toss a glass of wine in his face. From where she sat on the low wall, she could see Charlie inside standing at the buffet table, having bumped into one of the women he had fucked or was fucking or soon would be fucking—Berkeley was simply full of women like this, women so numerous they popped up in any movie line or in the vegetables at Andronico's or in the sea-kayaking section of REI. Charlie always struggled to introduce them. He couldn't always even recall their names, but his face had come alive with that special kind of interest when his search engine was engaged and he was drifting back and back and trying to fix on a couple of details, and she'd watch for the tiny smirk and for the slow quickening in the pulse that stood in his temple, and she'd sometimes see the quick shared glance of mutual recognition. His flagrancy carried its own attraction. Charlie sent out waves and waves of welcome, a woman was drenched in it, it was a radiance that was almost indiscriminate and simply expanded outward as from a large brick launched from the diving raft anchored in the deepest part of the flooded quarry. Anna didn't always care or couldn't figure out if she cared or only believed she ought to care, but they'd been trying to have a baby so that night it made her furious. She felt she might become insane, might drink and drink and never get enough, that she might lift two glasses to her gaping mouth at once or eat all the food set out on the table or that she might herself fuck the next person she ran into whether it was a man or a woman.

So she went to sit in the backyard, then Alec came along.

It may have been a matter of calculation, that Anna, feeling ruined by sex, set out then to wreck the next whole thing she saw and this was the Baxters' marriage. The true reason may have been as simple as this: it lay in the path of her destruction. But there was such simplicity to Alec, it seemed to her, in the plain way he showed both his desire and his disappointment, and so she'd begun to think of him.

And now after years of looking at one another across the room at the Empys' parties or the Chakravartys' parties, each knowing or almost knowing what the other one was thinking, this active waiting becoming part of the twisted rope of their lovemaking that now had everything wrapped up in it, including months and months during which she was so busy or distracted she never thought of him at all, waiting was built in. Waiting was part of the one long fuck they'd then initiated, that now entwined each in these days and nights of absence. The absence was the palpable thing they shared, the having and not having both being theirs, with the having now being what they could no longer live without. They could wait now because they were older and had learned to wait and their years of waiting had made them patient.

She was patient, she held his cock quietly in her mouth, she could do this for hours for him if this is what he wanted. She wrapped her fingers around his wrists and held his arms down at his sides to keep him there and still. She imagined Gina's watching and this excited her. Anna moved her mouth to show Gina the pleasure of kneeling before a man and allowing him to believe you were supplicant. She imagined Gina would not know this, that Alec was too large for most women and too gloomy and intense. Gina might resist him, Anna thought, or might be sullen, or might not want to lose herself to an enchantment. Anna wanted to hurt Gina, to teach her, wanted to make Gina watch the violence with which her husband was going to fuck a woman who was not his wife.

His cock lay quietly, resting, only her tongue and cheeks making the most subtle movements against the shape it held. His face was fraught, his cheeks sucked in. He had his eyes open, he took his breath in sharply, made one small cry.

Anna rested, leaning back against her own arms. "Here?" she said. He glanced around. She took his fingers in her mouth, moved her tongue over his fingerprints; his fingers were thick and long—she sucked them tasting her own glistening. He pulled to raise her; she stood, turned, brought him to the top of the stairs where he sat down out of view of the glass door.

She helped Alec untie his shoes. He took his shoes off, then his pants, shoved down his boxer shorts, kicked them away. He folded his suit pants over one arm, carrying his shoes in the other hand. The muscles of his ass were shapely.

They went down the hallway as quietly as if on tiptoe, Anna leading him to her bedroom at the back of the house where the windows faced south and east and there was a view of the bell tower on campus and the greening and oak rippled hills beyond, riffled at the top with the fringed stands of eucalyptus that moved like they were liquid. Each was comfortable now and safe and felt no awkwardness or strangeness, as if this was as it was meant to be. He sat on the unmade bed, lying back on the pillows so he could watch her.

She reached behind her back to unclasp her bra, looked at herself in the angled mirror on her grandmother's dresser and saw the underside of her luminous chin, eyes half shut, lips slightly parted, as beautiful to herself as she had ever been, if looking slightly messy and *gone*, like she was halfway drunk. She saw him watching her—wide hips, narrow waist, good breasts, belly and ass and thighs all firmly fleshed. Her hair was kinky, her throat and cheeks and breasts all slightly flushed.

"You have a nice long back," Alec told her. Anna closed her eyes; it was the sexiest thing a man had ever said to her.

"Know what I always wanted?" he asked.

"What?"

"I wanted to keep traveling," he said. His voice had been made soft by wistfulness. Anna was so moved to know this, the deepest secret of this man's broken heart. He lay back with his hands behind his neck, solemnly watching her.

"All right," she said to him. As Alec watched, she put her hand down and began to touch herself on the bump with her own wet fingers. She came to him so he could see, her own fingers there in the lips, the cleft. She twisted her pubic hair, pulling at it so she was open and could show him this. Let's go, her eyes urged him, let's go everywhere.

Alec's face was grim; he closed his eyes and swallowed as if this was somehow painful. She climbed onto the bed, pressing him back by the shoulders to keep him there, touching his nipples, his belly, his hips and balls. She took his penis in her hand, it was a little soft again. He lay on his back, legs apart, feet at a certain angle.

Alec was still wearing his dark socks. These were the long thin socks her father called his hose—they came halfway up his well-shaped calves. She pushed the socks down—they felt silky, seemed to slip with ease off his smooth dry skin. His feet were long and large, highly arched, each one heavy as she lifted it, weighed it. She knelt to cradle his foot in her lap, putting her finger between each toe. His mouth went slack and grave with the intimate feel of it.

He now wore only the undershirt, the same one her father wore to do yardwork in the summer when he came up during the last week of August to spend it with his family in East Eden. There was no washer or dryer at the cabin then, so she and her mother did the laundry by hand in the stone sink on the outside porch, then hung it on the clothesline strung out beyond the fruit trees, yellow-jackets swarming at ankle height right above the sweet mess made by the windfall peaches. Anna always was her mother's good girl. Her father bought these shirts at Brooks Brothers in Manhattan, she remembered. Girls in New Jersey called them the guinea tee; her father said *singlets*. Why did Anna's mind run like this during sex, to Gina's watching and to Charlie's other women and to the ones her father had who were somehow predictable and common and to her own mother's upset over her father's inevitable lack of better taste and judgment and why had sex never been *real* enough to really shut Anna's mind up before?

Alec lay back on the comforter, propped on pillows watching, his arms behind his head. His eyes were hazel, seemed to glint in the morning light. He was tenderly exposed, trusting. Anna smiled at him, she had a nice long back. She leaned over, began to touch the largeness of him, the smooth skin of it, the one vein standing up, the vague pulse there. The skin was taut and hairless, the same smooth inside/outside skin as mouth or throat or cunt or asshole, derived heartlike, gutlike, from so far within oneself, going so far back in the history of what a person is, back before eyes and therefore blind, before brain and perfectly wordless therefore and therefore free of guilt or shame. She wanted for once to be as plain as this, a simple thing in nature that was both beautiful and silent, something that existed for this alone and for him alone and for her own love of pleasure, and those things becoming the three winding strands of this one long rope. She wanted to live without the remove that language made, to smack at that skin until it was frayed and finally gone, to no longer have everything so *said* and therefore shadowed and so haunted.

She squeezed his balls, squeezed them until he groaned in a way that moved her. Her own face concentrated, came down into the small and perfect mirror of the serious look his had, and this was how they both knew power would pass back and forth between them.

He moved over on his side, turned her, watching her body as he positioned it. She lay beside him. She wanted to take his penis in her mouth and make him wait again for all those same long years, but he took her arms and raised her, positioned her now where he wanted her. He knelt and his face opened and his nostrils flared and he took her by the structure of her bones, his hands at the base of her skull, one set of fingers along her neck and jaw, and he pushed in so his penis went into the back of her throat and he was holding her roughly and with great and trembling strength and now he'd clearly had enough of waiting.

He held her hair at the nape of her neck and moved her as he wanted her to move in order to pace it. He moved, arching his back, watching, his face distorted, keeping his cock in so deeply and for so long she gagged, then drawing it back out again. He kept one hand at the back of her head, but slipped the fingers of the other hand down and in her. "I'll fuck you like this first," he said in his low calm voice, "then I'll shove my whole fist up."

He came as he said it, exploding into the back of her mouth. He had several long fingers in her and she came around them. She came, then came, falling away into the place where she was both intact and completely gone, never having had so much of someone all at once and in her and this is how she learned she had never before been filled.

—— 34 ——

The Sign You Stare at in Stores in Berkeley While Paying at the Register

This Is an Unreinforced Masonry Building
Which Under State of California Law
Constitutes a Severe Threat to Life Safety
in the Event of an Earthquake
of Moderate to High Magnitude.

A LEC'S EYES WERE tightly shut, the muscles around his mouth still taut, slightly twisted. She waited apprehensively; he looked agonized. Was it remorse over what they'd just done? But he opened his eyes and saw her and his face relaxed. He looked calm, even grateful. Seeing this, her lips trembled with strong emotion and she leaned over to kiss him.

"Are you all right?" Alec asked.

"Of course," Anna said. "What a question. Did you think I was somehow delicate?"

Anna got up from the bed and walked naked over to fold open the accordion doors—these closed off the kitchen alcove that lay along one wall of the bedroom and was where there was a sink. She let the water run over her hands, testing it as it cooled. She pushed her wet fingers back through her hair, filled a tall glass, carried it back to Alec.

"This is how I'm going to make a lot of money," Anna told him as she climbed back up onto the bed. She handed him the water, then watched him drink. "Isn't that about the best water you've ever tasted?" she asked. "I think the real future is in pure water. I'm serious, Alec," she said because he'd begun to smile at her. "You could bottle it and ship it east. You'd have to get a great label design, market it as Berkeley Tap." Anna took the glass and drank from it as if to test it. "BOTTLED AT THE SOURCE, its label would say."

"I think you're probably onto something," he said.

"I'd get people to do testimonials." He nodded. "Blurbs, you know, quotes."

East Bay water came from the Hetch Hetchy Reservoir in the Sierra above Yosemite. Their own fresh water that flowed from the snowpack in the Sierra down the Sacramento River delta was diverted south via the California Aqueduct to Los Angeles, where it was used to fill swimming pools and water millions of acres of lawns.

"Sorry about that," he said. He nodded behind him in order to indicate he meant their most recent intimate moment. "I didn't have anything."

"It's fine, Alec," she said. "I'm okay. Better than okay, actually."

"I didn't want you to get pregnant."

"That will not happen."

"It has," he said. "It did, to some of us."

Somehow, from someone—Serene or Veronique—Anna already knew this. "It's all right, really, Alec," she said. "All that's been taken care of." She was looking eastward out the window where the Campanile was chiming the hour of eleven. Anna would never again become pregnant, but she didn't know him well enough yet to be able to say this. Formality had come back, they were civilized again. It made her sad, that you could fuck and fuck and finally seem to get somewhere but you could never stay poised there at that far place of real intimacy where anything at all might be said or done—it had too much God and not enough self in it.

"Are you hungry?" she asked. "Shall I make coffee now?"

"You put a kitchen in your bedroom?"

"Not us, the people before. The people before rented the upstairs to students."

"What's that?" he asked. Alec was pointing at the iron Anna

used to caramelize the tops of the little individual desserts she long before stopped making—Charlie loved a perfect crème brûlée, said he could judge the quality of a restaurant by the musical tone the caramel made as he shattered it with the back of his well-tapped spoon. Anna's mother had given her this caramelizing iron along with nearly all the other fancy kitchen things Anna owned—the soufflé dishes in various sizes and the pizza stone and the tin she once used to bake madeleines. It was all part of Margaret Bell's wishfulness, that Anna have a more stately life than she herself had managed.

Anna took the iron up, felt its sturdy weight: the smooth wooden handle fit perfectly in the cleft of her palm.

"Looks medieval," he said.

"It does have a certain dark kind of heft, doesn't it?" she asked.

The iron was twenty inches long, bent at an angle; its head was solid and weighed nearly a half a pound. That weight, balanced by the fulcrum of the wrist, made it a perfect extension of the line of one's upper arm—the weight was distributed all along its length as it rested against her palm. Anna picked the iron up sometimes to offer herself some potential for violence, particularly when the anger she had recently stumbled into made her feel she might shake apart. The iron was at once so heavy and so light.

Anna showed him its weight by handing it to him. He felt it, then leaned over, kissed her deeply. Their eyes met as they sat back. It was astonishing how all proximate objects were now cathected, were now imbued with significance: how can our love make use of this? Amazing too that they'd each thought this, that each understood that the other thought this, that there might be in this unspoken understanding some way out of loneliness.

She smiled at him, then took her robe from the hook on the back of the closet door and went down the hall to the bathroom. There she peed, then sat with her arms across her belly as if she had menstrual cramps, stricken suddenly, rocking on the toilet, thinking, Oh Christ Jesus God, *now* what have we done?

It wasn't Gina she was thinking of, and of the pain they might cause her, but the faces of Alec's children. She was thinking of Cecily in particular. Anna was probably just Cecily's age when she came to know with certainty that her father was unfaithful to her mother, that he had a woman he was living with in town and that this is how her mother knew this one was suddenly more serious than the rest had been. How it became known to Anna was always something of a mystery since she couldn't remember any of this being actually spoken of or discussed.

What the drug companies needed to come up with, Anna often thought, was the little pill that combated fits of conscience. You could dissolve it under your tongue like nitroglycerine, and it would cause an instant loss of a little patch of specific memory, one small piece of the very recent past in which your life, progressing along one certain course, was all of a suddenly flung by events off in another, much altered direction. This pill would keep you from remembering how your selfish actions changed the lives of others. Global capitalists could use it, bosses who were downsizing, adulterers. You could dissolve a pill whenever the pounding of guilt and grief threaten to overwhelm. That pounding had begun in her; it was the pump of pure fear that was bearing down on her—in a moment it would overtake her.

Anna tried to breathe through it as she'd learned to breathe through the physical pain of childbirth, to find the hypnotized and abstracted place where sensation stood apart. Its name was panic, though she hadn't known that until Charlie left and Anna saw her life laid out and she noticed how alone she was now going to be. Until Charlie left, she'd believed her racing pulse and shallow breathing were merely death's percussion becoming part of her. These little deaths happened so frequently they seemed familiar, like the pounding of the Kodo drummers, *kodo* meaning *mother's heartbeat.*

She rocked and tried to pray aloud against the waves of it, prayed for her mother's God to come to occupy her heart and mind, taking the place of herself and *self* and *self*, and how she hated being so trapped by it. She'd sought to be passionate as another animal, forgetting beasts lack a sense of consequence.

Time was absolute and mathematical, was breath, and would go on and on, whether Anna was alive or dead, whether she and Alec had sex or not. Time was utterly neutral. Breath was a person's measure—so many breaths allotted, then knowledge and sensation are extinguished.

Anna breathed for a moment, stood up, washed her face, then brushed her teeth. The Four Confucian Principles were posted there on the Post-it. Her conscience nagged her: *Knowing Right from Wrong.*

Knowing Right from Wrong: Anna knew right from wrong but seemed to lack the moral strength to do anything about it. She needed to change the way she was leading her life. She needed to get going, to become active, but this day's work was already nearly finished: she had only the one thing left to do and this was getting rid of Alec.

She opened the cabinet, took a little bottle out, took one white pill, drinking tap water from the heel of her hand. She waited a moment to begin to breathe less desperately before she left the bathroom. She knew right from wrong: the right thing to do was to send Alec home, to make him promise he'd never come again.

Alec had straightened the bed and fluffed the pillows before he got back in. He opened the covers for her in welcome, making a tent—she could see that he'd taken off his undershirt and was now entirely naked. Her eyes stung. Flesh was weak, she thought, then backspaced and deleted: it was the conscience that was weak while the flesh was proving almighty.

Anna smiled wanly, dropped her robe, crawled in with him. Alec covered her carefully with first the sheet, then the comforter. He was patient, thorough, and this was its own nightmare: she could find no bottom to her feelings for him, no foothold or remove caused by suspicion or distaste—there was going to be no easy way to get out of this.

It may have been they slept, or they simply lay in bed wrapped together in the light from the east that filtered in through the open window. The muslin curtains lifted slightly out, settled stiffly back as if the world itself was breathing. She lay in his arms, feeling herself relax into his long body as he curled against her back. His breathing was slowing; she measured her breath to his so they could sleep as one thing united for this one brief time.

If this wasn't yet sleep, then it was the state that lay right at sleep's margin where the half-dreams open and beckon for you to come to them. She willed herself to be able to relax enough to go on out into the water, walking into it, her ankles, knees, the water was there at her fingertips. It was Sand Pond, her mother's house, the only place on earth Anna felt entirely safe.

She remembered that everyone she loved was safe and even happy—her mother was safe in East Eden and Maggie was safe at nursery school and she would be safe at the Empys' when Julie picked both girls up and took them home to play and Alec hadn't driven over so his car wouldn't be discovered so his life was still safe and had not yet been wrecked. Anna was in his arms—he held her and she was safe with him and he was a decent man who meant harm to neither her nor his wife and she'd taken the pill that, in a moment, might begin to calm her.

The last thing Anna saw before she fell asleep was the caramelizing iron. She didn't actually know him, she remembered, only intuited the twist of his soul, the way it would lie along the same twist as her own, how this was their beginning and this would probably be their end.

35

Cloud Chamber

AND NOW IT was springtime and because they were selfish and weak-willed and therefore unable yet to pull themselves apart, they went forward aimlessly. After three times they stopped pretending they were going to see one another only this final time and his visits then took on the pattern of the habitual.

He came first thing in the morning or at lunch once or twice a week during the hours Maggie was in school. He told his office he was out with clients or out of town or off visiting a building site, then drove to Andronico's and left the Fiat hidden on the street behind the parking lot. This was reckless, stupid, his car, with its personalized license plate, was easy to recognize. They were risking much too much.

They made love, then lay in bed to share a little breakfast or a little lunch. She was the perfect woman, who lived to cook for him. He was hungry, couldn't even remember when last he'd eaten. She told him all the secrets of her dark soul, her mute fury that her marriage to Charlie had ended as her own parents' had, that she'd seemed to learn nothing at all from her mother's example. She told him she never should have married and never would marry again, that she'd always understood the solitary nature of her maiden aunts, her grandmother's virginal sisters. Agnes and Maude lived in New Rochelle.

She told him of the pain she felt in growing up, that she was the tallest girl in middle school, got her period very early. She blushed, sweated; her lips twitched so badly when called upon she was sent to the speech therapist, who wanted to refer her for counseling. She told Alec this; she wanted to tell him everything—that her height was an agony, that her hair was white and frizzy, that she was fully formed in her body at age thirteen, with hips and breasts, and that boys teased her without mercy and that her own brother Davis was the worst of them.

She once thought of studying either architecture or medicine, she told Alec, had taken advanced math and science and mechanical drawing but had to drop out because she couldn't bear the pressure of being in a classroom dominated by boys who taunted. She was the only girl in the mechanical drawing class. Boys waited for her to look up; when she did, they mouthed words at her: *ass, boobs, tits, butt.* Words chosen to accuse her with the fact of her own anatomy, chosen to be assaultive. The boys pushed them at her when they saw they could make her color. She tried to keep her eyes down, tried to concentrate on the matters of the drawing. *Screw plate,* they mouthed. Shove it up your *hole.* These boys were pimpled, ugly, immature; they presumed Anna's interest in them and it was terrible that she was interested, that she did go home and imagine sex with one of them or with all of them. She imagined sex, though it also made her sick—pornographic language had always stirred her, had always had this dizzying effect.

Her brother was a year behind her in school, she told Alec. Davis was smart-mouthed, antic, had many friends, while Anna was so tall for a girl, she seemed freakish. Davis ignored her when they met in the hallway. Their father was almost never home by then, and Davis was completely out of their mother's control. He was younger than Anna but claimed to remember things she didn't; Anna didn't remember anything. She went from class to class with her books and notebook held to her front to try to hide herself; she kept her coat on all day long.

Anna Bell was the World's Whitest Black Person, Davis said. Her real father was Wilt Chamberlain. There was a time when she couldn't stand to hear the word *fuck* said aloud, so Davis said it constantly. *Fuck, fuck, fuck,* he said. He could have no idea how the vision of what that might mean swam up and overcame her, the sickening faces of the boys in her various classes, none of whom actually ever took a second to speak civilly to her, the chop and thrust of that Anglo-Saxon verb, the brutish smack of some of its nouns: *slap, stick, whip, slit.* The world was a movie made of blunt and soundless images: those same stinking and faceless boys becoming the herd of animals who fucked her in a barn against the bales of hay. She didn't like them. The boys she liked were in her English classes; the boys she liked were gay.

"Be nice to your sister," their mother ordered. "Your sister's sensitive."

"Aw, sure, Ma," Davis said. He reached out, cheerfully, ruffling their mother's head.

Her home life was a mess; she felt friendless at school. She found refuge in the discipline of a driven kind of scholarship. This was in Lakewood, New Jersey. Their father worked in Manhattan, came home increasingly infrequently. Davis was the drummer in a garage band, took drugs by the handfuls. Anna couldn't take drugs, couldn't even drink successfully, so afraid was she of total disintegration.

Davis now lived in Austin, Texas, the only academic Anna knew who carried a shotgun. He was a sociologist specializing in deviance, so specialized because, frankly—Davis himself said it—he happened to be one of them. The shotgun was a gift from the Hell's Angels. Davis once packed with the Angels while studying them. Anna and her brother were closer now. Davis called Charlie *that asshole.* Davis had a million frequent flier miles. He volunteered to use these miles to fly in, pepper Charlie's butt with buckshot.

Davis rode a Harley like in *Easy Rider*. Life was large from his vantage, a road movie starring him and Dennis Hopper and Peter Fonda and the Angels and filled with biker chicks and metal. Things had always happened to Davis. When he was in graduate school at UCLA, he had a summer job doing field work in a hospital in Long Beach and accidentally sparked a mob action to which riot police were called. Her brother told the story in a rapture of hilarity. The king of the Gypsies had been admitted with congestive heart failure—the whole tribe came to sit vigil.

More than a hundred Gypsies were in corridors stealing food and anything they could lay hands on—paper dressing gowns, cotton balls, boxes of latex gloves. There were little old Gypsies in Old World costumes, toothless and wizened as apple dolls. There were Kmart Gypsies, who almost looked like anyone; there were children and there were able-bodied men. The tribe was directed to the cafeteria that had been closed to others. The condiments, napkins, utensils, every single little half-and-half—the Gypsies stole all of this, anything that might be picked up and put in a pocket or handbag. Their king was already dead, of course, and had been for a while, but the hospital kept meeting and meeting trying to decide how to tell them this. It was a weekend, so the regular psychologist who did bereavement management was not available.

"They needed a grief counselor so they decided to send my brother Davis in," Anna told Alec. "You'd have to know my brother Davis—believe me, this wasn't the job for him. He's not someone who's big on tact. And he called everyone *Man* then, *Man* or *People*. Hey, People! he yelled. Hey, I need you to listen up. Your king? Hate to say it, Man, but, that's it: El Kingo's gone, zip, ka-puto! And what a long strange trip it's been."

No one had seen anything like it, more than a hundred Gypsies acting as one mass, screaming, rushing the door, keening, weeping, ripping at their clothes and faces, storming the corridors to find their king's body to drag it home. The chaos became huge, churning, operatic—Davis in its center, enjoying the spectacle.

The riot swirled around him, masses dressed in their identity outfits: hospital people in their uniforms who called the riot squad, who came with Gestapo shields and nightsticks and began battering Gypsies who could easily be identified because their faces were already gashed and bleeding and who, though armed with only the things they'd stolen, turned on the cops and the nurses and doctors and scratched and pelted them with plastic knives and stabbed them with surgical instruments still in antiseptic plastic wrappings. The most seriously hurt were dragged onto elevators that carried them right to Urgent Care to be first sedated then bandaged.

And Alec told Anna stories too. He told of the first girl who ever loved him: Layla Verdonner, who came to P.S. 135 in the middle of the school year. She arrived from Holland, spoke to no one, then lured Alec home to Hillside Avenue with the promise of chocolate pudding.

Her mother, Layla said, served real chocolate pudding the one correct way, still hot from the stove. It was made with Dutch cocoa and had cold thick cream stirred in. Layla was the girl for him: the thin, almost blue-white legs, the folded hands composed upon her desktop, the neatly turned-down anklets. It was her mother who had actually been hidden before Layla was even born, but Layla too was held captive in the attic that still seemed to wait for them.

The story told at the Queens Village Jewish Center was that Layla's mother, having lost her husband and her two boys in the camps, also lost her mind. Relief Services brought them out and put them into a furnished apartment. The ladies of Hadassah gave Mrs. Verdonner shoes, new reading glasses, tried to help her find a job.

Layla was what was then known as a bastard, but she was superior to Alec, superior to all Americans. She had her precise, accented speech, her autocratic attitude toward the correct method of making pudding. She sometimes let Alec come over, sometimes scorned him. He loved the rounded collars of her white blouses. He loved her snobbishness.

Their windows faced east, and Layla's mother used to stand for hours at her drawn drapes peeking out, wrapped in a blue-gray sweater that was too small for her. Hadassah bought her a new set of teeth, but these were Not Correct so Mrs. Verdonner set them on the windowsill in the kitchen. Alec thought they may have talked to her. It was the so-called Free World, but what meant this word *free*, she asked him. The sun was also Not Correct, the light's falling down in the wrong direction. It was moist, marine, ever-whitening, pressing strangely down into the neat Queens streets. These were greens she didn't recognize. She missed the look of certain streets as much as she missed her poor dead sons. She missed a good loaf of bread and a certain butcher shop more than she missed her husband.

Layla's mother stood watching the cape light arch over Long Island, the long hum and bending song of an unwelcome sun rising one more time. She stared back into the morning of her life toward the time when her sons might still be found alive or had not yet been born. She was looking backward. Alec was only nine or ten years old, yet he already understood this urge. He understood that there was a time when Mrs. Verdonner was not crazy. That was when she had a country, a house, a street, a family. There was history and a world and that world had a future and the chocolate pudding she made was somehow proof of it.

This was Queens Village, 1958. The streets were Gestapo-free, all had returned to normalcy and order. People smiled too much, Alec decided then, and he never revised this opinion. He took smiling to mean they were seriously frightened. His own mother was terrified, he noticed. She chirped like a bird, going "Yup! yup! yup!" People were afraid of the Bomb and of their own relatives turning out to be the next Julius and Ethel Rosenberg and of the power they'd already relinquished to the government. There was everything to fear including fear itself. President Eisenhower warned on television of the military-industrial complex. Their New Haven relatives hadn't yet de-Stalinized. Stuart worked in government. Alec was given a book about the life of Uncle Joe by his Great Aunt Sadie. His father took it down the alley to put it into someone else's ash can.

Mrs. Verdonner heaped the clothes given her by Relief in a pile in the middle of the street, added leaves, then dog shit. She peered out all day trying to decipher the manlike shapes in the forsythia, the sliver of day-blind moon, the paling light, this new wrong green. Layla begged, pleaded with her to remember they were *free*, safe here in America. The mother's eyes were blue, cold as gas jets. She folded her arms, was unpersuaded, still watched out the window, still waiting to be arrested.

She was one of the numbered ones, still possessed by history. Free World? She never heard of it.

36

Five-Year-Old,
Put Out on Highway,
Clings to Fence for Hours
Before Rescue

IT WAS A world beside the world in which they spoke in the short-hand way of twins who share a private language. They discussed such matters as the properties of the quantum and of the color green. Each knew something about green—about hue, saturation, brilliance—and neither could quite get over the pleasant shock of finding someone else who so deeply cared about this kind of thing.

What California lacked, he said, was variation in the color green. Green here was of a limited spectrum, so his eyes had waited all these years with their old Queens instinct for the spring that never came. Then he began to notice that these were desert colors, duskier and subtle.

Did he know, she whispered, that Van Gogh read green for blue? They had just made love; she was speaking directly into Alec's ear. Mmmmm, he said, less a sound than a pure vibration.

They talked about color and about the properties of light and of the Perfect Mirror into which light might vanish and never reappear—though theoretically impossible, researchers in Japan were very close to actually making one. They clipped items from the paper about this kind of thing. Each saved them for the other, secreting them away like the bright trinkets hoarded by magpies.

They shared updates on physics from the science pages, spoke of the Hubble telescope and its Deep Field images, the objects only now being identified. They talked about the Dark Zone beyond the edge of the visible universe and baby galaxies born out of star collision and about irrational numbers, such as the size of the object that is known as the square root of two. How had Alec been so lucky as to have found such a miracle, he asked, a woman who was not only good in bed but was interested in physics?

Perhaps Anna hadn't been *that* interested in such a concept as the size of the object that is the square root of two before but only because no one else before Alec ever reminded her that it was, like pi, endless—the idea of *endlessness* had now taken on heightened meaning.

Each avoided speaking much of the end of things, of his marriage or of her divorce or of mundane objects and occasions such as money or his need to put gas in his car or her need to take hers in for brakes or of what she was going to do with the sports car Charlie gave her. The Toyota was currently parked up the street from her house a ways, undriven and gathering dust.

They had sex and they ate what she made, sitting cross-legged in the bed, and they spoke of the search for intelligent life in the universe. This seemed to her to be just another name for the unending quest for God, she said. They spoke of their own religions and of their own parents and their various problems and of their kids and their past sex lives, and everything about themselves was suddenly much more interesting.

Alec didn't criticize Charlie except to say he couldn't understand how she'd stayed married for so long to a man who was so casually unfaithful. Jews were unfaithful, sure, just never casually so. Alec admitted he admired a certain casualness. Jews couldn't carry off casual, didn't do anything without the *oi vey* and the *oi vey is mir*. To be without guilt, he said, had always seemed so Christian to him—Christianity did seem to be a rather babyish religion to him because of this. What was the deal the Christers had with forgiveness. Jews didn't go by forgiveness—he, for instance, had pretended to forgive Gina though it was now clear he never had.

Also, Alec just didn't get the business with the Christian practice of *mindless* faith. What was the good of a God if not the back and forth—the Jewish God was one who liked to be yakked and yented at. And why did the Christers insist on portraying Their Lord as a kind of 911 Rescue Squad? The parents of this five-year-old, for instance, the little girl in the news story who'd been judged not sincere enough in her dedication to the Lord Her Savior, whose parents had dropped her off in the middle of the night on the meridian divider of an interstate highway, to live or die as the Lord saw fit, *and this really happened!* By morning—after clinging to the fence for hours—the child had to have her fingers forcibly pried open to get her to let loose of the chicken wire.

Well, what about Abraham and Isaac? Anna said, if they were discussing God's capacity for cruelty toward an innocent. And what possessed Alec anyway to imagine *she* might know anything about Jesus? Episcopalians didn't care about Jesus, they didn't read the Bible—they read the Book of Common Prayer. Besides, being Episcopalian had always actually seemed to her to have much more to do with table manners and the history of the kings and queens of England than with all the darker peoples running around in the Holy Lands.

It actually surprised Anna that Alec imagined she was "a Christian," she told him. One was *Protestant* when she was growing up in Nowhere, New Jersey, or one was Catholic—and Episcopalians were a subset of this since they thought of themselves as Anglo-Catholic—but no one she knew was "Christian." Christian meant being Born Again. Episcopalians were born once, then christened. She had no idea where all these Christians had come from, but it did seem like a rather recent development. According to Davis, many Christians lived in Texas, where they packed handguns and practiced execution as a sacrament.

Theirs was like a sexy childless marriage—it was fun and it

was selfish. He brought flowers. She cooked for him. He fussed over which airline she would take when flying back to spend the summer at her mother's. She was going to Sand Pond so Maggie could learn to swim. The legal part of Anna's divorce was nearly finished—Beemus's bumbling had evidently lulled Sheila Krasner into dropping her guard, and Anna was ending up with clear title to the house as part of the settlement. There were still a couple of leftover details. She and Alec didn't speak of the fall, or if, when she came back to Berkeley, she would be coming back to him.

Anna shopped. She cleaned house. She took down her curtains and washed and starched and ironed them so the light in the morning fell through stiffened muslin. They sent e-mails back and forth; these were erotic only in that his or her fingers had touched the keys that called for those specific letters, those spaces, those marks of punctuation:

This came. It was from Lewis Mumford:

The difficulties of transport and communication before 1850 acted as a selective screen, which permitted no more stimuli to reach a person than he could handle. A certain urgency was necessary before one received a call from a long distance or was compelled to make a long journey. This condition of slow physical locomotion kept intercourse down to a human scale and under definite control. Nowadays, the screen has vanished: the remote as close as the near; the ephemeral is as emphatic as the durable . . . the sudden annihilation of the usual perception of distance and closeness, the bursting of the iron bands that once made rigid the containers of knowledge, the trickling away of the perception of time and space . . . the widening crevices in what was believed, now here and there, the homely words of the language of time appear useless heaps of rubble.

This was sent in return:

What did one paranoid say to the other paranoid? I'm not following you—we just seem to have common interests.

They did have common interests. Water. Physics. Bird life in America. Colors, such as the color of black that was called crow-blue.

Neither was any longer young. It was remarkable to each that they'd met so far into their lives and kept having the same questions dawn: Had anyone before ever talked to them? Had anyone really listened?

— 37 —

Erotic Braille

TIME SURGED FORWARD during the spring they were together; time changed and each of them changed with it. Time, which had previously been frozen in each of their lives, now advanced and speeded up and was telescoped. It bounced as if it were light, went looping out with a slightly unsteady wobble. Time went out as a tide might go, and when it came flooding in, it brought love to them. Love lit the world, it turned her rooms bright, came to occupy all parts of Anna's small and restricted life. She marked the days of knowing him off on the calendar in her checkbook, either adding them or subtracting them from whatever total was actual.

The time they had been allotted was that one season, a springtime. Maybe it would be infinite. Did he know, she asked him, that Japanese had twenty-four different seasons?

Time was speeding through space at the same rate as the atomic matter the world was made of, hundreds of miles per hour. Time acted upon them, bent them; they were subject to the laws of gravity, were aging, were subject to particle decay. They were mortal and life was grave. Alec moved between the macro and the micro: the big life in the big house he'd built up the hill and the small life he had with Anna in her bed. The house on Descartes was singular, was not a house that a man like Alec could ever sell. He went back and forth; she existed in the one place only—her house where she slept and she dreamed of him and in which she waited as an empty shape.

What they required, she said, was the parallel world, and it already existed and it lay on the other side of the Perfect Mirror, where light vanished and did not reappear. Her life was more than half over, she spent so much of it asleep. So much time was wasted. Everyone deserved another chance to try to get it right this time.

She had always been attracted to the notion of dying and this was why. The two of them had died, she told him, and they'd been reincarnated and they now lay in bed in the world beside the world where all parts of them touched and were conjoined, their mouths and faces, their bellies and hands and genitals, and their eyes and ears were open to one another and their minds and hearts were eager and they didn't need to say anything at all because they already understood.

They lay in the world beside the world and now had an improved way of measuring the duration of a second—something else physicists were currently working on. Violence helped. Violence slowed time, made the details of the world more vivid.

They'd made love, he'd showered and dressed and he now lay back on the bed with her. He was fully clothed; she was still entirely naked. She was lying facedown on the rumpled sheets, her cheek cradled in her folded arms. His fingertips ran along the silky whiteness of her long back—there had never been skin like this. They had breakfast; he needed to get going. They spoke lightly of various things, their faces so close to one another's they seemed to share the same warm air. Her heart was still in rapture.

Anna still wanted him; she wanted certain things. Alec liked her to tell him what she wanted, to specifically ask, to say these things aloud and graphically so he could view it first in the shadowed stage of the pornographic imagination. She said things, was hesitant, still finding it difficult to be so nakedly revealed. She told him about the Frenchman at the roadhouse near the border of Canada who wanted to fuck her with a baseball bat.

He closed his eyes. Mmmmm, he said.

Alec had something important going on, needed to get out of there and go to work. She wanted one more story, something that might last until the next time they could be together. She wanted to know everything about him, everything about everyone he'd ever been with, everything he'd ever done with them.

There was one girl he knew when he was at Columbia—she was a waitress who became a daytime TV actress; he still saw her sometimes on commercials. She lived in Hell's Kitchen. He'd walked her home more than forty blocks from the club where they met. She didn't want him to know her real name, and she seemed to change it every week, each name striking him as being more and more fictitious. She was good-looking and she was kinky, he said, but he didn't really like her. She once had him tie her up and cover her head with a pillowcase before he got to fuck her.

Anna was listening carefully, eyes closed. Sweat stood on her upper lip.

Alec was resting back against the pillows, staring at the shapes of light and shadow that played across the ceiling. His hands were hooked behind his neck. He needed to get going. An atom is always moving. Had he mentioned the recent effort to stop the atom in its tracks by subduing it with lasers made of certain photons. An atom vibrates at hundreds of miles an hour even when chilled to Absolute Zero, he said. If they could arrest an atom—either by cold or by nuclear bombardment—it could be made to stop and lie still. If an atom would lie still, this would allow scientists to scrutinize its properties more thoroughly.

She leaned over, her eyes half-closed. She kissed him deeply, then offered her two crossed wrists to him. Arrest this, Anna said.

38

A St. Elizabeth's Watch

ANNA LAY ALONE in bed at night dreaming of Alec living just a ways up the hill from her. She dreamed of him and of him and Gina lying in bed together and of whether they slept coldly apart now that she was in their lives or whether they were still companionably entwined. She and Alec slept in a way that was as naked as they could get, as if they were trying to get as large an area of skin as they could manage to touch that of the other—Anna didn't imagine there were that many people in one's life with whom one might wish to merge.

Gina was fine-boned and pretty in a hard-faced, girlish way. She had very white straight teeth, but her smile was so small and grudging she rarely showed them. She was tough-natured, wise, had always seemed to Anna almost as proud of her misfortunes in childhood as she was of overcoming them. Veronique had told Anna the stories of Gina's childhood. Even when it was the fashion to boast about hardship, she hadn't boasted—still, everyone did seem to end up knowing most of the details.

She and Gina were friends in the Berkeley way of circumstance and mutual connectedness—they weren't closer because their kids didn't match in age or gender. Their relationship was *pleez*aunt, as Veronique would say. It wasn't a passionate friendship and they were not intimate with one another, though Anna now felt she knew Gina almost as well as she knew herself. She shared some of Alec's attitudes toward Gina, she found, and did think of her sometimes as being something akin to her own wife. Gina's work was good, intelligent, dogged. She was famously competitive with Alec, with everyone—though Alec didn't seem to actually notice this. Gina worked hard. She labored, it seemed to Anna, while Alec was effortlessly brilliant.

Alone at night, as gutted and empty as the shell of a burned-out house, Anna's pulse raced and she came alive with pain and she pulsed with an active sorrow not only for herself but for Gina and for the kids and what this love might do to all of them. She knew right from wrong but was still too selfish to get herself to behave like it. She saw her own childhood played out again, the love her father found in the other, more willing woman, the one who wasn't busy being rule-bound and thin and immaculate.

Anna was disembodied, felt her soul to hang loose as a kimono, her limbs gone bony, drawn out in sacrifice. She lay that way, arms outstretched, legs down and tensed, as if she had been stripped, skinned, raped, killed, but was somehow still alive and was now draped like a silken canopy over the marriage bed that was both her parents' and that of Alec and Gina Baxter.

Gina and Alec had been married in Queens by a rabbi, though Gina was already pregnant and hadn't technically had time to convert. Alec didn't believe in conversion to Judaism anyway. Jews were a people, he said, in the same way as were the Navajo. Jews use a canopy to create a space for marriage that is set apart and is held to be sacred. A marriage is only that one thing, a holy corner of the marketplace, one set aside from the rest of life as a spiritual room that no one else may occupy.

Now Anna hung there as that drape or canopy, there to watch the particularly sexy agony of Alec as he fucked this other woman.

Anna, eyes wide open in the dark, imagined Alec and Gina's love-making with such an active and participatory force that she seemed to be watching a silent film of it projected onto the contours and shadows of her own body. Anna had awakened him, she understood. There were times now when he fucked Gina while he thought of her.

In order to come back down the hill and to sleep inside her own skin in the covers of her own bed, Anna tried to imagine a more orderly progression for her life. Sheila Krasner was right: much of what was wrong with Anna had to do with her failure to ever earn any money. She had begun to think of selling the house—it wasn't a place she'd ever been happy until this last spring, and her love for Alec had built into it the agony of having to do without.

In order to distract herself Anna thought of various money-making schemes. She would design and market the St. Elizabeth's watch, she decided. This was the watch that not only told time and showed the date, but had etched into its crystal—in the tiniest, most Brontë-sisters-like letters—the name of the current president of the United States.

As her generation aged, Anna figured, more and more people would require this watch. Many people already did, particularly the disembodied ones, the poets and madmen, who seemed to live both inside and outside their skins. She needed a watch like this: she never left the house anymore without forgetting something she would absolutely need.

If you were a poet or madman and were slapped into a jail or hospital suffering from any number of mental or emotional incapacities, knowing the day's date and the name of the current president was how social workers determined you were enough in possession of your wits to walk the city streets. Anna would name the watch after the psychiatric hospital in Washington, D.C., where they kept Ezra Pound locked up for nearly thirteen years. It would sell well, she believed, in that it would be the right watch for these times—smart and funny, stylish and actually useful.

It was an early afternoon in the middle of April. Alec was on the phone in her bedroom talking to his office. They'd made love—he still had his glasses off. He was sitting in his boxer shorts in the big wicker chair in Anna's bedroom talking to Carlo about a trip they planned for the coming week. She got up and began to pull the bed together. In the wicker throne in his boxers he looked like Huey P. Newton in the Black Panther portrait.

Davis had that poster of Huey up on the wall of his bedroom when they were kids, also one of Eldridge Cleaver. No one ever infuriated their father as much as the Black Panthers—he seemed to think they had organized in order to enrage him. Frank Bell came home on weekends to their house in the suburbs to find music blaring and his wife drinking vermouth at the kitchen table while she played solitaire. There were revolutionary posters on the walls of the house Frank Bell bought and paid for, and his daughter was still in nightclothes and no one had even missed him.

He started bellowing almost as soon as he hit the door. "Hi, Dad," Anna stammered. "Would you like something to read?" she asked and, as if she was a stewardess, she offered him a book or magazine. He stormed off through the house, ordering Davis to get his hair cut, to turn the stereo down, to get his freeloading friends off the sofa in the finished basement. They were slovens, ingrates, they were going nowhere, would never amount to a hill of beans. Not one of them knew the meaning of work. Margaret stood, gripped one thin arm at the elbow with the hand of the other one, raised her chin. Work? she asked him coldly. Anna's father demanded that her mother quit medical school after her first year because the thought of being married to a doctor somehow emasculated him. He wanted her to stay home and raise the children.

Davis was like an ape, drugged and dreamily defiant; he made mocking noises at their dad, then ran out the back, took his car and drove off with his friends to the pizza place. Anna believed her father might kill him if he caught him, if they started fighting. She wanted her father to stop coming home, which he then abruptly did. He yelled this at Margaret the day he left: Each civilization meets its crisis in *every teenaged boy*. Anna had been thinking of it ever since.

Anna finished tidying the bed. She slipped her bathrobe on and went downstairs. A great sadness welled up in her. She walked barefoot out through the sunroom doors into the still wet yard—she left those doors standing open. She picked flowers for the lunch tray that she was putting together to bring back up to him and walked the wet brick path among the golden and blue-green tufts of ornamental grasses—Julie designed it. It was a drought garden, planted in a dirt mound held together by rocks—it held natives mostly, grasses, perennials, both fall- and spring-flowering bulbs.

Anna picked sweet peas for the pale blue vase—these pink, white and lavender stems were the last of them. They were lightly fragrant and were Cecily's favorite flower—Alec had told her this. The windows upstairs were open. She could hear him talking upstairs. He was going to New York and she wouldn't see him now for a week or more. Summer was racing toward them. Anna's divorce would be final in June. Maggie's nursery school was ending; she would be going to the French bilingual school in the fall where Alec and Gina had their son Peter. Maggie had been put in the same class with Clara Empy and Demian Chakravarty.

Neither she nor Alec spoke about the months of summer and what might lie ahead for them. Summer belonged to their children and to long days lying out by the swimming pool, to the outdoors, the sunshine, not things Anna and Alec would ever share.

Alec devoted himself to his family on weekends, busy with Peter's soccer schedule. Cecily was rowing crew, Alec up at dawn to drive her.

Maggie was now spending the greater part of one or both of the weekend days with Charlie, and the sudden silence of these childless weekends was as eerie as deafness, so loud was the clamor of the other families all around her. Anna became invisible without a child or husband. She became one of the women out on weekends doing things alone—she used to stare at them, envying their self-sufficiency, the way they seemed so calm and able to keep themselves so quietly together.

Anna had begun to go shopping early on Saturday morning to beat the crowd at the market at the Berkeley Bowl. She shopped by going slowly up and down the aisles in a love-struck daze, ignoring her shopping list. She then cooked for Alec in the afternoons so she could do something mindless while she thought of him, of the stories she wanted to tell him. Each had lived so long already, each had lots of stories the other had not yet heard.

She'd baked whole-wheat bread and poppy-seed cake, made lemon curd. The Saturday before, she made chutney, then chopped grapefruit rind for marmalade while listening to nothing except her own carefully tocking knife on the cutting board and the breathing tick of the empty church that was now her house, a place that—like her body—had never been more alive and well organized. The Hungarians were almost finished with the basement. The title had been transferred so the house was now Anna's alone.

She gardened, recycled, and while busy, Anna prayed, not for guidance, but for silence in which to work. She was too distracted to read or to write a line of poetry: his face swam before her, or a memorized aspect of the way his body worked, the line of his neck meeting his naked shoulder as he turned to look at her. She possessed Alec now, had him in eidetic memory, heard his voice, having memorized his word choice and its cadences.

Throughout the week he sent her e-mail from his office, often passages from his science texts. These were never signed. She found things in books she had to share and sent these back to him; these might be captions from plates in art books. These came and went as anonymous postings, were almost never in their own words, always the language of others that was somehow more succinct.

Now, standing at the sink in the downstairs kitchen, she filled the vase with water, then watched her hands, palms upward. There was so little respite from the loneliness. Nothing filled it except for work and reading, sex and talking.

Why was one marriage lost and another saved? There were some marriages, some that hadn't even looked particularly shaky, that the fire in the hills destroyed as surely as it burned the houses in which those marriages had existed. The insurance companies came forward with cash settlements that took into the accounting not just the houses and the furniture, but the housewares and linens and artwork, even dead cats and dogs. And more than a few of the couples looked at one another, then at the settlement, hundreds of thousands of dollars. Their middle-class lives assessed as being worth this implausible amount of money, with freedom beckoning, they sometimes just nodded, divided it equally since California was a community property state, and went off alone.

Anna had been just up the hill from Alec's house on that Sunday when the fire erupted in Vicente Canyon in October of 1991. She and Veronique were both newly pregnant—they had been out for a walk in the gusty morning along Grizzly Peak.

Anna was dressed in a big straw hat and dark glasses; her skin was pale from her smearing it with zinc oxide. It was noon. She and Veronique had walked and were back on Descartes, sitting outside on the deck, drinking iced herbal tea, eating something French Veronique's mother, who was visiting, had made for them. The hot wrong-way winds were gusting up again; these were unseasonable for October. Ravi and Charlie were off in Tilden on their mountain bikes. My God, Veronique said. What is that? She pointed to show Anna.

The cloud of smoke staining the sky to the south and east was so large, so dense, it was impossible for a moment to even get a sense of the scale of it. Then they saw two helicopters silently working against the smoke, dumping water on it as from thimbles— these helicopters were so dwarfed by the cloud's vastness they appeared only as the tiniest mechanical glints. The fire was obviously huge but also miles away. They couldn't hear sirens or the noise of the helicopters—it was clearly far off and being fought in an eerily perfect silence. Another disaster, as terrible perhaps as the earthquake but once again held at a distance from Anna, whose life's events happened without ever seeming to actually touch her.

The hot winds out of season whipped up the canyons and swept up the drying leaves—these lifted and swirled erratically and Veronique screamed out then that their husbands were on the trails that led right into it, and Anna held her and spoke to her and comforted her with logic, that the two were fast, that they'd know enough to turn around, that they'd be right back, that they would know not to ride into a firestorm, all the while ripped by the grief that ran through her that she too was pregnant and her husband too was riding there yet she didn't feel what she ought to feel. The grief was for herself: that she didn't love her husband as she ought to love him if she was having a baby with him, love him as Veronique did Ravi, physically, ardently, with this whole portion of the one person she would ever be, her single chance at a passionate existence.

Anna stood at her kitchen sink knowing that it was luck and chance that bent a life, sent it this way or that way, and that if the fifty-mile-an-hour winds that day had turned, her own life might now be so different. The winds that day drove the fire across two freeways and the Bart tracks and down to Lake Temescal and southward along the freeway on both sides into the hills above and then down into Montclair, and it also whipped this way from that first canyon, driving down along Ashby Avenue where they were able to stop it at the Claremont Hotel. The grand old hotel was gone, the news kept saying, but the hotel wasn't gone, simply cloaked in smoke so thick the news cameras couldn't see it.

The winds started one way, changed, turned. Had they not shifted, those winds might easily have found two small men on their silver bikes on a remote fire trail and pushed the fire there instead of back into the canyons where the eucalyptus stood ready as tons of oily fuel. The experiment of planting eucalyptus failed—the trees were now part of the revenge effect, nature scoffing at mankind's meddling. Eucalyptus had no purpose at all aside from providing fuel for an inferno. Tilden, Redwood, Joaquin Miller—each park was full of these trees, full too of starlings and English sparrows, imports that were all too successfully challenging the native species.

Had the Baxters' house burned that day, Gina and Alec's marriage—Anna was sure of this—would not have survived. If her work burned, Gina would have blamed him, would have left him, would have moved to New York where she would be an art star, better appreciated by better people. Work could be redone, lives remade, but the house was irreplaceable. Anna heard Gina when people praised the house too effusively. Sure, sure, Gina said, but it's such a monument to Alec's genius it's like living in Grant's Tomb with him.

Anna stood at the sink and remembered all the households lost to fire and to divorce and of the children of these houses that were torn apart and of the charred forests at the edge of deserts, all part of the water wars. California was a checkerboard chaos of water politics, Berkeley and Oakland unable to fight the fire in concert because their radio communications didn't interface and their hoses didn't match the diameter of the other's hydrants, the adapters somewhere in storage.

The burned hillsides were studded with so many thousands of stark chimneys it looked like war had come to the East Bay hills. Anna went with Julie to drive those desolate roads, thinking of the artwork lost and of the books left open on an armchair, only half-read or half-written. Nearly everyone who died in the fire was old, some found still curled upon their bedsprings. One policeman, one fireman and the younger ones, who—in the curious vanity of youth—had tried to save their cars that noon when the sky came down. There was a traffic jam high in the hills on the narrow streets that wound through Hiller Highlands, a development with greenways and hiking paths, where, in order to slow auto traffic, the planners put in cul-de-sacs.

Anna saw Julie and Carlo's house in the Oakland hills only once with the furniture moved in. The Empys lived in their new house for a total of fourteen days before it not so much burned as exploded, a big piece of the new refrigerator found almost two blocks downhill.

Gina had given them a housewarming gift of a metal sculpture that hung in their new bedroom above their new bed—one thing of Gina's that Anna wholeheartedly liked. It was in the shape of a seated woman's torso seen from behind from buttocks to neck, slightly larger than life. This piece was hollow, cast in bronze, darkly burnished. It was of the scarified back of a Sudanese woman of the Nuba tribe—row upon row of raised scars in a lacy pattern as precise as ironwork completely covered the body. It was edgy, more personal, more passionate, closer to something that might turn out to matter, Anna thought.

Gina called it Erotic Braille.

— 39 —

Redshift

Aₙₙₐ washed her face in the kitchen sink, then put a tray together to carry up to him. Alec was talking to his assistant. He was staring down at his feet and didn't look up at Anna as she came in. This was the first time this had ever happened. We shall grow old, she thought. We will not grow old together.

It may have been that the pain of seeing her now when he wouldn't see her for so long was too terrible for him, or he might be getting sick of her. This would eventually happen. He would grow tired of her and she would grow tired of him. He might leave Gina and marry Anna, but the inevitable would not be forestalled: love was by time eroded. People were vain and each was selfish and all bodies decayed and minds grew hazy. Anna was repetitive; she was tiresome in her same small and very predictable concerns, and Alec would be bored one day. She was almost eager for this time, as it would free them each from the current intensity, the ardor that she constantly felt hurt and ruled by.

Or Alec might simply have begun to be ashamed of himself and the lies he told. It shamed Anna that he was forced to lie to the

people he loved about where he was and the work he was suppos-
edly doing. He hung up, began to rub one hand across his face and
eyes. He looked very tired to her. He looked so apprehensive.

The phone rang. It still sat on his lap with the other hand resting on top of it—Alec was so startled he visibly jumped. Her heart
seized; they both stared at it. It was only Beemus, Anna knew, it
was always Beemus—that or Gina, inviting Alec in her husky voice
to come on home to her.

The machine answered, the tape swirled, clicked. "Pick it,
Anna! Do this! Pick it." Veronique waited now for Anna to do as
she was being ordered.

"I just drove by and I saw your cars so I know you *are* there."
Veronique waited. "You *are* there and I am coming in because if I
must do eeet then you must do eeet. We will pick our keeeed up
from school and go where the fishes swim round and round—what
is the name of it? If I must do it, then you must do it. *Cheezus!* Just
the thought of fishes makes me want to shoot myself." She waited.
"Anna, I *know* you are *not* out." She waited. "*All right!*" Veronique
finally hung up.

Neither of them could breathe or speak. *I know you* are *there*,
Veronique had said. They couldn't have felt more caught had she
said: *I know who is there with you and what you* are *doing*. Of all people, she and Alec knew, it would be Veronique who would drop by
unannounced, find the open doors downstairs and simply come upstairs uninvited. She'd been on the phone in her car, not even a
block away. Thees is a *vee*llawwge, Veronique told Anna one day as
she came up the driveway unannounced. Thees is ow one acts in a
*vee*llawwge.

"She means *aquarium*," Anna whispered.

The two kept staring at the phone believing it would ring
again, that Veronique was still there on the other end, that if they
spoke aloud while she was being recorded she would somehow
hear them.

When they finally did look at one another and she saw how

afraid Alec had become, her heart tightened just one notch against him. His eyes were wide, his cheeks looked slightly hollowed—this made him look so tired, so worn out. Anna would not know Alec when he was older, lost or lonely, frightened or confused.

She had made a salad for them with dried cranberries and smoked duck on mesclun, went to the little alcove to begin serving it. This was a beautiful salad, but the red and green of it made her eyes hurt—it looked so much like Christmas, another feast about which Anna always felt ambivalent. Christmas seemed to her to have been invented by the rich merchants to make others envy the goods they so effortlessly came by.

He poured himself a glass of wine, drank two big gulps down, filled the glass again. Then he asked her if she wanted some. Anna shook her head: "I don't drink," she told him. How was it possible that Alec didn't know this about her?

They said almost anything about sex but didn't speak of ordinary matters, of money or the future or what might happen after the summer, or the way Anna had begun to leave the room when he spoke on the phone to keep herself from hearing the lies he told. He lied to Gina, whom he loved, lied to his children when they asked what he'd done that day. He lied to Carlo, who was like a brother, and to Jerry Bloom, who was like a father.

Alec and Anna had been sleeping together for several months: they'd each confided this to exactly no one.

Dark over Black

T HEY SEEMED so criminal in their actions, so lawless and un-
bounded by convention, that Anna was only slightly surprised,
as she drove down her street one Saturday coming home from
shopping and running errands, to find her house crawling with police. It was late in the afternoon and there were two patrol cars in
front of the house, parked haphazardly, another halfway up the
driveway, all with new-star blue and infrared lights swirling to set
off migraine.

When the first car arrived in answer to the burglar alarm, one
cop explained, they found the sunroom doors standing open and
heard noises upstairs, so they called for backup. No one seemed to
be inside, he told her, but they were in there still searching from
room to room. There were a couple of lids to pots or pans that may
have fallen into the steel sink in the kitchen—this sound will trig-
ger the glass-breaking sensor in some systems. Did she have cats,
he asked her.

"No. But there are some Hungarians," Anna told him. "These
workers who come. But I didn't arm the system and they wouldn't

know to arm it. Anyway, this is Saturday and they would never come on a Saturday, would they?"

The policeman looked at Anna in the certain deep way people sometimes had of looking at her that made her refrain from saying the next thing that occurred to her, which was, Unless Saturday isn't Saturday to a Hungarian.

"Probably juveniles," he told her.

"Probably," Anna said, though there were no juveniles in her neighborhood and she had nothing in the house that they would want to steal. Charlie's electronic equipment had been moved from the garage room, and kids wouldn't break in to steal an art book, Anna knew, no matter how valuable. It also wasn't logical to imagine that kids would break in, then arm the alarm so it would go off with themselves inside. She had probably forgotten to lock the sunroom doors and a gust of wind must have blown the doors open, though there had been no wind and she hadn't armed the system. Still, a Pacific storm was forecast, she'd heard on the car radio, and she had just heard of lightning seeming to seek someone out, striking a man on a ladder under a cloudless Florida sky, with the electrical storm still ten miles offshore.

Anna hadn't seen Alec in a couple weeks. She was imagining their affair was over, that they'd finally been able to come to their senses. She was slightly relieved, passion being, well, so passionate, so all-consuming. As soon as she was sure it was really over, she could begin to count the days of agony and the days of missing him and eventually the longing would abate. She would come to days when she didn't think of him for hours; eventually there would be a string of days in which she didn't think of him at all.

Cops in Berkeley were well educated, well spoken, often graduates of Cal in Criminology. She now imagined *herself* to be a kind of study in criminology, guilty of thefts, of spiritual arsons and shopliftings, of the larceny she carried right below her heavy heart. She spoke with one cop, noticing how this act brought out all the guilt she'd ever felt, how too the junk of power he wore, the gun and cuffs, was sexy to her. She was thinking of this cop, trying to ignore the one who was crawling up the front stairs with a gun drawn. Anna was nonchalant because no one else seemed to think a policeman crawling up the stairs with gun drawn and the front door open was a very big deal—the one with her gun out happened to be a woman.

All this was being treated very casually—no one even kept his voice down—so it was clear they weren't trying to sneak up on the perpetrators. The one with the gun out was noisy herself, rattling all the noisy cop stuff hanging off her belt—nightstick and squeaking leather holster and squawking radio. They'd heard voices upstairs in the front bedroom, the cop on the porch explained. This was probably the kids who'd broken in and might be up there scared to death, unable to come down. Juveniles these days were sometimes armed. The cops often sent a woman in first so she could call out comfortingly—kids instinctively believed a woman was less likely to open fire on them. Kids believed it though this wasn't necessarily true.

Then the policewoman was back down the stairs, holstering her gun. "I almost shot your computer when it squawked at me," she said to Anna. "It seemed to say, 'Beam me up, Scotty'!"

"That's exactly what it does say," Anna told her. "It's the Star Trek screensaver. My former husband put it on my computer without asking me. He was afraid I'd burn lines into the back of the brain of the monitor like the shadows of corpses etched into the sidewalks of Hiroshima."

Facile, Anna thought. She hadn't spoken to an adult in days, so she was going on, saying all this with mindless ease. She, who no longer stuttered, now spoke with the flashy skill of a rodeo cowboy with a lariat roping nothing since the herd was forever gone.

The male cop was writing, had stopped listening, but the woman nodded. Anna spoke again, obviously doomed to be one of the garrulous ones babbling to strangers in checkout lines. "The timing mechanism has no patience with mind drift. If I sit there for just one second too long, the sound effects begin. You can shoot it if you want to—I actually wish you had."

"It's a power thing," the policewoman lowered her voice to say. "A guy's messing with your equipment? It gives them the illusion they have some kind of control over a situation. You can turn the sound off if you want."

"I can?"

"Sure," she said. "I'll show you if you like."

"Why do you suppose he never told me that?"

"General dickheadedness, I'd guess."

"False alarm," another of the cops was saying into the radio he had clipped to his shoulder. "Coded to the security system." He then began writing something up on the clipboard that looked very much like a ticket.

Coded to general dickheadedness, Anna thought. The new security system had never worked right, it was all complicated, system layered upon system, no longer the one beautiful and exterior logic, like that Dante mapped in his levels of heaven and hell, the map believed to show both the interior and the real world. It was all electronic solipsism, with the hard and software designers so far removed—the way an audiotape never fit into a tape deck in one consistent way a hand could memorize and mechanically learn and therefore do it mindlessly, as vinyl records once plunked simply down on a record changer ruled by simple rules of gravity. When a system became abstract, Anna's mind could no longer engage it. She came more simply armed: with the caramelizing iron she kept by her bedside, with the concrete anger that came from her rather classic disappointment.

"This is your free one," the policewoman was saying. "When it rings at the station house and there's no intercept, we're required to respond, so the city has to bill you. We give you one free one, then begin to charge a hundred dollars for each false alarm."

"One hundred dollars?" Anna said. "Then you won't be seeing me again."

— 41 —

The Revenge Effect

AFTER THEY LEFT, Anna brought the groceries in and put them away and went from the back to the front of the house admiring the dusky rooms lit only by light through their spotless windows. The house was hers alone. She had never owned a whole house before.

In the middle of the dining room table Anna found a dozen peonies in a tall glass vase that had not been there when she left to go shopping. Their beauty was staggering—they seemed to be opening as she watched.

The flowers were from Alec, had to be from Alec—peonies signifying what was stable and everlasting. Alec must have stopped by, must have triggered the alarm in trying to set it when he left. Setting the alarm as he went out in order to protect her did seem somehow so much like him. This was the kind of man he was; this showed why she had always known he would never leave his wife for her, yet still wanted to responsibly care for Anna in these small, symbolic ways.

Alec was both things, all things, a good husband, her lover. He was so civilized. He also sometimes hurt her during sex. He did it because Anna encouraged him to do so. She thought of that as she went upstairs, that it would be hard to do without the love of a man who was all things, so confidently extreme, so clear about what he wanted.

She stood at her computer staring into the black of the screen-saver on which the Starship *Enterprise* now traveled through Radio Galaxies in complete and utter silence. The temperature between stars was three degrees above Absolute Zero, Absolute Zero being as cold as anything could ever possibly get. He'd just sent her this news by e-mail. It stood for what they were when they weren't to-gether. The universe was flying away from whatever science might one day find to exist at its center. Science was the God this century worshiped, its newest creation myth.

The Milky Way and the Andromeda galaxies had recently been found to be on a collision course. Researchers now had evidence that black holes and other massive objects such as neutron stars drag space and time around with them as they rotate, a phenome-non they call "frame dragging."

Anna glanced at her clock—there was something very wrong with the time it kept. She stared at it as bewilderedly as Emily Dickinson might have before she learned the trick of telling time when she was fifteen years old. Most people over history have told time by the sun and by the clocks within their bodies—Anna wanted to live one day soon without a clock to wake her.

This clock was black, plastic, cheap but well designed with a clean, blank, modern face lacking numerals. It had only four tick marks, inscrutable silver hyphens at the twelve and three, the six and nine. James Joyce either so hated or so revered the hyphen that he used it in one word only, this being *no-one*—she would send this information to Alec if she could somehow find the quote. No-one aside from Alec had ever been amused to have this kind of news come to him unbidden. No-one aside from Alec had ever made her feel there was beauty and order and love in her dark longings, or that there might be poetic logic in the way her mind worked, a mind with this kind of broad-based, all-inclusive association, this dragging off a loopy frame.

Anna picked the clock up, staring hard at its face. There was something so very wrong, she needed to study it hard to make sense of it. Then she suddenly saw that the little word QUARTZ read upside down and backward. The clock had been resting upside down in its cradle. Time was still rushing forward as she watched, but it was exactly six and a half hours off, being dragged forward but wrenched off the frame of time mankind set down arbitrarily at some point, then made into law.

Where had that time gone? Down with the great slow sweep of molasses, spiraling down what cosmic drain? Could there have been some kind of Supernatural Intervention that had worked to bring Anna to this juncture? What was the point of it? What was she supposed to learn?

She stared hard into the black of the clock's face to try to see it. Her life was no longer operating according to the rules and laws set out by her mother's church. Episcopalians worshiped the body wrong, she thought, worshiped the sex of No Sex, which was like a life spent owning property as an absentee landlord.

There was drag in the frame of time, then the old Episcopal rules of No Sex but for procreation flopped, redshifted so now it was Sex All the Time.

It just sounded much more crazy for a person to say she longed to follow a traditional religious practice with its notions of right and wrong and of sin and redemption than to claim she'd just witnessed time stolen by aliens. Someone brought Anna twelve white peonies edged with the palest pink, traded these for six and one-half hours of one Saturday—a poem might rest there somewhere in the mathematical equation. Six and a half hours over N plus or minus peonies was the only kind of fraction this would, one day, ever amount to: the time Anna once spent in recovery from her lost marriage. Their love was doomed, had an edge of violence, wasn't yet destructive. It wasn't yet destructive, she thought, because there was still the search for God in it.

Had someone actually been in Anna's house? Her hands were cold, her underarms went clammy. She had the iron she kept on her bedside table. She had anger, her wits. She had the up-and-down spine of her own self-righteousness. She felt briefly haunted, then reason came flooding in: it was a chain of events that had happened in coincidence, that Alec brought flowers, triggered the alarm, that the policewoman knocked the clock over as she sat at the computer to turn the sound off, then put it back together wrong. Event simply followed event along a life's course. The storytelling came afterward. It was up to the storyteller then to make it seem neat and orderly, to convincingly deliver Anna to the moment when it would seem perfectly necessary to her that she leave and never see him again.

$$—\ 42\ —$$

Typhoon Coming On

S HE WAS STILL thinking of the clock's time being stolen then returned to her by turning it right side up and of the Little Ice
Age she had already lived through and how during it she'd gotten
some writing done, and of the coming and going of various glacia-
tions, and of what hour it might be in Antarctica where all the lon-
gitudinal lines converged, when the phone began to ring.

It was Alec and he was up the street in the café at the French
Hotel. He'd been shopping at Andronico's Park and Rob. He wondered if Anna and Maggie might want to wander up and run into
him and he could buy Anna that coffee he still owed her. Maggie
could probably use a hot chockit.

"Well," Anna said. She breathed, trying to keep the walls of her
stomach and bowel from shuddering—she had just been working
on getting her body numb. "I, of course, would love to, but I'm
afraid our little chaperone has gone off to spend the night at her father's, so we'd probably better decide to take a rain check. I mean
realistically, Alec? You know? Knowing the two of us?"

"Gone?" Alec said.

Less than five minutes later he was at Anna's front door, his sides heaving, having sprinted the blocks between them. "What," she asked, "do you think we're doing, Alec? We need to actually sit and talk about this and what's going to happen to each of us."

He couldn't seem to answer. He was winded, and his face and shirt were spattered with big drops from the rain that had just begun to pelt down. These huge storms thundered in regularly off the overheated Pacific, their rains ruining the plantings in the half-rebuilt hillsides of the burned-out canyons. The underground creeks and sewers of Berkeley had backed up, the soil was saturated, runoff gushed through manholes, the mud in the bay fanned out in a blond alluvia. Inland, in the Sacramento Delta, hundreds of thousands of acres of farmland were under water, millions of dollars in croplands drowned. Drought, quake, fire, flood: a Biblical cycle of California's disasters. Why, she wondered, did anyone want to live here?

Anna let Alec in—how could she do otherwise? Her having no will to resist him was part of the compact they'd made, their specific clockwork. He kissed her face, her neck, her mouth, half-holding her body up to his, one hand beneath her thigh, so her hips and belly were raised to him. She was wearing jeans, a shirt Charlie once gave her as a joke on which were written these words: A TEE SHIRT NAMED DESIRE.

They stood in the entryway, their bodies entangled, with the hall lights on. Danger surrounded them, heightened their lovemaking, made sex better, as did Anna's passivity and the way she placed herself in the path of Alec's selfishness. It was raining hard and noisily, but people still walked by on their way up to dinner in the restaurants and cafés on Shattuck Avenue. The light in the entry was the only one on. The rest of the downstairs was sucked into sudden darkness.

Anna waited to be swept away, her protests nullified. She couldn't help but be distracted by thoughts of her house, how it had begun to seem like an exoskeleton that she was growing, as she-crabs make new hard shells after the time of molting.

She kissed him but her mind still roamed: a house with peonies, how good and thick the quiet was, how far she'd had to travel in order to come to it. A house going suddenly dark like this reminded Anna of the winter her mother spent drinking too much vermouth by herself at the kitchen table. That was the year her father asked for a divorce in order to marry the woman who'd been his secretary for a dozen years, his mistress for ten of these. Her parents' divorce was the first ever in Anna's family. There were elderly aunts still appalled by the fact of it.

Anna kissed him, her body warming to him, grateful he'd come back to her. Her mind watched them. It was sexy to watch them, his rapturous intention, his ability to so concentrate, hers to become so completely pliable and vacant.

"I got in last night. I couldn't wait until next week to see you," he said.

"Let's just hurry, Alec, all right? Where did you park? They tow, you know, at the Park and Shop after an hour." She was in drift, thinking of Gina being left, of her own mother at the kitchen table getting quietly drunk, this being Margaret's sole avenue of defiance, how a woman acted inward, taking whatever blows there were into the softness of her body, while a man might more easily go out and commit his hate upon the world.

Anna's body let him, let him, let him draw her on and up the stairs, but the major part of her attention had gone home, was now drifting through the rooms of a darkened house turning lights on for her mother so she could find her way to bed.

43

The Search for Intelligent Life
in the Universe

ALEC FLICKED ON the overhead as they came into her bedroom—they'd never made love in the dark. Anna had socks on, no shoes. He kissed her, pushed her back onto the bed, pulled at her pants, its zipper; he yanked her jeans off, pulled her panties down. He put her panties in her mouth so she could taste the way she tasted.

Anna had nice full breasts; they hung down a little, were sore sometimes during her period. He pushed her bra up off them, pulled her shirt off. Her eyes were large, expressive. He liked to see reaction, his own power shown back to him.

He leaned forward holding her breasts in each of his moving hands, was on her then, breathing hard against her hair, brought his face to her belly, his mouth to her breast and nipple, bit her. She thought of the long needle she once gave him, his pricking her there with it—remembering this, she started to rise to him. He was hungry, needy, nothing about him was gentle. This was what Anna loved in him, also what she hated.

Alec moved down along the midline of her naked belly with his lips and teeth, pulled at her pubic hair to open her to his teeth and tongue. He found her bump and lips, his fingers opened her, she stayed as he showed her, poised just as he placed her. He told her in short words that were the code they used for his command: stand, sit, kneel, he'd say, and she'd wordlessly do these things.

Alec stood. She watched him, watched him, her eyes hooded, her body heavy and inert, lying before him like gravity. He began to look around. She saw he was going to make something with her body, use it as part of his construction. He planned all this when he was away, remembering the height of her bed, her weight, the way he would place her, correct for the discrepancy. He began to systematically gather pillows from the top of the bed.

He placed pillows as he wanted them, stacking these along the edge of the mattresses. He reached to move her, putting her hips along the edge on the pillows so she was at the right height for him. He placed her arms above her head, told her to keep them there. Anna floated above them, watching.

Alec was still fully dressed. She watched him as he methodically unbuckled his belt. His hand slowed on the buckle. She watched him. Their eyes caught. She moaned the slightest moan—she was being caught up now, as a car on the roller coaster is caught on a hook at a certain place in the track and will then be ratcheted up. It caught her, dragged her, body first. His big hand worked his button, the zipper. His hands, his voice, were huge and beautiful; she felt them fill the deepest parts of her. Alec dropped his pants and undershorts but didn't otherwise undress.

His penis, solidly engorged, stood out from beneath his shirttails. He stroked it absently as he looked around, casting his eyes over the pillows, the bedding, to see what else he might need, his eyes coming back now and then to assess the shape Anna's body made.

"Here," he said, moving her up and toward himself by taking her by the hips. Then his concentration broke. He smiled, leaned forward, touched her lips with his knuckles, "God," he said, "I love you so," and she squeezed her eyes shut against the blinding pain of that and the sound that rose in her throat. Love was anguish, was something they would never get free of.

"Here," he said, "Scooch up, good." He held her; her hips were tipped forward and raised. "Now, spread," he told her.

She opened her legs to him, her arms still poised above her head. He pushed her legs down, open, knees bent. He pressed, touched her, watched her eyes as he did this to see what would move her. She was helpless, open, his.

His long fingers moved in and out of her. His eyes narrowed as he opened her, bent over just a little, shoved his penis in, his face closed down, was sucked back into itself. "My God," he said.

She cried out with the heat of that first thrust—her cry excited him.

The lights were on, the curtains open. The widows on Anna's block might see if they were interested in watching. God too was watching, Anna thought, before remembering there wasn't One. There was only the fact of their two bodies, the urge and what the two of them made of it, the this and this and this.

—— 44 ——

The Uncertainty Principle

THE STORYTELLING IMPULSE, Anna noticed, pretended to go forward but actually worked backward. It was the net cast back over a life or world in order to connect events, choose, bring coherence, an appearance of logic and order to what otherwise might seem a random chaos. It gave shape, provided the vast mess with the look of an internal logic that seemed as neat as clockwork: if B follows A, then C follows D.

Alec told her the story of Timmy while they lay together in her bed. Anna played the movie of that event on the ceiling of her bedroom, lit with white and moving orbs that were sunlight reflecting off the birdbath. She listened to him, and because she was beginning the practice of trying to hate him, she listened carefully to the story for a tone of self-justification. She needed to hate him in order to get free.

It was the winter of the first big rains. Cecily was a toddler; Gina had started back to school at the California College of Arts and Crafts in Oakland. She had gone from architecture to fine art, was finishing her degree at CCAC in painting. Alec had left Cal and was trying to get his practice going. Life was difficult in every way—she was torn between wanting to be back in the excitement of her artistic promise and becoming more entrenched in the domestic by having another baby. She wanted another baby because she didn't want Cecily to go on seeming like an accident. She wanted another baby so her new family wouldn't mirror the fact that she was an only child, believing another baby could break the curse of her own childhood. She wanted the geometrics changed from the triangle she'd had growing up to something more like a parallelogram; something with four sides, Gina thought, might prove to be a more stable form.

They were still on Oxford Street, not yet dreaming of Descartes. Alec had his one-man office in the low-rent part of University, in that little Moderne tile-faced storefront down the block from Ristorante Venezia next to the violin shop, empty now. He had his models set out in the deep recesses of the plate-glass windows. He worked standing up at the drawing table he still had. He would walk home for lunch to see Gina when the weather was good.

It rained, he remembered, for weeks without letup—Gina was going crazy, stuck as she was in the house with a toddler, having no time to get any of her own work done. Gina drove Cecily around in the Dodge to get her to go to sleep, took her to the indoor malls to let her run up and down the wheelchair ramps and to the University Art Museum to run through the sloping galleries. That was when Gina decided she was a better painter than Hans Hofmann. She was a better painter intrinsically, though she hadn't yet learned how to paint. Gina was working like a maniac. She painted downstairs in an in-law apartment in the basement built back into the hill so the light was lousy, even on a sunny day. They didn't have money for a studio, didn't have money to hire a sitter—she tricked Cecily into sleeping so she could get an extra hour in. Alec couldn't see why she needed to add another child to these pressures and burdens.

The house was already too small, then the rains began. The sky didn't clear for months. Their neighbor's sister came from Argentina to help with his children. Angela expected the normal summer of January and February in the Southern Hemisphere, couldn't speak a word of English, was too depressed to learn, took pills one day in an accidental overdose. Gina drove her to the ER at Alta Bates and her brother sent her home.

Alec walked home at night to the ungodly mess in the living room made by Cecily's play group, the toys and food left strewn around. His life was in freefall: he'd tumbled out of Columbia, arrived at Cal and had ended up somehow in a small cold dump on the Left Coast of Nowhere, still waiting for a phone call from the good father he never had.

It seemed such a vast dull wilderness to him at times. There were no paintings in the art museums, no important theater, no new buildings he honestly admired. The best work in the Bay Area was modest and residential and had all been done so long before. The best work by modernists was in Los Angeles, was being done by those who followed Neutra and Wright, but that was a city Alec actively hated. He had been passed over for tenure at Cal. Even two years after Charles Moore left, Alec was still expecting the call that would ask him to come back to New Haven. This was an irrational hope since Alec had yet to do any kind of remarkable work and Moore had only known him to nod to in the halls.

Then one morning he awoke to the radio report that one of his former colleagues, a China scholar at Cal, had been killed in the night when the hillside behind his house collapsed and buried it. Alec lay on the damp sheets looking at the geometries of the face of Gina, who seemed both too young and too old for him. She said *git it* and *ohrnge* for *arange* and *ant* for *awnt*. He thought of Professor Wing Li Po, who survived the Cultural Revolution, got to the Gold Mountain only to be buried in his bed beneath a sea of mud and books. Alec wasn't up to this. He couldn't make enough money to take care of a wife and kid. He was a failure and was filled with dread for his future.

And what was he doing here at the melting edge of the continent living atop a strike-slip fault? He easily could imagine being buried beneath his own stacks of books—he read the spines to himself in the half light only because he had memorized their order on the shelf—*A Pattern Language, Michael Graves, Wright's Usonian Houses.* Whatever pressed on his chest gained weight.

If awake, Gina was talking. She was talking, yakking, hawking him, wanting another baby, needing another baby, to undo the old bad magic. Actually, he said to her, we happen to *need* another baby about like we *need* a hole in the head. Where did she imagine the money for all this was going to come from? He turned sarcastic, taunting. She said he had started to do crazy things, doodling his name in Cyrillic on a napkin instead of talking to her in a restaurant like a normal person. He was also yelling at her, she said, bellowing when he got in from work and found the glass table in the living room smeared with shmutz and pawprints from the little kids: *Never again!* he was supposed to once have bellowed—Alec believed it, he supposed. It sounded somewhat like him, though he had no memory of actually having said it.

He had just begun working with Carlo, who was still single, as Alec should have been. Carlo was free to travel to visit his family in England and in Italy, free to relocate to New Haven or Manhattan. Free to come and go and frequently visit in L.A., where Frank Gehry and Frank Israel were doing some interesting things. Gina wouldn't go there, wouldn't actually go anywhere. She had her dead mother and her dead father planted in the cemetery, the one you got to by driving down Pleasant Valley. It was all Pleasant this or that around here: Pleasant Hills and Pleasant Grove. The very word made his teeth ache in the way of cotton candy at Coney Island.

Gina couldn't travel because of her painting and the baby; she couldn't move because she had her network of school friends and art friends and mom friends, women named Yasmeen and Brittle and Sod, women who suffered from allergies to house dust or houseguests, all of them self-proclaimed survivors of this and that.

"Oh, fuck you, Alec," she'd begun to say.

Alec's future was finished, while Carlo's stretched out before him like velvet gliding along the tight rump of a beautiful woman. Carlo went places, dated various ones—his taste in women was achingly exquisite. Alec watched him jealously. His own life had compacted down into an existence, a same deadly present, attending the same goddamned Berkeley party at which people discussed a few things: public versus private schools, the capabilities of their personal computers, the safety of their Volvos. Or they tried to tell you the whole plot of a movie in their largely incomprehensible foreign accents.

Once when someone asked him what *he* thought, Alec said, Frankly, I was just thinking how much I'd like for someone to shoot me so I won't have to take part in this conversation.

He was of course quite drunk. Gina gave him a poisoned look.

He'd actually been thinking about Carlo's women friends, especially the long-legged blonde in a little black dress and black hose and pneumatic shoes who was flirting with Alec from across the table. She had taken one shoe off and had put her stockinged foot up into Alec's lap, where he secretly cradled it back against his stiffening cock.

In those days he always felt strapped, robbed, chintzed. He watched himself begin to go into panic mode while spending, to irrationally stock up on paper products or to charge cheap junk off late-night TV—he once bought the Ginsu knives, put them on his credit card. Alec already felt haunted by the father who wasn't even dead. He was losing faith in himself, in everything he'd hope for. Alec knew he was objectively more talented than many Cal had retained. He watched who it was they did promote—it was as bad as Yale, not one was Jewish. This was their loss. Cal lost Alec, but they'd lost Charles Moore too. Alec was ashamed of himself. He'd knocked a student up. Still, he did then go ahead and do the honorable thing by marrying her.

He and Gina caught the other staring at one another in the night-blacked mirror of their living room window, each wondering if the other was them who they might have freely chosen, each probably thinking, Maybe not.

He blamed her, but blamed himself more. His heart actually went out to her—she needed the more stable forms so a Queens boy would appeal. Gina acted tough but didn't really know the first thing about how to take care of herself: her baggy cotton underwear and the fact that she didn't even know how to put her bra on right, having had no mother to show her. Instead of putting her arms into the straps, then reaching up behind to fasten it like a normal female, Gina stood staring down at the mechanism, hooking it at her waist as if it was a puzzle she had to solve. She fastened it, then moved it all the way around so she could push herself awkwardly into it.

He may have said *never again* but he didn't mean it, very obviously. He may have said he wanted no more babies until they *could afford it*—this is what he'd meant, at least. He may have complained that he'd never been to India or hadn't yet seen the Centre Pompidou. She hated traveling even then. He wanted to take Gina on the real honeymoon they missed because she was so sick when they spent those few days at Wellfleet. He understood that on the Caribbean Islands or anywhere else along the Equator the sun plunged suddenly down like Icarus without a transitional dusk or twilight. He only wanted to show her the falling of the most swift night.

He'd begun imagining traveling to Italy with the long-legged girl Carlo was no longer dating, to envision his escape from the milk stink in the Dodge station wagon, the smear of gummed cookies on glass tabletops, the cracker crumbs being continually ground into the leather seats of the chrome chairs designed by Mies van der Rohe.

Gina was always witchy, could probably read his mind. She narrowed her eyes at him: Fine, she told him, you go do what you need to do and I'll get my own stuff done and maybe we'll hook up later when it's more convenient.

She was so Californian, so intrinsically hip and cool about the fact that their marriage was falling apart. It was nothing, a spat, an extended low-grade argument that lasted a couple of weeks, a month or two at most. Alec wasn't cool at all. He may have said no to a baby but he clearly hadn't meant it. He was a Queens boy, a family man.

The rains continued, that winter becoming the wettest on record. It rained for twenty-eight days without ceasing. Books in the basement molded. The water table rose. They slept in the same bed but never reached across the clammy distance, speaking only in cold courtesy. December became January that eroded into February. The Sacramento and American Rivers overflowed their levies. More lives were lost.

Gina seemed so tough, but had been harmed so deeply and so early and was still so easily wounded. She was an orphan who didn't always dry herself thoroughly after she bathed. The wet of her pubic hair dampened her underpants. He was almost ten years older. He'd been in the world, he could teach her things.

Gina's face swam as he sat working at his drafting table, her big eyes watching him as they once had from the back of the classroom, her hamburger shoes, the femininity that she warded off so successfully until he made a house for her and she felt safe in it.

He blamed her though he knew she was as ambivalent as he was, hadn't set out to trap him. They were careless, so passionate, reason was simply overwhelmed.

He sat working as rain washed the plate-glass windows in great sheets, and suddenly understood it: he'd been cruel to her, withholding. She needed him to *want* to marry her—this is what a new baby would do. The night before she and Alec married in Queens, an old aunt from New Haven—a Bolshie and true vulgarian—began to talk at the rehearsal party about *shiksas*. You hadda watch out for a *shiksa* because that item came with the *goyishe hartz*.

"Excuse me?" Gina asked. It may have been that she had honestly never heard the term before.

"Cold fish," the aunt retorted. Stuart and Viv were dumbfounded, stumbling, such words of derogation, they told Gina, were never uttered in their carefully tolerant household. Gina looked up the word, she told Alec later. *Shiksa* derived from the German for *blemished*.

Gina was an orphan who didn't hold herself in high regard and so believed he'd married her not for love but because he was Jewish and bound by duty to marry the blemished girl he had knocked up. He knew it now: Their needing another baby, he understood was a matter of spiritual calculus. Another baby who was wanted and planned for would subtract all the other negatives, split the two of them off from the sad path her parents' lives had taken. They would be intentional.

They'd do it right this time, he thought. Go away to a Caribbean island where the sun fell straight into the sea, have candlelight and romance and she'd slip her shoe off at dinner and he'd cradle her foot against his balls and they'd make each other hot by talking about the ways they might fuck, get the check, rush off.

Alec was so excited by realizing he actually had what he wanted that he locked the office without calling first, wanting to rush home to demonstrate his desire for her. He took his umbrella and set out, up University to Shattuck, winding up Oxford in the soaking rain. Cars whooshed by him. The floods swept up onto the sidewalk, drenching his slacks and shoes. He was a neat man but didn't care. Alec's heart overfilled with goodness: he was a family man, he had a wife and infant daughter, and his love for them had conquered selfishness so he'd left the Dodge home for Gina to use.

The house was brown-shingled and stood on the uphill side of Oxford above Indian Rock. She was a scrambler, able to work so few hours in her painting studio she rented time in slots to other students from CCAC, so Alec wasn't altogether surprised to see the battered VW bug sitting in their driveway. DEFY AUTHORITY, one bumper sticker read. Another said ATOMKRAFT? NEIN, DANKE!

The rest was simply harder to factor: that Gina was standing outside in the steady rain at the door to the studio with water dripping from the peak of the hood of her blue parka, face wet, her legs bare. She had been laughing, he supposed, or crying. She stood rattling the handle of the glass door to the studio on the street floor of the house, pounding on the glass, calling for the person inside to unlock it. It was a baby trick, locking someone out, so Alec knew it had to be Cecily—she was a toddler. But why was Gina dressed the way she was?

Then Gina turned, saw him; her face changed in a way that no amount of time passing would ever undo. Alec saw her fear of him, the tall dark man striding up the walkway—he was a monster, everything a woman dreaded. It would have been easy enough to strike her. She was trapped back against the garbage cans with nowhere to go.

Time froze then, went glacial. Seconds expanded. He saw it all in perfect detail, her hands that were small and wet, how they clutched childishly at the front of the parka to keep it closed—she was wearing nothing at all beneath it, he saw, and his heart overwelled with pity for her little body, its silliness, its frailty. Only the rain stood between them. Her bare legs were stuck down into huge red rubber rain boots much too large for her.

"Alec," she said, moving back from the door, moving back into the recess that was the other door into the basement. "This is not what you think. Believe me, Alec. This is *nothing*, I swear to you. I was modeling for him, Alec, posing, like I used to do in college? Nothing is going on here, Alec. Don't go crazy with this. A person has choices. You can honestly choose to not go crazy here. I was *modeling* for him, like I did for the life-drawing classes to earn money when I was in school."

He saw him through the window: it was the boy she'd met at CCAC. Gina thought Timmy was amusing; Alec had always hated him. Alec had no use for the Satellite Male. She let Timmy use the studio but didn't charge him because he never had any money. This was because Timmy was a mooch and loser. He snuck around, coming over only when he knew Alec wasn't home.

Alec's rage was a perfect thing, towering, reasonable, cold. He could murder the boy, even kill the both of them and get away with it, he knew—the cops would understand it. They were like the guys he grew up with in the neighborhood—that you could kill a wife who was fucking around was another of the rules in Queens. This boychik didn't deserve to live on purely aesthetic grounds: the greasy blond hair, the shitty posture. He was one of the fashionably pseudo-homo types who came off opportunistically bi so women felt so safe with them when he was actually the most ruthless kind of predator. How tediously predictable this shit was, how Oedipal, how Iago!.

Alec glanced at Gina. The pathos, really, that the attentions of a little creep could make her look so flushed and alive.

They each heard Cecily calling for her mother from inside of the house. Alec could actually hear his daughter twice, once in the room above and then again on the baby monitor Gina kept in the painting studio. Timmy was trapped in there, having locked this woman, a mother, his kindly benefactor, outside in the rain as some kind of twisted joke. Alec looked at her—wife, orphan, mother of his child.

Alec became perfectly cold. He raised one long leg, aimed, kicked the glass door apart right at the doorknob, aimed perfectly, recoiling just so, and was therefore uncut. Timmy was trying to push up a window that was fixed open a few inches with crime nails. His shirt was open, his jeans big and loose and hanging off his hipbones. Where did they get these half-dressed slobs?

Alec strode to him, grabbed him by the hair at the nape of his neck and by the waistband of his baggy pants. Timmy was long, stringy, but didn't weigh anything. Alec tossed him in a heap in the corner. "Stay," he ordered as if Timmy were a dog. The kid reeked of turp and the sweet stink of marijuana smoke, his face gone white. Timmy's eyes gave off that flinty video-cameraed sheen that came from being really, really loaded.

Timmy curled on the floor to guard himself. Alec's rage was beautiful, just as judicial as when he smacked his cousin Pauly, shoved him face first in the snow bank, then hauled him out and patiently ran him, fully dressed, under the warm water in the shower, before he got him to sit corrected in warm pajamas to write out this pledge: "I, Paul S. Dershowitz, do solemnly swear never to throw ice balls vichiously as it might hurt someone."

Alec went to the easel to look at the canvas, took his reading glasses out of his suit pocket. The nude was recognizably Gina, head tipped back, legs spread, the flesh done in ripe swatches. "You fucking little shit," Alec said. He picked up a palette knife, but the edge wasn't going to be sharp enough. Alec looked at it carefully, appraisingly—the work was good. The boy was talented and he'd clearly studied his Lucian Freud, his Francis Bacon. "Too bad," Alec said aloud. He went to get Gina's matte knife. She used this to nick the fabric in order to start the rip in the canvas she bought by the roll and stretched herself. Her clothes and hair in those days often smelled to him like canvas dust, like sizing and gesso. He strode back to Timmy's painting and began to stab at it.

Cecily was crying on the intercom.

"Don't hurt him," Gina said. "If you hurt him, I'll leave you."

"*You'll* leave *me?*" Alec stopped in order to ask her.

"Why can't you listen, Alec. He didn't *do* anything to me. We didn't *do* anything. He wanted to paint me, he asked me to sit for him. He was doing it for us in trade—he was going to give me the canvas."

"Oh, I'm absolutely sure he was," Alec told her. He was peering over his glasses. He went back to slashing at the picture.

"It wasn't sex, Alec."

Alec turned and stared at her over his reading glasses. "Gina," he said, "this kind of thing is *always* sex."

"You don't kill a person over a painting."

"Oh no?" he asked. He continued hacking the picture up. He was in a kind of rapture: the boy was good, good, good, he thought as he stabbed it. He was good and Alec was a failure and his wife, in her disloyalty, had exposed this to the world.

Gina abandoned Timmy, went upstairs to Cecily. That's what saved their marriage, Alec later thought.

"Hey, no really, it's cool, man. No, really."

Alec turned to look at him. Timmy had gotten up. "Picture was turning out shitty anyways, so who gives a fuck." He shrugged elaborately, was slinking over to Alec, one hand shoved down into his pants pocket to show he meant no harm, the other extended as if to shake hands with him.

Alec blinked, took his glasses off, put them carefully into the paint tray of the easel, turned, lay one big paw on Timmy's shoulder so he could carefully aim, hauled off, struck him. The blow caught Timmy on the hard orbit of his eyebrow and cheekbone. He staggered backward, hit the wall and slid so he was sitting in the splintered wood and shards of glass from the kicked-in door. He was barefoot, Alec saw. The red rain boots—like those of a huge child's—were his, quite obviously.

"You *asshole!*" Timmy yelled indignantly. He stared down at his bleeding feet. "You hit me! I'm cut. You wrecked my painting, man. I'm gonna fucking *sue* you!"

"Oh," Alec breathed, as he walked toward him, "I so sincerely hope you do."

4.

On the Mystical Shape
of the Godhead

The increase of disorder or entropy with time is one example of what is called an arrow of time, something that distinguishes the past from the future. . . . Why does disorder increase in the same direction of time as that which the universe expands?

STEPHEN W. HAWKING, A Brief History of Time

45

This Do Not Work and It Do Not Play

When yelled at by clients given to raging, Do you know who I am? on the telephone, Alec had begun to gaze off toward his far wall—he kept it largely blank for just this kind of staring. He'd hung a print, one of the numbered but untitled Rothkos from his last and most bleak period—Alec thought of that time as Dark over Black—on a bulletin board where he also tacked obituaries. His current favorite was that of Blanche Hunter Stern, who had been voted Miss Sunset District in 1928. The language was perfumed by nostalgia, sweet and dense as cake.

Oh, no, please! Oh, do rave on, Carlo might have said aloud to this client, one of the several they had who was not just rich but *rich*! Alec had just read that 124 of the world's richest people owned more than everything owned by all the peoples and the governments of the world's forty-five poorest countries, and it could be that this guy was one of them.

These people were part of the mushroom cloud that was global capitalism in which all corporations merged into the same few people and they went ever upward to sit on the right hand of God in heaven where they became One, having achieved Singularity.

Alec put the *rich* man on the speakerphone so the man could somehow cosmically hear his own foolishness, then set about tidying up his desk. His eyes fell on a handwritten note on his bulletin board, stuck there with a pushpin, something he and Jerry Bloom had found taped to a slot machine in Reno. THIS DO NOT WORK AND IT DO NOT PLAY.

"This do not work and it do not play," he read aloud.

"What?" the *rich* man said—his voice bounced around all the corners of Alec's office in the way a rich man liked his voice to do.

Alec, startled, hit the button and picked up the handset, then became transfixed by the shape of it, thinking: this *lack* or *absence*. The client had begun talking again.

Didn't a person like this stop to consider the cost in man hours before he called long-distance? Alec had better things to do than pretend to listen to him. With deregulation, phone minutes had become just much too cheap and there were too many people in the world and they were all talking on the phone that minute or forwarding this or that unfunny joke by e-mail; everyone was simply much too close at hand and not the slightest bit particular. How did anybody hope to ever get anything done? Couldn't this man be quiet now? Conversations lasted way too long. Language was now the same flimsy junk as what everyone bought by the tons and tons in the millions of aisles in all the tens of thousands of malls and Wal-Marts and superstores where Americans shopped and shopped with carts overgrown by giantism into personal handcarts, this crap lugged home, kept for a short while, then carted off to the bay, where it was shoveled in as landfill. His next-door neighbor, Cliff Peech, had made a cool couple of million manufacturing extra large-sized household HandiCans. They were equipped with handles so the garbage trucks could lift and dump without any of the contents touching human hands.

So much junk was bought and sold—people could just buy it, then drive it straight to the water and push it in without ever bringing it home, thereby cutting out one whole level of bullshit. Words were junk, as infinite as stars, and they were being uttered and said and written that very moment, tapped in, put out, *sent,* going out into the ether that was either nowhere or was the porno chat room where the lid was completely off but no actual intimacy of the mouth-to-mouth or the skin-on-skin would ever transpire. What he needed was what—before Anna—he used to lie on his chaise and long for. He thought of this as Sex with an Actual Person. He'd sent Anna an e-mail that morning, but he needed now to go see her, needed to speak with her, not electronically, but face-to-face, in their mother tongue, with their lips nearly touching.

His assistant Sandy buzzed him the moment he got off to remind Alec of his meeting with Carlo, also to say the registrar had called from Lawrence Hall to say the class in sunsets had been canceled again so she was crediting the charges to Alec's credit card. "Sorry," Sandy added. "I know how much you were looking forward to it."

Alec felt the old sorrow welling up. His tears might fall onto the blueprints spread out on his worktable: Was this to be his contribution? Two kids and the one big house that was so good he was now doomed to build it over and over again?

He had the newspaper article he'd knifed out with his X-Acto blade to go on his Blanche Hunter Stern Memorial bulletin board.

An earthquake in Assisi yesterday killed four men who were examining the basilica after an earlier tremor had cracked a fresco of St. Francis. The second quake destroyed that fresco and others, and dust billowed up in the church.

He was not to mark himself in grief—so instructed the Torah. He was not to gash himself with mourning, or Alec might, just then, have struck his face with his glass paperweight, while keening and saying these words: Giotto, Pietro Lorenzetti, Cimabue.

"You read it," Alec said to Carlo a few minutes later. They were staring dully at a thick packet of pages that lay equidistant between them on the conference table, pages held together with the biggest paper clip—a Bull Dog clip, much bigger than any paper clip would have dreamed of being when Alec was a kid. More Big Dick-ism, Alec thought.

"You read it and tell me what it says." Alec pushed the pages more toward Carlo, took his glasses off. He put his cheek down on the cool of the marble. The table was Italian: pure, clean, classical. He and Anna could run away, go off and live in Tuscany.

After a moment of Alec's lie-down, Carlo cleared his throat and remarked, "One of us is probably going to have to decide to be the artistic one." Carlo waited. "One artistic?" he asked. "The other the reasonable businessman?" He picked the pages up, riffled them, set the packet back down again. "We could flip for it?"

"I'm in trouble," Alec told him. His cheek still lay on the hard cold stone. Carlo waited.

"I've fallen in love with a woman not my wife," Alec said. He watched the molecules of his breath fog the glassy surface.

"I know," Carlo said.

Alec sat up and stared at him indignantly. "What do you mean, you *know*?" he asked. "You can't know, Carlo. How can you *know* if I haven't told you?"

"Well, firstly, you're pathetic—just look at you."

Alec put his head down again. After a moment's rest he riffled through the pages, looking at them from the same flat plane. They measured nearly a quarter inch. This was a modified policy that would provide their company with its very intricate liability insur-ance, protecting them against malpractice claims. It was statisti-cally impossible, their broker said, that they would *not* now be sued for architectural malpractice.

The pages were black with type in the ugliest of faces, set with tiny margins: no human wrote these words, Alec could see, and no human would ever read them until a house fell in or burned up or was swept away by mud and the claim reached out and through and touched everyone and finally was brought back to them. Then the words would be combed with the avidity of the office staff at École Bilingue searching the kids' scalps for lice.

He and Carlo were going to be sued. They would be sued sooner rather than later. They would be sued because they had malpractice insurance and they worked for rich people and rich people all had lawyers who needed to earn more money and everyone had unreasonable expectations, these days, about what was and was not preventable and because Alec's and Carlo's insurance company was going to settle any claim. Alec's father was right: everything did cost you money, especially having money. They were going to have to hire a lawyer, a specialist in this kind of thing, to protect them from the people who were protecting them.

"Secondly," Carlo added gently, "Julie tells me this is so and I have learned to listen to my wife."

Alec sat up, pushing the pages across at Carlo. "Here," he said. "Fair's fair. You do it this time, what do you think? And you can take the next turn too."

It suddenly seemed vitally important that he go in and tap out another e-mail to Anna regarding the earthquake in Italy—it was imperative. He needed her to have all the words he ever knew, to have her eyes running over them, for her to be able to say them in the clear voice of her mind, the voice he found very pure and musical: "The Basilica of St. Francis of Assisi contained the most important and extensive early Renaissance decorative cycles in Italy outside the Sistine Chapel, where, art historians agree, Italian painting was born."

"And dust billowed up in the church," he said, to excuse himself, grabbing his suit coat off the rack.

Carlo cleared his throat.

"Everyone knows then?" Alec asked as he got to the door.

"Did you honestly expect it not to show?"

"Everyone?" he asked again.

"Well," he said, "I suppose that would depend on what you mean by everyone?"

"The women?" he asked.

Carlo nodded. "No one told Julie," he said. "It was just that Anna had begun, well, radiating happiness."

"Veronique?" Alec asked. He said this name because he couldn't bring himself to pronounce the two syllables that belonged to Gina.

"I don't think so, but who can say?"

They both waited, listened.

"She knows," Alec decided. "That woman knows everything." He had to go see Anna. He was nearly to the door before he thought to ask, "How did you figure it was the two of us?"

"Simple logic," Carlo told him. "Easy to deduce, actually, since neither of you has ever much bothered to speak to anybody else."

46

Absolute Zero

SHE WAITED, LYING flat-out facedown on the bed. He'd asked her to wait; she was very good at it. He was doing things, bringing things he thought they might need. He picked up the caramelizing iron, the sash to her white bathrobe, a jar of waxy cream.

She offered her wrists to him and he tied them with one end of the bathrobe, secured the other, which he knotted, by closing it in the sash of the window at the head of the bed. Their eyes met over the iron—the shaft of it was bright black, its wooden handle blond and smoothly polished. He waxed the handle carefully with the fragrant cream, placed the iron on the nightstand, began to undo his belt.

"Turn back over," he said.

She lay on the sheet, head turned, faced away from him. He was all things to her, all men she'd known, all she would ever know, and she was all women. She was herself and she was Gina and she was the kinky one in Hell's Kitchen that he'd fucked with her head covered by a pillowcase. She had been transported, was in the trance of it. She heard him slipping his belt through its loops, sitting on the creaking chair to remove his shoes. He unzipped his pants, slipped out of them—she heard the soft sound as he folded them, his walking over to hang them on a hanger on the knob of the folding closet, then his footsteps as he came back to her. Her face was still averted.

"How many?" he asked.

"Ten," she said. She waited, the word cathected. Numbers were pure sex to them. There was the faint whoosh as the leather was raised, the higher whirl as it flew, cutting the air as he brought it down on her, then the loud wet smack as it struck. Heat jumped, spilled out, spread, was rapturous; she moved against the agony that bloomed, turned sweet, lessened. Then nothing for a minute, then the burn that began to burn more deeply, into the muscle and toward the bone.

"Count," he said.

"Nine," she said to him.

She waited for it to come. It was as carefully placed and well considered as he considered everything, how he'd built his house and how he'd made his life and how he'd come to love a woman who would be leaving him. Each had always known it.

There was the whiz of its singing, the slap, its sting, her cry, then the deeper burning. Then a softer one and another soft one, then a waiting. It was music, it was lovely, he was perfect at it, he moved them patiently over her. He could do it forever if he wanted—raise his arm and lower it until he tired of it. He moved them over her covering her with heat; it was all part of one song, the stinging, her counting, waiting. Finished, he shoved the window up, didn't free her wrists.

"Now kneel," he said. Anna knelt on the bed with her head down, bottom up, her head cradled forward, resting on her elbows. Soft air moved in through the open windows, was cooling the heat of her thighs and buttocks. She waited. He held her by the hips in either of his two big hands. The girl in Hell's Kitchen once asked him to fuck her with his whole hand.

His fingers found her clitoris, moved it; he shoved his thumb into her ass, put two fingers in her cunt, fucked her slowly, exploringly.

He stopped, moved away, opened the jar again, asked for her hands. She rested forward on her cheek and shoulder, put her hands back between her knees. Alec put some of the cream on her fingers and held them against his cock tip—the waxiness melted between them, into him. He smoothed it into himself, then began doing this to her, doing it carefully as if polishing a beloved object, the hood of her clitoris, her lips, the puckered rim of her anus. He pulled her hips to move her toward him. The bed shuddered as he climbed up onto it to kneel behind her.

She waited for the smooth shape of the polished wooden handle. Instead he touched her with his finger, entered, shoving in past the sphincter that locked tightly down to keep everything out and so was like her soul. She needed him, needed this violation. He turned, pushed himself in and out of her, then removed his finger.

She felt the bluntness of Alec's cock bump at her. Her cunt was an open wetness that throbbed now wanting him, his fist, his arm, his entire person that would be the merging that was the opposite of birth. He wanted this smaller place, its tightness, also to give the pain of it to her, ripping her, the pain and the sexiness of asking her to suffer it for him. She'd asked—he made her wait. She'd asked for it knowing it would change her; she wanted to be changed by him, for his imprint to stay on her no matter where she went.

"You need to scooch back," he said. She reached out and brought pillows to her stomach to arrange herself. "Good," he said, "now press back into me."

The pain was searing, she couldn't help but move forward to get away from it. "I can't do this."

He had softened. "Say *no*," he told her.

"No," she repeated. "Don't," she said. "I can't."

No was what he needed. *No* hardened him, made him into the long black stick that finally stuck. He held her hips and shoved up deeply in and it was better then.

They waited.

"Are you all right?" he asked after a small moment. He said this in his real voice, not the altered one he used for sex, the voice that became thick and ropey.

"Don't move just yet."

Anna needed to wait, to be able to relax, to let the feeling spread. She was holy, her body holy, her asshole holy, holy as the earth to which she was being united by virtue of death and dirt and shit and by this which was the opposite of birth. She needed to wait while she got used to feeling illuminated, full, bright with the feeling that stood right at the edge of pain but did no longer really partake of it. Their love was drastic, risky. It was singular, there would be no other. The daytime sky outside was bright as heaven, stars lay in their infinitude on just the other side of the thin glaze of vanishing atmosphere. Her asshole: one light within such enormous darkness.

"All right," she finally said.

"Okay. Now press back into me."

Time stopped, might or might not ever begin again. Numbers changed, became erotic. She began to count the long slow strokes he took; she was counting, waiting, needing to come to the place where the pain would open out and become wordless and soundless and she would need more rather than less of him.

"Here," he said. "Give me your hand again." She reached back to give it to him. He had the jar open, put the cream on her fingers, held her fingers with his fingers atop them, placing them down against her clitoris, now bulging, heated, throbbing. He moved her fingers there; he'd stopped with his penis shoved deeply inside her.

She moved and moved and began to move on her own and began to feel it then. She was opening as if she was a flower. The peony stood for what was everlasting. She was becoming known to him, he to her, as completely known as she'd ever known another person. She needed to stop thinking. She had become the silent earth, also its vaulted heavens. She was changed now, was nothing but the shape he made; she could feel him in every part of her, in the architecture of her body.

"Can I come now?" she asked, but she was already coming. She came hard in both cunt and ass and he came as she did and they were a single thing in coming, a single pulsing, one pulse, first bright then bright then dimming.

47

One New

And it wasn't just a house's size, Gina once told Anna, but the pretense it made to permanence. A building wouldn't last, but it did want to pretend it would. A house took so long to build, cost so much, depended on so many other people for its making. The architect was really the most tragic of artists, she thought; everything he did was so publicly displayed, set out to be judged and ridiculed. He might have to drive by it again and again and see its strengths and weaknesses and the way it became old so soon or dated and still stood there in all its shame and failure.

It was estimated, Gina told Anna, that the average viewer in an art museum looks at a piece for eleven seconds. Someone clocked it with a stopwatch. The visual arts showed, were set out, displayed. Anna was lucky to be a poet, she said, because writing was so much more hidden, so much harder, really, for the other person to ever get at. Reading just took so much more time.

Time was the money of the nineties, its drug, its currency, and there was no one in Berkeley as busy as Gina. She was accelerated in her ascendancy. Of all their friends, they agreed, it was Gina who was going to make it. Because of this a vein of envy ran

through the women in their circle; it was delicate, barely percepti-
ble, an antique tracery. Gina had what they all wanted: kids and
husband, the house and the career. She had also eerily ceased to age.

Julie sometimes called Gina Baxter our *prodigious* friend.
Veronique once left this message on Anna's machine: "Oh, and I
ave one other new"—this was the singular of *news*. "*She* is having
another show, can you *belive* it? What eees the matter with theees
woman?" Veronique hadn't even needed to say who it was she was
referring to.

Alec called Gina a scrambler; he admired her. Anna admired
her too. How could you not admire her? She was like the home
team you couldn't help rooting for. She would let nothing stop her.
She'd hauled herself up from the house on McGee, the place where
her father lost the keys to the car, never bothered to replace them,
so the old Studebaker rotted on its tires and weeds grew up
through the floorboards.

Gina didn't get sick or nap or waste a day nursing a bad mood
or a hangover. Her canvases were large, she worked indoors. She
wasn't one to sketch, so she didn't travel well. She had worries, it
was work that saved her. It was when the kids were little she realized she could barely endure vacations—she was just too anxious to
relax and put her feet up anymore. They went away for two weeks,
she always said, and she fell four or five weeks behind.

Home with two little kids, Gina had no time to paint but
painted anyway. She took classes in drawing, painting, glassblowing,
printmaking, changed from CCAC to the San Francisco Art Institute, studied under Joan Brown and Manuel Neri. She used resin
and plaster and various metals in her castings. She used her life, her
own childhood tragedy, as if it was physical matter.

Her childhood was a disaster, and she had long ago become determined that her children would suffer none of that. She would,
she told her friends whenever a couple split, do anything she
needed to in order to avoid divorce. Her voice was low. She completely meant it.

The jealousy of Gina showed only in little things—the tiny glee that ran through their circle that spring when it was rumored that Alec was seeing Anna, the one small fissure in the so-far-perfect edifice known in Berkeley as the Baxter House.

Gina never worked harder than she did that spring. She was talking seriously with Dolora Conningham—everyone met Dolora at that party Gina gave for her. Dolora was a high-powered some-one from somewhere amazingly important.

Serene called with an even newer *new*: the Whitney was buying a piece of Gina's—it was part of the video thing she called "Bungalow."

Why is it, Anna asked, that Gina's success always seems to convince the rest of us that we've already failed?

Ah well, Serene answered, Remember what Balzac says, that fame's the only sunshine of the dead.

48

And the Dust Billowed
Up in the Church

A WEEK BEFORE the kids got out of school for the summer,
Gina phoned to ask Anna out to lunch. Gina never went out
to lunch anymore, she told Anna. She'd dropped off the face
of the earth, had been working day and night getting her show
together, hadn't seen Anna, hadn't seen anyone. She just heard
from Veronique that Anna was selling the house. They needed to
catch up.

Anna was so flustered by this call she had to slow down and
speak deliberately to avoid stammering. Her lips, her entire face,
felt suddenly huge and rubbery. She slowed down, lowered her
voice in both volume and in range, spoke slowly, but her mind was
in a wild tumble. What did this mean? That Gina knew? Her voice
was entirely friendly. Did it mean she didn't know or that she knew
and didn't care?

They spoke lightly of various things: the new head at the
French school, Veronique's being pregnant again, Carlo's buying
the sports car from Anna as a surprise for Julie's birthday. She
heard herself speaking slowly, even humorously, but when she got

off the phone, she noticed that she'd been holding the phone so tightly the muscle in her upper arm had begun to cramp. They had agreed to meet at Chez Panisse.

Nor could Alec decipher it. He'd believed, when Gina mentioned it, he heard Gina say she and Anna were going out for *lunch and a shave.*

Alec was standing at the sink in the kitchen drinking a glass of water when Gina told him this—he spat water against the splashboard, then nearly choked trying to draw his next breath. *You what?* he would have bellowed at her in any other circumstance. How *could* women be so insane? His mind reeled, a kaleidoscope porno of skin-flick images, mouths and limbs, their intersection, the cunt lips and asses of these two women whose bodies—both his, not his—he knew so well. He hovered above them looking down as they lay together naked to have their bikini wax, if this is what having "a shave" might mean? His soul was the small brown thing that witnessed from the ceiling, blinded, a nothing, only fur and a heartbeat. Men were nothing, unnecessary. Women went off, spoke their truer secrets each to each. They would have lunch together—might they talk about him? Waxing? It was California that invented this type of thing. This plagued him until Alec had a chance to go sneak a look at Gina's datebook to see when this bizarre event was booked to happen. Alec had misheard, as usual. In her messy lefthanded scrawl Gina had jotted, Anna, lunch @ the Chez.

Of course, the Chez—Alec heard it all over again.

"Neither French, neither English" is what Veronique had to say about this particular construction.

Anna had been rereading her introduction to Confucianism—it was astonishing the degree to which she often misunderstood the most basic things about any kind of spiritual practice. She read as a Yankee, a Calvinist, believing she needed to *improve.* She needed to plan and adjust, then go and do. She needed to accomplish, she believed, needed to get better organized, as if her spiritual life were the kind of business plan devised in the MBA program at Wharton. She needed to study the Four Principles, to study hard, then practice, eventually might learn to incorporate them into all parts of her being.

Confucianism had no tense like the future perfect. This was it, her one life. Courtesy, sympathy, shame, and knowing right from wrong are already innately part of it. These traits were what made a person human. Anna needed to run a few errands. She needed to walk up to Shattuck and buy cut flowers for the dining room. The real estate open house was the next day.

She bathed, began to dress for her luncheon date. Every article of clothing she brought out of her closet looked gauzy and transparent. Her skin was hot, seemed to still burn from the last time Alec touched her. Veronique said she could immediately tell whether a woman was well or poorly fucked—the idiom in French was more delicate: *mal baisée*, poorly kissed. Anna had told her nothing. Still, Veronique now looked at her differently.

California, that spring, was poised in a moment free of F.E.M.A. disaster. The work on the house was finished, its title transferred. Anna was legally divorced. The inflationary bubble of the Bay Area real estate market was shimmering and pure. It was like the stock market, where the baby businessmen were getting richer by the hour in the pump and thrust of the engine of the American economy.

Anna needed to go there armed. As she was sitting at the vanity in her bedroom putting in her earrings, turning her head this way and that way, trying to assess the swish and dangle, the broker on Hopkins Street called. She needed to tell her that although the house hadn't yet been officially listed, a client and his agent were coming into her office in a half a minute in order to present an offer.

— 49 —

The Mystery and Order of
the Universe

It is related, O King, that the wife then uttered some words over the lake, and the fish began to dance, and at that instant the spell was lifted, and the townspeople resumed their usual activities and returned to their buying and their selling.

ANONYMOUS

S*O IN THE Nuba tribe a woman's marital and maternal status is actually written on her body.* Gina wasn't really shouting at Anna, but her voice did seem to have a precise geography and was the territory Anna had now entered.

Anna felt polarized to Gina, as if she were True North, as if Anna might look down or look away but could do nothing about the thin and quavering needle of her rapt attention. No one else seemed to matter so entirely.

They were in the upstairs café. Anna tried to sip her water, but her lips, as she touched them to the water glass, had begun to tremble. She had on a beautiful dress that was hand-painted in washes of gray and blue, the colors of weather. One very good thing about being tall, Anna knew, was that it allowed a person to wear clothes well.

Gina had a husky voice, grave and surprising in a woman who was so physically childlike. She'd brought a portfolio of drawings and photos to show Anna. She'd brought these because Anna'd mentioned how much she loved the piece Gina gave to Carlo and

Julie, how it had come to stand for everything lost in the wildfire. At the words "everything lost" Anna felt her throat begin to ache. The photos were of the research Gina did on scarification of the Nuba tribeswomen.

These women, who live in the southern part of the Sudan, receive their final set of scars after weaning their first child. While the patterning of scars is begun at puberty, it wasn't until after childbirth that a woman ascended to the position of actual and legitimate wife, when the scars adorn much of her body, including the entire back. Because the process is expensive, the scars denote caste as well as marital status.

Anna looked at the photos, courteously, as if this might be mildly interesting if it weren't so far beneath her. She glanced around the restaurant, looking for the famous people who were always there but whom Anna would inevitably fail to recognize. Famous people ate at Chez Panisse so often one felt almost famous just to be there breathing the air of them. Her eyes came back to Gina.

Gina was dressed stylishly in a silk top that showed the muscles of her arms and shoulders. She opened her purse, took out the most startling glasses in order to read the menu. The lenses were little rectangles that seemed to be made of sheer panes of completely see-through glass, these affixed to her face by only the thinnest silver wire that ran back into her hair behind small, perfectly shaped ears, the lobes of which were not pierced. Gina's dark hair was slicked straight back. It looked wet, but when her head moved, the comb lines didn't.

They talked about food for a moment, what each would like, how hungry they were, what they might get to share.

She started in again, tapping the photograph. If he wishes to keep his wife, Gina was saying, the Nuba tribesman has to pay materially while her bond to him is made with pain—this is a custom untouched by a thousand years, she mentioned.

At the word *pain*, Anna's eyes widened, the room bounced and began to shimmer oddly. Sweat pearled on her upper lip. Anna touched her lip with the tip of her tongue, tasting the salt of it. Gina watched her through the wobble with half-shut, heavily lidded eyes; she seemed to somehow know her. Anna was more than listening—she was rapt, transfixed.

The pattern is made by a specialist in cicatrization—this is what the making of keloids or raised scars is called. This specialist is always another woman—some are justly famous for their artistry. This is the most important art of the Nuba, who are nomadic, the scarring of the skin of its women its most enduring medium. Women come from far away to seek out the best artists. The better the artist, the more spiritually connected she is assumed to be. The scarring is painstaking. The artist catches the skin of the back with a hooked thorn, pulls it up to just the right height, then slits the epidermis. Gina seemed to whisper if she spoke at all. It takes hours and hours. If the wounds heal properly, this beautiful pattern of keloids appears. Gina spread her hand over the color xerox of the photograph as if she herself had made the pattern.

The wife spends the days after the procedure in isolation. She goes off to pray the surgery has gone well. Conditions are primitive, things can, do go wrong. When things go wrong, it's read as a spiritual calamity.

Anna had begun actively searching for something wrong, some flaw or imperfection that would free her from this woman's spell. Her eyes fell on Gina's hands—they were small and hard and as wrinkled as a crone's, with paint worked deeply into the cracks of them. These were a worker's hands. Anna looked down at her own. She admired her own hands, which were long and aristocratic like her mother's. When in the throes of the most acute self-hatred, the beauty of her own hands seemed to offer one small reason she might go ahead and live.

"We forget how basic makeup is, that the word *cosmetics* derives from *cosmos*. These are cosmetic scars in the most real sense," Gina said. "The geometry of the scars is a mirror of the Nuba notion of the order and harmony of the universe." She raised her eyes to Anna's. As they looked at one another, Anna felt her face heating up again. Gina knew nothing, she knew everything. How had they even begun talking about these things? Anna wondered. Had they even taken a minute to greet one another—she couldn't quite remember.

Anna glanced down at the painty hands, the hard look the skin had from its years of baths in paints and solvents, saw the fan of fine wrinkles splintering outward at the corners of Gina's eyes. She was squinting, staring off, as if toward Africa.

Berkeley was the town that had helped transform the world by listening to the wisdom of its youth—now this youth was growing old. Gina was aging, Anna saw; they all were aging, Gina was no different, she was going to die like everybody else. Death underlay every act, Anna thought, all art, all sex that had a prayer of meaning anything, having a name for it is both mankind's curse and its blessing.

Gina knew this material inside and out—it had to be part of a lecture she gave at the Art Institute, where she was now teaching, Anna realized, where a class like this would give the Goths a sense of historical legitimacy.

"The Nuba designs are like clothes that fit the body perfectly," Gina said, showing the parallel lines beading along the woman's shoulders, then dipping inward toward the spine. Gina moved her fingers along the line of the back. "The Nuba have names for not only all the muscles of the body but for all the depressions and declivities between each muscle—no other language is so rich in this knowledge, better able to detail the inches of specific surface, to name the skin in this intimate way. The keloids are spaced along a horizontal line that curves according to the individual's musculature. They rise, harden as they heal, becoming about the size and shape of pearls embedded within the skin." The Nuba's back was so dark it looked honestly black.

"No longer nursing a child," Gina went on to say, "no longer prohibited from intercourse, a married woman signals by her scarring that she is again available by being made erotically exciting to touch."

"Caucasian skin just doesn't scar like this." She raised her eyes to Anna's, whose vision had begun to pop and dazzle. "More's the pity," Gina added.

Their eyes locked, each knowing below knowing just what the other knew. Anna's lips were open, she nodded slightly, having agreed to that which had no need of being spoken.

And there was the bounce and warp in the air and light of the café when the gods looked down and life was suddenly completely what it is and shows as such. Their food arrived; never was food so beautiful, the people more beautiful, both patrons and servers, both women and men. Color sparkled as if they were stoned or drunk. Voices came and went like music offered, snatched away.

They had a pleasant lunch: two salads, one of three citruses, mint and avocado, the other of smoky bacon and the slightly bitter frisée. They had the goat cheese calzone, having easily agreed to share everything. They ordered coffee, the peach ice cream. It came with thin, fragile almond cookies, drizzled out like lace, then frozen by the heat of baking. Anna was going to miss living in a town where people knew how to eat.

Chez Panisse honestly was the crossroads of this town, their village, the place where, if you waited, everyone would eventually come along, even the president of the United States.

They spoke then of their children and of their work and of the school, Anna telling Gina what she'd said to no one else, that her daughter wasn't going to be going to the École, since Anna and Maggie were moving to New York to be near Anna's mother.

Alec's name was mentioned by Gina three times, casually. Anna said his name not at all.

Gina paid—she insisted, though Anna had a huge wad of money. She had cash because she had sold the van that morning to a Vietnamese man named Howie, who gave her thousands of dollars in twenties and fifties.

She and Gina kissed in parting, which was a bit like kissing oneself, since they'd eaten the same things. They held one another tightly in saying goodbye—Anna had to shut her eyes against the pain that came bounding out of nowhere.

Anna walked home past the French Hotel, where therapists and writers and computer programmers sit drinking coffee all day beside Andronico's dumpsters. While he lived, this is where you might find Eldridge Cleaver, who had his Bible since he'd become a Christian minister. Nowhere did people talk as they did in Berkeley—the world Anna and Alec had was made of it.

She walked past the cars in the lot of the Park and Shop, crossed Cedar, noting the stores one by one, saying their names to herself in order to remember them. She turned right at Virginia Cleaners.

Home, Anna went to the shelves to look up the Nuba in her book on African art. She became transfixed again by the photographs that lay alongside the text, identical to some of the xeroxed images Gina had. This was the state where Anna floated outside her body—it was exactly to be in the heightened place that meant she was in the possession of a poem. Anna didn't ever own a poem to write it—the work was the master, she its instrument.

She remembered what she was doing, roused herself, went upstairs to type. She hadn't written anything in a long, long time.

She typed these words, copying them directly from the book:

Although various groups in the Sudan engage in the "personal art" of body painting and scarification, none do so as elaborately or as often as the Southeastern Nuba. This may be due to their geographic isolation from Christian missionaries during the colonial period; even now, they are relatively unimpressed by Islam and by a central government that would rather not be reminded of tribal differences.

At birth a Nuba child's body is oiled (having the skin oiled makes one culturally normal, a sort of proper "dress" among these otherwise naked people) and red or yellow ocher, depending on clan membership, is put on the infant's head.

While adorning the body is itself painfully initiatory—as in the application of tattoos (among lighter-skinned peoples) or the cutting of keloid scars (among the darker-skinned, upon whose skin tattoos do not show up well)—*we feel the importance of waking up out of the dream of nature, how difficult it is to do this, and what a high price must be paid without much complaint, for complaining comes from the infantile psyche that the initiate is trying to leave behind.*

Displayed is a highly visible, collectively sanctioned record of pain successfully endured for the sake of psychological adulthood.

The italics, she typed, are mine. But there was something else, she thought, something she was forgetting to tell him. Anna waited. Certain phrases occurred, none adequate.

She pressed Send.

—— 50 ——

The Physics of Sunset

The type of nest a particular species builds is determined by heredity, the raw materials available, the nest site, the experience and ability of the builder, and—perhaps—by imitation of older birds.

LESTER L. SHORT
The Lives of Birds: Birds of the World and Their Behavior

ALL IS LOST to him, gone, can be regained now only in memory. Time is thick as ice, moves, has turned, backs up, carves valley, pushes mountains aside. He now remembers more than perfectly—he relives. The years empty out, he comes to the cabin he and Gina rented from a hunchback and his wife in Wellfleet on Cape Cod. The man was a painter, shortened, twisted, who, by rights, should have been some kind of Lautrecky genius as recompense for the way he was physically canted and wrung. But life is not fair and though Alec can still see him, he can also see his painting, which was nothing better than mediocre. He cannot recall this man's name, a name that will not *live*.

The artist and his wife lived in a beautiful setup, a cluster of cabins they called Pilgrim Pines. They also seemed to have been given the gift of domestic happiness. They were utterly devoted, Alec noticed, blindly in love. These two seemed to think of love as an abundance, and were charmed by the idea of Gina and Alec's being on their honeymoon. They seemed to have forgotten that people on their honeymoon often like to be left alone.

They tried to keep their distance in the mornings, but would show up together at noon to try to get Alec and Gina to come out and enjoy the place, to ride the bikes they'd be more than happy to lend them, to get them to walk on the best seashell beach or to come out to play doubles on the weedy tennis court—all part of the honeymoon package at Pilgrim Pines. There was something about the purity of their expectations that brought out the worst of Alec and Gina's joint cynicism.

"Jesus," Alec asked. "Tennis with those two? What a nightmare."

"Tell them!" Gina groaned.

"I do, they just keep asking."

"Tell them anything," she said. "Tell them I died."

This was in April on spring break from classes at Cal and the weather was chancy, most days cold and rainy, the sky close in the way of the East, its air being weightier than in the West, more moist and dense. One late afternoon with the sky threatening to clear, the painter and his wife showed up on the porch of the little cabin with a picnic basket and a hand-drawn map. Their faces were so bright it almost hurt to witness them. Gina and Alec *had* to take these things, had to go off *right then* to this one specific spot. They pointed down the road, showed on the map where they were meant to park. Alec and Gina needed to leave right then, they had to go! or they'd miss the sunset.

This was another bad day for Gina, who was almost four months pregnant yet still had morning sickness. Some days she was sick the whole time she was awake. The artist and his wife were like twin suns on the porch, their enthusiasm blinding them to Alec and Gina's distress. Dutifully, and not to be disappointing, Alec and Gina took the basket and the map from them and got some woolen blankets from a chest and loaded them in the car. They drove down the narrow road, needing to go and act like newlyweds.

"We're headed west, then?" Gina asked him. They were driving through a tunnel of sticklike branches that hadn't begun yet to leaf out. The woods seemed woven into a soft gray thicket above their heads, like smoke, he thought, or death. She was still so young—Alec kept forgetting this. She'd hardly been out of Berkeley. Alec was so moved to think he had married her, that she was pregnant, that they were now to be a family.

It was a cold day in April with flurries—a real snow was threatening. The heater in the little piece of junk they'd rented made a whirling noise but put out no heat. She was mottled with fatigue and rolling waves of nausea. Why exactly, she asked, did we let them talk us into this?

Alec pulled the car into a sandy clearing on the water overlooking Cape Cod Bay. It was here they needed to park to see it. The sun, they'd been told, was going to blaze out when it hit, merging with its own reflection on the water.

"Shook foil," Alec said.

"What?" she asked. Her little face sometimes looked elfin to him, as if she might sprout the soft horn bumps at the moment of her next enchantment.

"Gerard Manley Hopkins," Alec said. "One of your people, I believe."

"What's *that* supposed to mean, Alec?" she asked. "He was British Catholic, wasn't he? He lived in the mid to late nineteenth century—how exactly, does that make him one of *my* people?"

He didn't answer. "Might be 'God's Grandeur,' " Alec said.

Alec had become preoccupied with the length of his legs and torso and the matter of the track the car seat rode on and the seat being moved back as far as it could be made to go. He was always concerned with the matter of his limbs, what to do with the length of them. He twisted to reach through into the back. He took the champagne from the picnic basket, began unwrapping its foil, untwisting its soft wire, concentrating then on the heaviness of the bottle and the way the closing wire was at once malleable and resistant. He popped the cork, making the face that exaggerated his effort, this for Gina's benefit.

Life was, for him, always the same ordeal, this valiant struggle toward mastery. Each day Alec had to begin anew, as the physical awkwardness threatened to overtake him—he had to shift and alter the world in order to try to find both the equipment and the open area where he might have room to accomplish any one of life's small tasks. Pouring the golden bubbling light was the work at hand, it went well, champagne came out flowing liquidly. Alec had long before decided gravity and light were time's most beautiful objects. He watched as the sparkling wine sought its level in the bathos of the two plastic glasses.

"But that would make it dawn?" he asked. He looked at Gina, who didn't answer him.

Neither had mentioned the most obvious thing, what they'd been too kind to tell the innkeepers: The spectacle of a sun setting into the water was absolutely commonplace on the coast where they lived; they actually saw it nearly every day from their own living room on Oxford Street—saw it, that is, if they took a moment to look at it.

They waited.

She was thirsty, but there was nothing else in the basket to drink and she wouldn't take the glass he poured for her, so he drank that off. Then Alec sipped his own champagne, ever the sophisticate.

They waited beneath an Atlantic sky so quilted with darkness the bottoms of the clouds seemed heavy-bellied as they bumped along the tops of the spindly, well-spaced trees. The grayness was becoming so complete Alec could no longer make out the sun's trajectory and it was getting hard to read. He looked again at the map—it was not well drawn. How did this man dare call himself an artist when he had no respect for basic letter forms?

It was so cold their breathing showed as plumes. Gina didn't have proper clothing for the winter and had pulled the sleeves of one of his big woolen sweaters over her bluish hands. They'd said they loved one another, but neither was certain they really were in love. They didn't know one another well enough yet to tell if they were even going to enjoy being in the other's company. And going out to view a sunset? Again, what was it this was supposed to make them *feel?*

Behind the clouds and hidden from their sight, the sun was clearly sinking, light being visibly leeched from the thin stand of pines and birch saplings in the sandy clearing. Alec waited for the darkness that was so often present in his chest to be lifted away from him. He waited, breathed, sighed deeply, and was suddenly surprisingly filled with the hope that the pledges and vows they'd made might be honestly realized.

My wife, he thought. He reached out to Gina, took her hand in his. She was so cold her skin had taken on a waxy look. Her cold knuckles were surprisingly sharp. She shuddered—he felt it roll through her—then she opened her hand and turned it over. Their palms were both smooth, he could feel the slight friction of the two different textures.

They waited, watched, and the clouds suddenly eased and the gold-white and silver of an astonishing light streamed out as from under the opening door of heaven and the world was wild with it.

So it is here and now, he thought, that my life begins.

ACKNOWLEDGMENTS

My THANKS TO these friends for their close readings: Carole Koda, Saskia Hamilton, Trish Hoard, Alice Powers, Brenda Hillman, Bob Hass, Karsten Pruess, Jan Wurm, and Ross Feld. And to Annie Lamott, for that one loving, yearlong gift, a special thanks. And to Robin Desser—whose insight, diligence and wisdom guided the making and remaking of this book—my eternal gratitude.

Printed in the United States
by Baker & Taylor Publisher Services